CRAZY LOVE

FISH.
Net.
Combat.
Boots.
Lightning.
Bolt.

From where Dylan was sitting in the plane seat next to her, he could see Skeeter's tattoo zipping up her leg and the zigzag just above the hip-hugging waistband of her skirt. The highly stylized line of ink appeared again higher up, zooming out from under her tank top with another zigzag on her shoulder blade, following the curve of a tiny pink bra strap down to the kind of curves that made it impossible for him to sleep at night.

All of it was mesmerizing, but he'd gotten stuck on one small spot less than two inches in width, a break in the bolt, a small spot on her upper thigh where there was no ink.

Black.

Ops.

Afghanistan.

Mission.

Skeeter.

Skinned.

He took another slow sip of coffee.

There it was, staring him in the face, the perfect example of everything he'd been trying to say last night, of every reason he'd had for not bringing her with him, which didn't exactly explain why she was within touching distance at 30,000 feet, working on her laptop and smelling like the sugar she'd long since licked off her lips—sweet.

Very sweet.

Edible—and he knew right where he wanted to start, a little fantasy of his he probably wasn't going to get a chance to indulge, not in a 747, not even in first-class. If he was down to his last few hours on earth, it might be nice to check out with one shred of integrity still intact.

Or not.

The tank top was stretchy white lace. Her shoulders were bare, the right one practically touching him—a silky soft, creamy smooth shoulder with that slinky little pink bra strap running over the top curve.

He was trying not to think about it.

He shifted in his seat to get an extra quarter inch of distance between them and looked at his watch. Thirty-six hours left before his week was up.

Thirty-six hours.

That really wasn't much. Not in the broad scheme of things. He should probably make love to her. So what if he lost his last shred of integrity? He at least would have had her, and there wasn't a doubt in his mind that she was worth more than anything he had in his bag of tricks—including his last shred of integrity.

CRAZY LOVE

Tara
Janzen

A DELL BOOK

CRAZY LOVE
A Dell Book / July 2006

Published by
Bantam Dell
A Division of Random House, Inc.
New York, New York

This is a work of fiction. Names, characters, places, and
incidents either are the product of the author's imagination or
are used fictitiously. Any resemblance to actual persons, living
or dead, events, or locales is entirely coincidental.

Dell is a registered trademark of Random House, Inc., and the
colophon is a trademark of Random House, Inc.

ISBN-10: 0-440-24278-9
ISBN-13: 978-0-440-24278-9

Printed in the United States of America
Published simultaneously in Canada

www.bantamdell.com

OPM 10 9 8 7 6 5 4 3 2 1

AUTHOR'S NOTE

Anyone familiar with the beautiful city of Denver, Colorado, will notice that I changed a few parts of downtown to suit the story. Most notably, I took Steele Street and turned it into an alley in lower downtown, a restored historic neighborhood in the heart of Denver known as LoDo.

CRAZY
LOVE

CHAPTER

P INK.
   Sweater.
   Short.
   Skirt.
   Long.
   Legs.
Dylan Hart flipped his cell phone shut and rubbed his hand over his forehead, trying not to stare at the girl on the other side of the office. She was out to slay him, his nemesis, the bane of his existence—Skeeter Bang, five feet eight inches of blond bombshell leaning over a computer.
   Jail.

Bait.

She knocked a cigarette out of the pack of Mexican Faros on the desk and struck a match off her belt.

"Put that out," he ordered. She knew there was no smoking in the office.

"Make me," she said, then stuck the Faro between her lips and inhaled, holding the match to the end of the cigarette. A billow of smoke came out of her mouth when she exhaled.

Make me?

Dylan was the boss of 738 Steele Street in Denver, Colorado, second in command of Special Defense Force, SDF, a group of tough-as-nails black ops shadow warriors who specialized in doing the Department of Defense's dirty work.

Make me?

"Put out the damn cigarette, Skeeter," the man working at the last computer said. "And if you bend over that desk one more time, I'm going to paddle you."

Thank you, Superman, Dylan thought.

The girl was out of control, but Superman, a.k.a. Christian Hawkins, had kicked more ass and taken more names than most men alive. He could handle Skeeter Bang, and honest to God, they had bigger problems, much bigger, like the phone call he'd just gotten from General Grant—and of course, there was still that little problem of the death sentence he'd picked up on his last mission. Wouldn't want to forget about that now, would he?

Yes. Actually, he would, but forgetting about it wasn't very goddamn likely.

"Skeeter," Hawkins warned her again.

And the chit put it out, just like that, without batting an eyelash or missing a beat. Though who the hell would know if Skeeter batted her eyelashes? The girl *always* wore sunglasses, and a damn ball cap Dylan was about ready to burn, literally, put it in a trash can and blast it with a flamethrower.

He was hardly ever at Steele Street to see her, and then even when he *was* there, he couldn't actually see her—which was all for the best. Just the way he liked it.

Except now he had this walking time bomb thing happening, and if it turned out that things weren't going to go his way and the whole damn shooting match was about to be over, well, maybe he should tell her how he felt.

Or maybe not.

Shit. He was such an idiot. He shouldn't have come home. He should have just toughed it out in Indonesia.

"So what did General Grant want?" Hawkins asked, gesturing at the cell phone Dylan still held in his hand. General Richard "Buck" Grant was SDF's commanding officer at the Department of Defense,

DOD. He deployed them, paid them, and made sure damn few people beyond the secretary of defense had a clue what they did for a living. They trained at Quantico and Fort Bragg, lived in Denver, flew out of Peterson AFB or Buckley, and were the only group of special forces operators in the world with a twenty-year-old girl on their team, even if she was only the office manager and their computer tech.

She also just happened to be one of the best auto mechanics they'd ever had at Steele Street— which was saying a lot, considering that most of SDF was made up of a bunch of former juvenile delinquent car thieves who'd stolen, chopped, and rebuilt more cars than anyone else in the history of Denver. To the cops and the gangs, the short alley called Steele Street in lower downtown was still synonymous with grand theft auto, no matter that none of the guys had stolen a car in years.

Guys—that was his point. Every teenage thief at Steele Street had been a guy. General Grant had started SDF with those same guys, until three years ago, when Hawkins had dragged home a spooky, baby-faced street rat with long blond hair and twenty stitches holding her face together.

Geezus. They all needed their heads examined.

"Dylan?"

He jerked his attention back to Hawkins. The expression on his friend's face told him he'd been caught red-handed, staring at her ass again. *Dammit.* He hadn't hardly noticed her the first two years she'd been at Steele Street—and then one day, he had noticed her, noticed that suddenly she had more curves than a Camaro, that her stringy blond hair had turned into a platinum waterfall, and that though she was still spooky as hell, she wasn't spooked anymore. She'd been standing on her own two feet—in combat boots, no less—with confidence radiating off her like a supernova.

He'd been noticing her ever since. He couldn't seem to help himself, which pissed him off to no end.

Ignoring Hawkins's knowing grin, he cleared his throat.

"Grant's concerned about some documents he saw at Senator Whitfield's mansion tonight." "Concerned" was putting it mildly. "Apoplectic" was more like it—which meant maybe Dylan ought to stop getting distracted by Skeeter's butt and start focusing on the job he got paid to do.

"I thought he was on his way to the London conference tonight," Hawkins said.

"Whitfield's was his last stop. He's headed to the airport now, but he's pretty damn sure the documents are exactly what the guys on the E-ring of the Pentagon are afraid they are—the Godwin file."

"And that warranted an immediate phone call to us?"

"Yes," Dylan said. The general knew better than

to drag his feet on something as volatile as the Godwin file, if what he'd seen really was the Godwin file. Some people doubted that the documents actually existed. Others prayed every night that they didn't.

"So what does he want us to do?"

"Steal the file." That was the mission. Steal the damn thing and bury it, before it blew up the careers of half a dozen congressmen and another half-dozen major players at the Pentagon.

"From Senator Whitfield?" Hawkins's gaze sharpened with interest.

Dylan knew it sounded nuts. Stealing from a U.S. senator was the kind of mission guaranteed to get somebody's ass thrown in Leavenworth, even if the thieves worked for the Department of Defense—*especially* if they worked for the DOD. On top of all the regular "thou shalt not steal" laws, federal law explicitly forbade the use of military personnel for operations within the United States. More than once, though, when a situation had gotten sticky enough, Grant had shuffled him and a couple of the guys through the FBI's payroll so they could follow through on a mission without having their backsides completely exposed.

Grant hadn't mentioned any shuffling tonight, but Dylan knew their commanding officer always did his best to cover their asses and their tracks. Of course, under normal circumstances, Buck Grant and

Arthur Whitfield were on the same side, America's side, and under normal circumstances, U.S. Army generals did not go around authorizing the theft of top-secret documents from senators—but nothing about the Godwin file was normal.

It was a legend, a myth, a time bomb that had been lurking in the murky waters of the Defense Department's rumor mill for over a decade. It was the bogeyman sitting at the intersection of U.S. foreign policy and clandestine operations, and if the rumors were true, it had been a death warrant for a CIA agent and the U.S. ambassador under his protection, just the sort of dirty laundry nobody wanted aired, especially the people whose names were on the orders.

"Whitfield has an appointment to see the Chairman of the Joint Chiefs of Staff Monday morning at nine A.M. Grant wants the file to disappear before the meeting."

"So we're heading to Washington, D.C."

"I am." It was a one-man job, and despite certain god-awful inconveniences in his current situation, he preferred to keep it that way. His luck had been running nothing but bad lately. Either that or he'd hit the top spot on some real mover and shaker's shit list, because things that shouldn't ever go wrong had gone wrong in Jakarta.

"You're going to need somebody to watch your back," Hawkins said.

"Creed and his team aren't due back until Sunday." Which meant backup was a luxury he didn't have.

"They might make it by tomorrow night."

"By tomorrow night, the deed will be done, and I'll be on my way home."

"You should still have somebody with you," Hawkins insisted.

"And that would be?" Dylan asked, giving the other man's leg a pointed look. A cast went from just below Hawkins's knee to down around his foot. The broken ankle was compliments of a successful mission six weeks ago in Afghanistan that had netted the U.S. armed forces a long-sought-after terrorist leader. No one was naming names at this point. Hawkins, with two other SDF operators, Creed Rivera and Kid Chaos, had done their jobs so well, word had yet to leak out that the terrorist leader was even missing, let alone that he was sitting in a cell in Guantanamo Bay.

In answer, Hawkins flicked his gaze toward Skeeter.

A shiver of alarm skittered down Dylan's spine. Hawkins couldn't be serious. Skeeter? On a mission?

No way in hell.

Especially one of his missions, which all required deception, deceit, discretion, and stealth of the highest order, not to mention plenty of sheer, unadulterated nerve. He was a thief, the best. Big things, little things, cars, computer chips, ideas and identities, fingerprints, information, jewels, gems, high-tech junk, a nuclear warhead out of Tajikistan, or seventeen million dollars out of an Indonesian warlord's black money slush fund, whatever General Grant wanted, Dylan delivered. Those were the terms of his freedom, and they hadn't changed in the nine years since the general had first proposed SDF to the U.S. secretary of defense. An elite force of highly expendable men had appealed to the man who had been the secretary then and to the two who had followed. SDF had a commendable reputation, but dozens of successful missions hadn't changed Dylan's situation. The other members of SDF, most of whom had been in the military, could come and go as they pleased, but he was always on borrowed time. The CIA still wanted his ass in a federal prison for his involvement in a dicey operation in Moscow back when he'd been a green kid smart enough to get what he wanted, but not smart enough to stay out of trouble while doing it. To date, the agency had consistently been outgunned by General Grant and Dylan's benefactor in the State Department, a man code-named White Rook. It was a situation Dylan wasn't going to allow to change. He'd be damned if he went to prison, which meant he couldn't afford failure, ever.

So he didn't fail, ever.

He shot Hawkins a cold look and silently shook

his head. He wasn't taking Skeeter to Washington with him. He wasn't that insane, or that selfish. Not yet.

"Don't talk about me behind my back like I'm not in the room," she said, continuing to tap on the computer's keyboard without so much as glancing over her shoulder.

Dylan swore under his breath. The girl *was* spooky. Neither he nor Hawkins had said a word, but she knew.

"You're not going," he said clearly, not wanting there to be any doubt in anybody's mind, most of all his own.

"She's good," Hawkins insisted. "Steady as a rock and practically invisible when she wants to be."

And when would that be? Dylan wondered, arching his eyebrow at his friend.

Hawkins didn't blink, and against his better judgment, Dylan let his gaze slide back to Skeeter.

Forget it. She was outrageous, the cosmic opposite of invisible. Her pink sweater was sleeveless, practically Day-Glo, and absolutely, positively laminated to her body. Her black leather miniskirt hugged her hips like a second skin. She had Chinese tattoos inked into the upper part of her right arm. Underneath her black tights, a lightning-bolt tattoo streaked up her leg from her ankle and shot over her hip, up under her arm, up around her back, and down over the top of her shoulder. He'd never seen the whole thing, couldn't see it now, but he knew it was there. She had that perfectly silky, perfectly straight, perfectly maddening platinum blond pony-tail that went all the way to her butt, and every day she managed to work a little chain mail into her out-fit. Today it was her belt and a knife sheath. Add the mirrored sunglasses and the ball cap and she was nothing short of a piece of work.

A piece of work with a button nose and the soft-est, most perfect skin he'd ever seen on a woman. She was built like a centerfold, dressed like a Goth princess, and had the face of a cherub. Every time he looked at her, he felt like the world's biggest fool.

So he tried not to look, tried not to come home very often. Hell, he hadn't been to Denver five times in the last seven months, but he'd already overstayed his welcome tonight. He could tell by the pain running down the middle of his chest. She gave him heartburn.

At least that's what he called it.

"No," he said. Hawkins was crazy if he thought she was invisible. Dylan saw her everywhere he went, from Bangkok to Paris, from L.A. to the Beltway. He saw her in his sleep. He'd spent one night in her company last January, chasing Creed Rivera across the city through the blizzard of the century, and he honest to God hadn't been the same since. Hour after hour of talking with her, being with her, and damn near dying of fear for her life had only exacerbated his incredibly inconvenient obsession. He was so out of line to want her the way he did.

"She can shoot and loot," Hawkins said.

The hell she could.

"Who has she ever shot?" he asked, then didn't wait for Hawkins to tell him, because he already knew. "No one, that's who."

It was impossible. Office managers and computer techs did not go out on missions, not even with an outlaw outfit like SDF. Sure, he'd taken her with him to find Creed that night, but only as a computer tech, not as an operator. And yes, things had gotten out of hand, and yes, she'd gotten into trouble up to her neck and gotten back out all on her own, but none of it had been planned.

Again, Hawkins didn't blink, just held his gaze, steady and sure, until Dylan finally got the message. Another shiver of alarm raced down his spine and damn near stopped his heart cold.

"What's been going on around here?" he asked, very quietly, very calmly, very certain he wasn't going to like the answer.

"It's a natural progression," Hawkins said, unperturbed. "She's been training for almost three years, and she's good, really good."

"Where was she good?" He couldn't believe this.

"Colombia. Kid and I took her with us as backup

on the Personal Security Detail we did for Occidental Petroleum in Bogotá."

"The one where two members of the National Revolutionary Forces were killed during a kidnap attempt?" He'd read the report, which hadn't had Skeeter's name on it anywhere. The FNG's—Fucking New Guy's—name, Travis James, had been on the report, but not Skeeter's.

Hawkins nodded, then hit a couple of keys on his computer when it beeped.

"She got the first kill," he said, looking back to Dylan.

Dylan, who couldn't breathe.

"They were waiting for us in the lobby of the hotel we were using as a safe house," Hawkins continued. "It was close-quarters combat, textbook CQC. She beat Kid on the draw, which neither you nor I could do on our best day."

She'd beaten Kid Chaos on the draw—and Dylan still couldn't breathe. She'd been in battle, with people shooting at her, trying to kill her.

"Has she been anyplace else?" he asked, his voice still so very calm.

To his credit, Hawkins finally looked uncomfortable. "Kabul."

"Afghanistan?" he asked, just in case, unbeknownst to him, there was a Kabul, Kansas, or a Kabul, Kentucky, like there was a Paris in Texas.

"Mostly just in Kabul, but a little bit up the Gayan Valley toward the Pakistani border."

Dylan's gaze went back to Hawkins's cast. "Where you almost got blown to smithereens?"

Hawkins shook his head. "We'd sent her back to the capital before we went up into the mountains."

"But she saw action."

It wasn't a question. He could see the truth on Hawkins's face.

"An ambush. The special forces soldiers we were with weren't too happy to have her along, and the Afghan militia guys were downright horrified, but when the Taliban hit, she didn't hesitate. The girl kicks ass, Dylan. She can hold her own, and she can certainly watch your back in Washington, where she's a damn sight more likely to get hit on than hit."

Unlike Skeeter, Dylan made no claims of clairvoyance, but he'd just gotten a very bad vibe.

"Hit?" he asked, working hard not to choke on the word.

"Skinned," she broke into the conversation, turning around and giving him the full benefit of her mirrored gaze.

Skinned. His heart lurched to a stop, then started back up on a ragged beat.

"It burned my pants, grazed my leg, and was gone. I didn't even feel it," she finished.

Bullshit.

He shifted his attention back to Hawkins. He'd

trusted Christian Hawkins with his life more times than he could count, real "end of the line, so help me God" times—but he no longer trusted the man with hers.

It was a wrenching realization.

For seventeen years, trusting Christian Hawkins had been the bedrock of his life. They'd been to hell and back, firefight hell where the odds had been against their chances of survival, the hell of losing two of their SDF brothers, and the black hell where a man was more dangerous to himself than anybody else on the planet. They'd pulled each other back from the razor's edge more than once, and once was all it took to cement a bond that went deeper than blood. If asked, Dylan would have said nothing would ever come between them, nothing could shake their friendship. They were solid.

But Skeeter had gotten "skinned" on a black ops mission in Afghanistan, of all the goddamn places for her to be, and Dylan's trust in Hawkins's judgment was shaken to the core. He'd known Christian was training her, and he'd known that what had started as a course in self-defense had turned into something far more demanding, far more serious. The girl had proven adept, skilled, and too uniquely suited to the clandestine world in which they worked not to be brought deeper into the fold.

But not as an operator in the line of fire. Never as an operator. Hawkins should have known that.

Keeping himself carefully under control, Dylan slowly rose from his chair. He was going into his office, his private office, where he could close the door and drink himself under his desk.

He didn't have a choice.

He couldn't afford to say something he was bound to regret, not where Hawkins was concerned, and his nerves were just a bit on edge. He needed a break, a vacation, something, before he snapped, and if he was still alive after he took care of General Grant's Godwin file disaster, he was going to disappear for a while, go someplace and see if he could get his head back on straight. Skeeter Bang was not for him, and he needed to convince himself of the fact before he did something irredeemably stupid. He had enough sins on his head without adding her to the list.

At the door to his office, he stopped and turned, his gaze meeting her damned mirrored sunglasses. It was probably a bad idea, but he had to say something—just a little something straight from the heart.

"I think it might be best if—" He stopped, recognizing a weak start when he got off to one. What he needed was to be honest, forceful but kind. He needed to use the authority of his position, and yet be reasonable.

"If I ever . . . *ever* . . . hear of you going out on another mission," he began again. "So help me God,

Skeeter Jeanne Bang, I'll bust you back down to grease monkey so fast, it'll make your head spin, and then I'll ship you up to Commerce City to work in the garage, sweeping floors for Johnny Ramos."

His words fell into an abyss of silence.

Okay, so it had been a carefully modulated threat, but it felt good, and he would deliver on it in a heartbeat. Guaranteed. And if he did say so himself, he was pretty damned impressed with how calm and steady he'd kept his voice. Listening to him, no one would ever guess how badly his heartburn was suddenly acting up. The pain was like a knife in his chest, and the nausea was about ready to double him over.

He turned to go. She'd killed a man and been hit by a bullet, and he needed a drink.

"Screw you."

He froze where he stood, his hand on the doorknob.

Screw you?

He wanted to paddle her himself, then shake her, then sit her down in a chair and explain to her why she must never, ever get herself in a situation where she could be shot at again—and then throw himself at her feet. It was all so tragically stupid, he couldn't bear it. He'd never been a sap over a woman, and she barely qualified for the designation. He knew exactly how much older he was than her, to the day, and he couldn't quite fathom his fascination. He'd never been attracted to younger women. So what was different about her . . . except everything?

Screw you?

He wasn't going to dignify the remark with a reply. He didn't dare, not when he'd fantasized about it more ways than she could possibly imagine. Scotch on the rocks was what he needed, something cold and serious. He did not need an argument with a tattooed, clairvoyant street rat who just happened to be the woman of his dreams.

CHAPTER

2

S KEETER WATCHED Dylan disappear into his office, her jaw so tight she couldn't speak, her hands clenched at her sides.

Commerce City, her ass. Johnny could sweep his own damn floors. SDF and Steele Street didn't run by themselves, and Dylan knew it as well as she did. He couldn't replace her in a month of Sundays, if ever.

"Well, that went pretty well," Hawkins said, turning back to his desk and continuing with the automobile inventory they'd been working on when Dylan had shown up. Typically, they'd had more acquisitions than sales so far this year, and even with seven floors of garage space, Steele Street was running out of places to put cars. Some of their stock had to go, and after half a day of careful deliberation, the two of them had narrowed the To Go list down to one nondescript, late-model Buick they called Sheila, the same name they used for all their nondescript, late-model Buicks. They had to do better—but not tonight. She was done, finished, out of there.

Almost.

"He's such a *jerk*," she said, her gaze still fixed on Dylan's office door.

"Sometimes."

She wanted to throw something at that door, like one of her boots. That ought to get his attention, a big old black mark on his pristine office door. He hadn't been home for two hours, and he'd already locked himself away—*double damn it all*. Things were supposed to be different this time.

"Why did you have to go and tell him about Afghanistan? That wasn't the plan." She turned on Hawkins, so frustrated, and angry, and hurt, she could bust. "The plan was just to tell him how good I was in Colombia. Let him warm up to the idea of me being part of the team. Remember?"

"Dylan's the boss." Hawkins's computer beeped again, and he tapped a couple more keys. "He needed to know, and the timing was right."

"No, it wasn't." Nothing was right. She was staring at Dylan's closed office door again, just like the last time he'd come home, and the time before that, and the time before that. It was almost more than she could bear. "You didn't tell him about Travis, and he was in Colombia, right next to me."

"Dylan has already okayed Travis for active duty."

Shock stunned her into dead silence, and for a long moment all she could do was stare at Hawkins. *Travis? Active for SDF? Unfreakingbelievable.*

"When?" she demanded to know, finally finding her voice. She was the one who had trained the angel boy. So how in the hell had he gotten authorized for duty before she had?

"Three weeks ago," Hawkins said.

And Travis hadn't told her. *Dammit.* She ought to—

"Hey, wait a minute," she said, startled out of one thought and slammed straight into another—another unfreakingbelievable thought. "Don't tell me Travis isn't visiting his cousin in San Francisco."

"Travis isn't visiting his cousin in San Francisco."

Double dammit.

"He's with Creed, isn't he?" She couldn't believe he'd lied to her. "In Colombia." But of course he'd lied to her. Travis James was too good a friend to deliberately hurt her feelings—and her feelings were hurt. Big-time.

"Yes," Hawkins said, not sounding the least bit concerned with her feelings. "He is."

Damn Dylan Hart. That man *really* needed to learn to appreciate her talents.

"I'm going to Washington." And by God, she was.

"Not without Dylan taking you, you aren't."

The hell she wasn't. She didn't need Dylan Hart to steal the Godwin file, and wouldn't that just fry his *machismo*, if she beat him to Whitfield's and stole the damn papers right out from under—

"Don't," Superman said.

Startled out of yet another thought, she jerked her head around. "Don't what?" *Geez*. What an amazing idea, an amazing plan. She could break into Whitfield's, snatch the Godwin file, and be back in time for—

"Don't think what you're thinking." Hawkins looked up from the keyboard. "Back up and rewind, Baby Bang. You're not going to Washington, not without Dylan's approval."

"Yes, I am." It was too perfect, the ultimate coup, the—

"No, you're not," he said, his steady gaze adding enough weight to his words to make a girl think twice.

But damn. It would be so easy.

"I could." Honestly, she didn't have a doubt in her mind.

"I know you could," he agreed. "And you're too good to spend the rest of your life knocking around the office, but it's got to be by the book from here on out."

"What book?" SDF didn't have a book.

"The Skeeter Jeanne Bang Rule Book, all eight volumes of it."

Except for that book. *Dammit*.

"He'll come around," Hawkins said. "Just give it a little time. Let me talk to him tonight."

Time. She let her gaze go back to Dylan's door. She'd run out of time—again. *Damn him*. He'd closed himself into his private office, and if everything went the way it usually did, that was it. He'd be gone in the morning, and she wouldn't see him again for weeks, months.

Suddenly, it wasn't almost more than she could bear, it was *way* more than she could bear.

"Talk all you want. I'm out of here," she said, turning on her heel and heading for the door that led to the garage. It was eight o'clock on a Friday night, and she was going to blow off some steam. All she needed was a fast car, nerves of steel, and to throw down some cash at the Midnight Doubles.

The car was waiting for her out in the bay. The cash was in her hip pocket, and her nerves were pure titanium alloy. Just let the rice-car boys try to mess with her tonight. She'd bury them up to their eyeballs in asphalt.

———

DYLAN'S office was a refuge of near-Zen simplicity, containing a desk with two black laptops, a lamp, and a phone. The bookcases and file drawers were made out of beech and matched the desk and the door. Pale green woven-grass wallpaper covered the walls. There were no photographs, no plants, no loose supplies scattered anywhere.

The main office, where everybody worked, was full of high-tech equipment and gadgetry and enough Scandinavian-designed furniture to host a team meeting with a cocktail party on the side. There was only one chair in Dylan's office—for a reason.

He settled into that chair with a bottle of Scotch and a glass of ice he set on the desk. The bottle was almost empty, which didn't bode well for his plans.

Neither did the sudden roar and rumble coming from the garage. The ice in the glass shimmied. The floor hummed, and the walls shook with the power of the engine *somebody* was firing up out in the bays.

"*Sonuvabitch,*" he muttered, lofting himself out of the chair. Dylan couldn't recognize every single car Steele Street owned by the sound of their engine—but he recognized this one. It was unmistakable, and it wasn't supposed to exist. He'd personally given the destruction order back in January, and the best damn mechanic they had was supposed to have obeyed.

Instead, she was out in the garage giving it gas and making the whole place rattle.

The girl was *completely* out of control. Somebody needed to take her in hand, rein her in, put a leash on her, *something*, and it obviously wasn't going to be Superman.

He jerked the door open.

"Where in the hell is she going?"

Hawkins checked his watch, then looked up. "At eight o'clock on a Friday night in August, I'd say she's going to the Midnight Doubles."

"Driving Mercy?" He couldn't believe it.

"That would be my guess," Hawkins said, oddly undisturbed by a situation that Dylan found damn near apocalyptic—Skeeter racing Mercy against a bunch of idiot weekend road warriors who didn't know their torque from their alternators. He'd done his share of street racing, and it was a freaking free-for-all. The miracle was that more people didn't go down in flames.

He tightened his hold on the bottle of Scotch. "She was supposed to tear that engine down last January," he said as calmly as possible. "I gave a direct order."

Mercy was a monster, a 1969 Chevy Nova with a 427 and a zero to sixty of under four seconds, and that was before Skeeter and Creed had modified her. With high-octane gas and ten pounds of boost, the dynamic duo had gotten the Nova up to 700 hp, making her absofuckinglutely lethal on the streets.

"It would take a papal bull to get Skeeter to destroy Mercy," Hawkins said.

"She isn't Catholic," he said, feeling another nerve snap and unravel and go straight down the toilet.

"She's not stupid, either, Dylan." Hawkins turned back to the computer. "You need to give her a chance. You need to stop staring at her ass and take her to Washington, D.C."

Well, that was pretty close to the last damn thing he wanted to hear—and it was wrong, to boot. What he needed, what he really needed, was to take her to bed, but he wasn't going to do that, either. As a matter of fact, he wasn't going to think about it anymore. He was done, finished, moving on.

"Call her and tell her to get her butt out of that car and back up to this office." That's what he needed to do—give orders. And what everybody else needed to do was obey them.

But once again, it didn't look like he was going to get what he needed.

The look Hawkins gave him said he was completely deluded. "You must have her confused with the other Skeeter Jeanne, the one who does what I tell her to do, because the one out there"—he gestured toward the windows overlooking the garage—"that one pretty much does whatever the hell she wants to do, especially when she's off the clock."

As if to prove his point, a pair of tires started winding up out in the garage. Within seconds a cloud of smoke rolled against the windows.

Sonuvabitch.

Dylan strode over and looked down at the rows of cars filling the bays. They were some of Steele Street's finest—Trina, his AC/Cobra roadster; half a dozen of Quinn's Camaros; a lot of classic muscle from the late sixties and early seventies, including Hawkins's 1971 Dodge Challenger, the mighty Roxanne; and in the middle of them all, Skeeter, tempting fate, God, and the wrath of the ventilation system.

Mercy was screaming when Skeeter finally released her brakes and tore down the garage, burning rubber all the way, heading for the freight elevator.

Dylan's heart lodged in his throat. *Fuck.*

The building wasn't long enough for that freaking trick.

Sure, he'd done it, which was why he could hardly breathe. At sixteen, he'd come within inches of dying in flight, airborne behind the wheel of a fastback Shelby Mustang.

At the last possible second, Skeeter eased down on the brakes and downshifted, driving Mercy home. The Nova slid into the freight elevator like warm butter, no danger, no drama—except for the heart attack she'd given him.

Okay. That was it. She was done. Finished. He was clipping her wings.

He looked back at Hawkins, who tossed him a set of keys.

"You'd better take Roxanne," Hawkins said. "Where Skeeter's going is no place for a nice girl like Trina."

Skeeter wasn't going anywhere, Dylan could A-1 guarantee it, but he took the keys anyway.

Anybody who wanted to play chicken with the seventh floor ended up in the old freight elevator, the one that looked like an upended Gothic catwalk clinging to the outside of the building, the one that took fifteen minutes to reach street level. The new elevator on the other side of the building would get him there in two.

HAWKINS felt the rattle of the door when it slammed, and he heard Dylan slip on the first stair and swear.

Christ. He released a weary sigh and let his head drop down on the desk.

The boss had it bad, but no worse than Baby Bang.

A year ago, he would have murdered Dylan in his sleep if he'd messed around with Skeeter. But a lot had changed in the last twelve months—most of all Skeeter. She wasn't the same girl she'd been. She was stronger, inside and out. Sometimes he looked at her and wasn't sure what he'd created, or if he'd had a damn thing to do with her transformation.

Oh, he took full credit for her four-inch groups with a .45 at twenty-five yards. And her deadly roundhouse kick—that was all his. She could break a guy's balls without breaking a sweat, because he'd taught her how. But there was no way on earth to teach someone how to beat Kid Chaos on the draw. That was pure mad instinct. He'd never seen anybody beat Kid on the draw, not and double-tap a guy who was shooting back.

Skeeter had done it with split-second timing, two shots to the chest on her first mission. She'd been just as effective in Afghanistan.

He hadn't been lying when he'd said she was too good not to be utilized. She was an instant advantage on the playing field, an instant leveler when the odds were against them, and she needed to be at Dylan's back when he went up against Whitfield's security. If Grant wanted the Godwin file bad enough to sic SDF on a U.S. senator, it had to be something worth protecting. The mission wouldn't be a walk in the park. They never were, no matter how simple they looked at the outset, and he'd be damned if he let the boss go in alone when Skeeter was ready, willing, and able. Dylan had been walking the razor's edge these last few months, taking the kind of chances Hawkins thought they'd talked each other out of a long time ago, like the job he'd just pulled off in Jakarta. The boss had been a little short on details, but Hawkins knew Jemaah Islamiah, an Indonesian terrorist group, wasn't to be fucked with, and he knew that over the course of his last mission, Dylan had single-handedly gang-banged every cell of Jemaah tangos from the Bay of Bengal to the Banda Sea, diverting seventeen million dollars of their high-grade heroin slush fund into a numbered Swiss bank account owned by the Indonesian government, for which favor the Indonesians had vowed eternal gratitude to the United States.

A useful thing, seventeen million dollars' worth of eternal gratitude—so was teamwork, damned useful, but Dylan seemed to have forgotten all about teamwork. He'd always been SDF's lone wolf, but the boss had been working without a net all year, and it was taking a toll. He looked like hell, pure, unadulterated, rehashed, warmed-over, rode-hard-and-put-away-wet hell. Dylan was falling apart, whether he knew it or not, and Hawkins wasn't going to let it get him hurt, not on Hawkins's watch—and at Steele Street, every watch was his watch.

With a couple of keystrokes, he closed the inventory program and opened a coded e-mail account. Sure enough, General Grant had sent a few files. Hawkins opened the first one and started downloading the attachments. As always, he was impressed with the general's intel. If SDF had a secret weapon, it was their commanding officer. From what he was seeing, it looked like Grant had raided the Secret Service's files. Detailed diagrams of the Whitfield mansion flashed on the screen, along with diagrams of the security system and Grant's notes on the safe he'd seen in Whitfield's office.

Last, but not least, was a memo detailing an invitation that would be waiting for Dylan at his hotel. Senator and Mrs. Arthur Whitfield were hosting a reception for the British ambassador tomorrow night. Dylan would be going as Michael Deakins, a State Department aide assigned to the ambassador.

White Rook. No one else could have arranged such a perfect cover at a moment's notice, and Hawkins didn't have a doubt in the world that given a few more moments, White Rook could arrange another.

He typed in his request, then sat back in his chair to wait.

He didn't have to wait long. In a couple of minutes, he got confirmation: Mr. Michael Deakins would be taking his wife, Jeanette, to the party.

A grin curved the corners of his mouth. Dylan had better batten down his hatches, because Skeeter looked good in Versace. Damn good.

CHAPTER

3

DENVER WAS her city.

From LoDo to the suburbs, Skeeter had tagged it a thousand times. Anyone who'd been on the streets or in the alleys had seen SB303 spray-painted on a wall somewhere.

But that was all in the past.

She ruled with a new kind of power now, the power of hard-won skill and the undeniable power of 427 cubic inches of displacement. She ruled Mercy, and Mercy ruled the streets, especially the two-mile stretch of abandoned highway east of the city known as the Doubles.

She slowly drove the Nova toward the middle of

the cars parked alongside the rubber-marked pavement. There were close to a hundred vehicles lining the sides of the highway, and people started gathering around her long before she pulled the car to a stop.

"Hey, Skeeter," somebody yelled.

"Hey. It's Skeeter Bang," another guy called out.

"*Shit*," someone swore.

Skeeter grinned. Anyone expecting to make some cash tonight wouldn't be glad to see her or Mercy, but for the most part, she didn't pay the crowd any mind. The racing hadn't started yet. Bets were still being laid down, with bottles of beer, half-smoked joints, and a drugstore's worth of chemicals changing hands along with the money. Music blasted out of dozens of cars along the strip.

The Midnight Doubles were as much a party as a car race, with no rules for either, but head to head at over a hundred miles per hour was no place to be paired with a drunk, or somebody too stoned to stay on top of their game. Skeeter always checked out the drivers even more than she did the cars.

Tonight's crowd looked like they'd started the party early—maybe too early. B. B. Heaney had already blown his engine. Smoke was pouring out from under his Mustang's hood. The rice boys were gunning up and down the highway, but nobody was setting anything off yet, and from the looks of Rob North and the girl hanging all over him and his

Hemi 'Cuda, racing was the last thing on his mind. Gino Cuchara and his crew looked ready to go, but Skeeter wouldn't race Gino. He got mean when he lost, and Skeeter didn't think his girlfriend could take too many more beatings—and why that was her problem, she didn't know. Lots of people got beaten all the time.

She'd been beaten. It was a weird thing for a kid—and not at all what she wanted to be thinking about tonight.

Cripes. She let out a sigh and tucked a loose strand of hair behind her ear, then gently touched the scar that began at the corner of her eye. It went for five long, jagged inches, up through her eyebrow and across her forehead. It didn't hurt anymore, hadn't for a long time, but she didn't like looking at it and knew nobody else did, either, so she wore her hat and her sunglasses and did her best to forget the night Superman had carried her out of that flophouse on Wazee Street, both of them soaked in her blood.

Geez. Her life was weird. She was weird.

And she'd outgrown the Doubles.

She'd known it before she'd gotten halfway out of town.

She pulled to a stop at the end of the line and cut Mercy's engine. Reaching across the seat, she picked up her pack of Faros and knocked one out, then slipped the pack between her belt and her skirt. Her small stash of kitchen matches was in her back pocket, and after striking one across her belt, she lit up.

Oh, yeah. That helps, she thought, letting out a billow of smoke.

It was a crappy habit, but she couldn't say she didn't like it, or that she probably wouldn't try quitting again pretty soon—just not tonight.

Leaning forward, she draped herself over the steering wheel, took another long drag, and watched the crowd.

She didn't belong here, not anymore, not after Colombia, not after Afghanistan. She belonged with Superman, and Kid, and Creed. She belonged on active duty with Travis, dammit, and she belonged with Dylan—maybe not the way she wanted, but professionally she belonged with him, and stomping off into the night was not the way to prove it.

Screw you?

What in the world had she been thinking?

Nothing, that's what. She hadn't been thinking at all. She'd let her emotions get the better of her common sense and said something incredibly juvenile to the one person on earth she most wanted to treat her like an adult.

Screw you?

Double freaking cripes. She dropped her forehead down on the steering wheel. Even a simple heist needed planning, intel, equipment. She could have helped get it all together, maybe impressed the hell out of him, maybe earned herself a slot on the mission. Hawkins wanted someone in Washington to watch Dylan's back, and she could do it. Helping SDF's boss steal the Godwin file was the perfect opportunity for her to prove herself to him. All she had to do was get him to take her to Washington, D.C.

Right, she thought.

A heavy sigh escaped her, and she scanned the crowd again. She hadn't driven all the way out to the Doubles to smoke cigarettes and get all maudlin, and she hadn't really driven out here to kick Rob North's or B. B. Heaney's butt in the quarter mile. She needed something, and when she saw Johnny Ramos heading her way, she knew she'd found it—spooky or not, weird or not, like every other girl on the planet, sometimes she needed somebody to pour her heart out to, sometimes she needed a friend.

DYLAN pulled Roxanne to a stop well down in the pack, being sure to keep out of everyone's headlights. Hawkins's Challenger was a legend at the Midnight Doubles.

Christ. The Doubles.

He looked around at the cars and the kids, at the drugs and the trouble just waiting to happen, and had to ask himself what in the hell he was doing there.

Unfortunately, the answer was pretty damn simple—Skeeter Bang.

Curiosity and women were a combination that had gotten him in plenty of trouble over the years, but he'd still given in to it, because he was damned curious about her, about her friends and how she spent her time, about what she liked and where she went. He knew what she did for SDF—or at least he'd thought he'd known, up until Hawkins had dropped his H-bombs.

Shit. He hated to even think about people shooting at her. She could die on a mission. It happened, which was all the reason he needed not to take her to Washington with him.

Yeah, he knew the chances were a hundred to one against even a single shot being fired on the Godwin file heist, a thousand to one—unlike his odds tonight, which were running a hundred to one in favor of his heartburn getting a whole helluva lot worse before it got any better.

He leaned forward over the steering wheel, staring out the windshield, his gaze narrowing.

Sonuvabitch. A tall, dark-haired kid was walking up to Mercy, and Skeeter was getting out with a smile on her face, looking damn glad to see him. Even from the back, something about the guy looked familiar, but it wasn't until he wrapped his arms around Skeeter and turned sideways that Dylan recognized him. Johnny Ramos. *Sonuvabitch*. The kid was here, and he had his hands all over her.

All over—around her waist, sliding up the middle of her back, squeezing her upper arms, coming to rest on her hips. *Geezus*. He went for her ass, a move Dylan would have put money on, but Skeeter caught his hand and gave him a little punch. The kid grinned.

Dylan's jaw locked.

Eighteen, that's how old Johnny was, and at the rate he was going, he'd be damn lucky to see nineteen.

Which was ridiculous. Dylan had no claim on her, and she didn't need him to handle Johnny Ramos. He'd seen her spar with Hawkins, and if she didn't like Ramos grabbing her ass, she could break him in half.

But she wasn't breaking anything—except his heart.

He swore under his breath. He was too old for this, chasing after girls in cars and losing out to a freaking teenager.

He didn't fire up Roxanne, though, and he didn't look away. He watched Johnny hold her, watched them talk, watched Skeeter's lips move, her head resting on Johnny's shoulder. He waited and watched as a tear rolled out from under her mirrored sunglasses and made a wet track on her baby soft cheek—watched Johnny wipe it off with the pad of his thumb.

Fuck. He'd done that to her. Dylan knew it as well as he knew how stupid it was to be sitting in the dark watching this little drama play itself out.

Crying. Because he'd been a bastard and shut her down.

She'd be twenty-one on Sunday. He'd already bought her a dozen presents, things from all over the world, but only one would have his name on it—a set of spinners for Babycakes, her '65 Shelby-Mustang GT 350. It was sacrilege, putting spinners on a classic, but he knew Skeeter would love them, and they'd look great on the Mustang, pure pimping.

He wished to hell she was driving the Shelby tonight. Mercy had earned her name because she had none. The garages at Steele Street were full of beasts, but the Nova was Godzilla on wheels, fire-breathing, a barely street legal force of destruction. The last thing he wanted to see was Skeeter going head to head with Mercy against one of the Midnight Doubles road warriors, most of whom looked like they spent as much time altering their brain chemistry as they did altering their cars. That would be even worse than what he was seeing now—Skeeter and Johnny plastered against each other.

It shouldn't hurt as much as it did.

He pushed himself back into the seat.

She was his. He didn't know where he'd gotten such a crazy idea, but it had been in his head for months, dogging him, and avoiding her wasn't helping matters. He was worse off now than he'd been in January.

He needed to change tactics. He needed a new plan.

He needed, somehow, to figure out a way to work her out of his system without taking her clothes off, because that would be easy—easy for him and real hard on her. If he put his mind to it, he could have her in his bed tonight. He was so fucking smooth, and she was so freaking young, and he knew how she looked at him from behind those damn sunglasses. But he also knew himself, and once he'd had her, his obsession would be over. He'd move on, and there she'd be at Steele Street, hurt and disillusioned, every time he came home, every time he showed up to put a mission together.

He honest to God didn't think he could face her under those circumstances, or if he'd get much of a chance to face anything under those circumstances. Hawkins would murder him in his sleep if he hurt her like that, and Creed would be the one handing him the knife. Kid would hold Dylan down so Superman could get a good clean cut, right through the old jugular, and he wouldn't blame any of them. They all loved her—and all he did was want her.

Swearing under his breath, he lifted his hips off

the seat and dug a roll of antacids out of his pocket. She was killing him. He threw half a dozen of the chewable tablets in his mouth, not knowing why he bothered. They never helped.

Christ. Her shoulders were shaking, and Johnny was rocking her back and forth, and Dylan had to wonder just how much worse this whole scene was going to get—and whether or not he was going to be able to handle it without getting out of the car and going over to her.

He tossed back a couple more antacids and washed them down with a swig of Scotch out of the bottle he'd brought with him.

Fuck. There was another way.

Before he could think the damn thing through and admit what a shit-for-brains idea it was, he dug his phone out of his other pocket and flipped it open.

"Uptown Autos. Superman here," Hawkins answered.

"In your dreams."

Hawkins let out a short laugh. "Don't tell me you lost her."

"No. I'm at the Doubles, and Mercy's parked up the line."

"And Skeeter?"

"Laminated to Johnny Ramos." Like plastic wrap on Jell-O, a real airtight seal.

"You want me to get a bucket of water?"

Yes. "Call her. Tell her she's in."

"Good idea" was all Hawkins said after a slight pause, as if Dylan hadn't just reversed his earlier decision by a full one hundred and eighty degrees, as if it really was a good idea—which it wasn't. He just didn't know what in the hell else to do with her.

"The Godwin file isn't a combat mission," he said, as if that made his change of mind perfectly reasonable, perfectly justifiable.

"No, it isn't," Hawkins agreed, still so damnably calm.

"I'll set her up as surveillance." And the job was CONUS, in the continental United States. Even if things went bad, they wouldn't get too bad, not on a fairly straightforward heist, and nothing like what he'd been up against halfway around the world these last few months, where things had gone bad more times than he cared to remember, especially in Indonesia. He was either slipping, or he was being set up, and he hadn't been able to figure out which.

"She's good at surveillance," Hawkins said. "Hold on. I'm calling her on the other line."

Up ahead, Skeeter had broken free of Johnny and reached into Mercy to get her phone. Dylan couldn't hear what Hawkins was saying, but he saw Skeeter wipe the back of her hand across her cheek, saw her straighten up, take a stance—take another step away from Johnny.

Good. That was better. He felt a measure of his own tension dissipate, felt the pain in his gut ease. Yeah, this could work. This was *going to* work.

Then suddenly it wasn't working at all.

Skeeter looked down the line, sliding her gaze over the cars parked at the side of the road until she landed on Roxanne.

Goddammit.

"What are you doing?" he asked Hawkins.

"This is your chance to be the good guy, Dylan," Superman said. "Run with it."

The last thing Dylan heard over the phone was Hawkins hanging up.

Run with it. Right.

She started across the drag strip, her strides long and forceful, her hips swaying inside the little scrap of black leather she called a skirt, and he swore again. Face time had not been in his plan. But she was going to be in his face in sixty seconds or less, with the high ground in her favor if he didn't get out of the car.

Dammit. He shoved Roxanne's door open and slid out from behind the wheel. When Skeeter stepped off the pavement, he was ready, standing next to the Challenger, waiting. He was the boss, he reminded himself. He was the adult, and he was in charge.

"Sir," she said, coming to a stop in front of him

and, of all the unexpected things, sticking her hand out.

"Uh, Skeeter," he said, taking her hand in his and giving it a firm shake. Sir? From the girl who not an hour ago had told him to go screw himself?

"Superman said you wanted to see me." She took an at-ease stance that only upped his unease. Hip-shot attitude was her normal pose.

But he could live with this. Sure he could. As a matter of fact, he liked it—a lot. Polite condescension to his authority was exactly the right mind-set for her to be cultivating. She was a smart girl. He should have known she would figure it out. She'd just needed a little nudge in the right direction. Obviously, his ultimatum had been the perfect course of action to take. He'd finally gotten something from her he wanted—submission.

Yeah. He could live with that.

Feeling better about his decision to bring her in on the job, he allowed himself to relax half a degree.

"I gave the Godwin mission another look," he told her. "And I can use you in Washington."

Her reaction was instantaneous, and if at any time in the last three years he had realized what a magical effect those words would have, he would have been using them every day. He would have made stuff up just to say them, bent over backward to create all sorts of scenarios just so he could say "I can use you in Washington" and watch the world's most amazing smile break across her face—those soft lips curving, a blush coming into her cheeks, her whole countenance suddenly and unequivocally radiating happiness.

Hell. Hawkins had been right. Being the good guy definitely came with some perks. He should have tried it earlier, instead of specializing in being such a coldhearted son of a bitch.

"That's great," she said, the breathless catch in her voice being another unexpected perk, the way it wrapped around his heart and slid down to his groin—which was exactly the kind of reaction to her he was trying to avoid.

"I'm glad you think so," he said, allowing his smile to broaden even as he told himself to take it easy. A breathless and submissive Skeeter Bang was not a breathless, submissive, and naked Skeeter Bang—and it wasn't going to be. Ever.

"I won't let you down."

"I'm sure you won't." And he was. She was perfect for the job. "I need a driver."

"A driver?" She sounded somewhat surprised.

He nodded, damn pleased with his solution to tonight's mess. "You'll be responsible for all our transportation in Washington—from the airport to the hotel, to the Whitfield mansion, where you will station yourself with the car for surveillance of the area while I lift the Godwin file, and then from the Whitfield mansion back to the hotel, and from there to the airport. If things go as planned, we should be home sometime late tomorrow night. You can also drive us from Steele Street to Denver International." He added the last as a bonus. She deserved it.

"You want me to drive you around Washington, D.C., and wait in the car at Whitfield's?"

"Yes." He nodded again, figuring that pretty much summed it up. "You will, of course, be armed." Another little bonus he felt justified in offering. The girl knew her way around a pistol. That was for damn sure.

"I see," she said, glancing back over her shoulder for a brief second before bringing her attention back to him. "And you're sure I can handle all this?"

"Absolutely."

"Because I wouldn't want you to have any doubts."

"I don't," he assured her.

"Well, good. That's great, Mr. Hart," she said, pulling out a pack of cigarettes from where she had them tucked into her belt and knocking one into her hand. "But I've got to confess, I have a couple of concerns."

Sir *and* Mr. Hart. There had been a time, a brief time last January, when she'd called him Dylan, but he was willing to pay the price of familiarity if it kept her safe.

"And what would those be?" He watched as she

put the cigarette in her mouth, tucked the pack of Faros back into her belt, and then struck a match off her knife sheath. Cupping her hand around the flame, she held it to the cigarette and inhaled.

It annoyed the hell out of him, the whole damn smoking thing, and he was just about to mention it, politely of course, when she looked up and exhaled a small, perfect smoke ring right at him. It floated through the night air, getting bigger and bigger, until it wreathed his face and broke up.

Geezus. A smoke ring. In his face.

He was no longer annoyed. Oh, hell no. He was so relieved, it was all he could do not to grin. Drag-strip girls blowing smoke rings were not girls on the verge of tears.

"I think it's important that we trust each other," she said, finishing her exhale and flicking the short end of ash off her cigarette.

Trust? Now, there was a double dog dare if he'd ever heard one.

"Trust each other's decisions," she continued. "If we're going to be a team."

"I trust you." And he did—to drive him around Washington, D.C., and drive him crazy. If that was the dare, he was in, probably in over his head, but as long as she wasn't crying, he could take a little craziness.

Geezus. A smoke ring.

"Good. That's good," she said, her gaze straying

over his shoulder. She gave someone a quick lift of her head, and he got a bad feeling—a feeling that only got worse when he heard some monster engine start up down the line.

"And your other concern? You said you had a couple." It took everything he had not to look and see who she'd signaled.

She paused for a second before speaking. "I think you'll feel more comfortable working with me if you concentrate on my skills rather than my age, if you just forget how old I am."

Not bloody damn likely. Not with that face.

"Sure. Good idea."

"And you shouldn't think of me as a girl. Ever," she said, looking him as straight in the eye as someone in mirrored sunglasses could, which was surprisingly straight. He could feel her gaze holding his. "I don't want you trying to take care of me when you need to be taking care of yourself."

Not think of her as a girl.

Right.

Using every ounce of restraint he had, he kept his gaze from dropping down the front of her, down the curves of her breasts, down her slim hips, down the endless length of her legs, and he was still doomed. He'd worked with women in the field and never given sex a thought, but he wasn't going to forget Skeeter Bang was a girl—ever.

"Do your job. Drive the car. And we won't have

any problems," he said, his voice calm and steady, so steady, he almost believed it himself.

"Great. Then we're okay to go."

"Okay to go," he agreed. "We'll have a mission briefing at eight o'clock. In the morning." That was early . . . but maybe not early enough. "With a pre-briefing meeting at seven-thirty." That was really early. Honestly, she should just pack up Mercy and go home, which had absolutely nothing to do with her age or gender, or how much he trusted her.

Liar. He didn't trust her as far as he could throw her right now, not with the big boys starting their engines and Mercy sitting on the other side of the strip, looking like she could eat every car at the Doubles and still have room for dessert.

But he didn't think leaving was what Skeeter had in mind.

Her next words proved it.

"I'll see you at the office, then, seven-thirty A.M. sharp." She stuck out her hand again, and he took it for another firm shake, working hard not to just pack her up and take her home. "Thank you for the opportunity, sir. You won't regret it."

He already did, but before he could voice his concerns, she was off, striding back toward Mercy.

He did look over his shoulder then, and sure enough, there was a guy down the line with a shit-eating grin on his face, watching her, a big guy in a muscle shirt, with a bald head. The man was leaning on a cherry red, 1970 Hemi 'Cuda, and when he straightened up and opened the hood, Dylan's bad feeling got even worse.

He knew what was going to happen next, and every one of his instincts told him to stop it, to grab her and stop it before it got started.

"Hey, Johnny!" he heard her shout, her voice unmistakable.

He turned back to the strip and saw her walking up the double yellow stripe running down the middle of the road, one long-legged stride after another, headed for the Nova.

"Pop the hood and break out the ice!"

Ice. *Goddammit*.

"What about the meats?" Johnny hollered back, and Dylan could have wrung his neck.

"Change 'em," she said.

Dammit.

She'd come ready to tear the place up, with ice to cool down her intake, and Mercy's slicks to put more rubber on the road, and he was going to have to stand there and watch it all happen. Trust, she'd said. Trust her to make the right decision—like eating a goddamn Hemi-powered Barracuda at the Midnight Doubles.

HE WANTED a driver? Well, hell, Skeeter would show him a driver. She'd take Mercy and drive Rob North's 'Cuda straight into the ground.

He wanted her to sit and wait outside Whitfield's while he did the mission alone? Well, hell, nobody did sit and wait better than she did. She'd been sitting and waiting for seven months for a chance like he'd just given her.

And she wasn't going to blow it. Hell, no. But neither was she going to roll over and play dead. He was going to have to get another girl for that gig—like one of his MBA, Ph.D., fashion model look-alike girlfriends. He had a million of them, without a street rat in the bunch. There were no bad girls in his lineup, only the cream of the American social strata. And that was the reality check she needed. Dylan Hart was never going to be hers.

Never.

But from the first moment she'd seen him, when she'd still looked like something out of a freak show, with the stitches running across her forehead, her one eye blackened, and her lip swollen, and him looking like a poster boy for a polo club, she'd been in love—stupid, calf-eyed, unrequited love.

He was the most physically arresting man she'd ever seen, his face the stone-cold definition of hard-edged elegance, his dark hair silky and always perfectly cut, the broadness of his shoulders accentuated by the lean musculature of his body. He was the brains behind SDF, the boy who'd started the chop shop on Steele Street with a crew of teenage car thieves. He was the boss, and he was a mystery, his past nonexistent. There was no Dylan Hart, no birth certificate, no medical records, no Social Security number, no anything anywhere before he'd been sixteen and gotten arrested for grand theft auto—nothing except a faint trail she'd followed to a name, five million dollars, and a seventeen-year-old scandal.

The name was Liam Dylan Magnuson, the money had never been found, and the date coincided with when Dylan had shown up in Denver, but she had not been able to make a positive connection between

Liam Dylan Magnuson and her Dylan Hart, nothing she could take to the bank, or to Superman for confirmation.

Her Dylan Hart—she let out a small snort. He wasn't ever going to be hers. Not in this life, and probably not in the next.

Cripes. Just what she needed, more bad news.

She dropped her cigarette on the asphalt and ground it out with the toe of her boot. He'd made it clear what he thought of her—incompetent. *Geez.* Sit and wait in the car while he stole the Godwin file.

He either hadn't been listening back at the office, or he didn't want to believe she'd comported herself with commendable professionalism her first two times out with Superman. He saw her as a child, but if he stuck around, that was going to change.

No child could have built Mercy. No child could take Rob North in the quarter mile. It took more than guts and speed to get the Nova to the finish line in one piece and ahead of the competition. It took skill and the lightning-quick reflexes she'd honed against Superman. It took some brains.

She checked the ice pack Johnny had put on the intake, then knelt next to him at Mercy's left rear wheel to help with the lug nuts. After they'd switched out the tires, she started her final check of the car.

THE half inch of Scotch in the bottom of Dylan's bottle wasn't nearly enough to get him drunk, which was fine. No matter what happened in the next twelve seconds, he still had to drive home.

Twelve fucking seconds—or less. He knew what Mercy could do.

The Nova and the 'Cuda were on the line, clouds of smoke lingering over the tires the drivers had heated up during their burnouts, the engines rumbling, chassis shaking with barely suppressed energy. There were no lights at the Doubles. Cars staged on a white stripe painted across the asphalt. They launched at the drop of a flag.

His gaze went from the muscled skinhead piloting the 'Cuda to Skeeter in Mercy, and something tightened in his chest. She was otherworldly beautiful, sitting in the black beast, her skin porcelain in the glare of a hundred headlights, her expression calm, her focus unerring. The ball cap and her sunglasses had been jettisoned in the pre-race preparations, allowing him a rare and wondrous glimpse of what she really looked like—and she looked like an angel, her face framed by platinum blond bangs chopped into half a dozen different lengths, the rest of her hair bluntly cut in longer and longer layers until it all went up into the ponytail that hung over her shoulder. But it was her face that did him in, every time. He lusted after her body, but he was a fool for that face, the innocence and the violence of it never failing to turn him inside out.

And she was ready to rumble, one hand on the wheel, the other on Mercy's shifter.

Trust, he thought, taking another swallow of Scotch.

Trust her not to annihilate herself.

The flag dropped. His heart stopped. Time slowed.

He felt the roll of the throttle in his pulse, felt the power surge of 427 cubic inches of displacement let loose. The 'Cuda's tires spun for the barest fraction of a second, and the race was lost. Skeeter's launch was solid, pure. She hit sixty miles per hour in under four seconds, over a hundred miles per hour well before the finish line, fast enough to give the spectators whiplash. She held to her lane like an arrow, so straight, so clean, so motherfreaking quick, like a cat off the line, the Hemi 'Cuda on her ass the whole way.

There was no luck involved.

It was all engineering, mechanics, skill, and nerve, the last of which he seemed to have in damn short supply when it came to watching her race. *Jesus.* The hand he had around the bottle was shaking. He'd rather endure the elevator trick five times a day than see her go up against some unknown street delinquent again, ever.

He needed to find her another hobby—like covert ops.

Okay. That was good. That plan was already in place. Taking her to Washington and parking her in a senator's driveway was probably as close as he was going to get to keeping her out of trouble.

Great.

He took the last swallow of Scotch and headed back to Roxanne. For once, it seemed he'd made the right decision when it came to little Miss Hell-on-Wheels.

CHAPTER 5

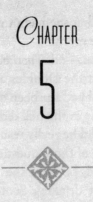

OR NOT. Dylan thought for the hundredth time in the last ten hours—including all the wee hours of the night during which he'd gotten damn little sleep and a little too much of his second bottle of Scotch.

He was sitting perfectly still at the conference table in SDF's main office, waiting for the briefing to begin, his sunglasses firmly in place, trying to keep his head from going off like a Titan missile, and trying to keep from staring at Skeeter as she downed her third doughnut.

He was failing on all counts, and the whole doughnut thing was making him queasy, not to mention the fact that she hadn't gotten home until four o'clock in the morning.

Four o'clock A.M.—*ante meridiem*.

He'd left her at the Doubles about ten o'clock. So what in the hell had she been doing between ten and four? And how in the hell did she look so fresh and rested—and did he really want to know the answer to either one of those questions?

No, he decided, because she obviously hadn't been up all night drinking Scotch and worrying about somebody. That's what he'd done, and he looked like hell.

Christ. He'd been insane to give in to all that juvenile angst at the track last night. He had no business taking her anywhere.

And now she had sugar on her nose, and on her lips. It was enough to fry a couple more dozen of his brain cells—and his brain cells were in damn short supply this morning. Great. Running out of brain cells, running out of nerve, he should never have come home.

"Goddammit, Dylan," Hawkins said from across the room. "Goddammit."

Well, that didn't sound very auspicious.

With effort, he slanted his gaze toward the fax machine, where Hawkins was reading a transmission as it came over the line.

Superman did not look happy.

"It's a goddamn commendation from the secretary of defense." Hawkins pulled the fax free, still reading. "A goddamn commendation."

Shit. That's all he needed at eight o'clock in the morning.

"Jakarta . . . Jemaah," Hawkins muttered, scanning the page. "Valor in action under the direst circumstances . . . tenacity . . . subsequent es—"

Abruptly, Hawkins stopped, his gaze frozen to the page. Then he shot a rapier-sharp glance across the office.

"Escape"—that was the word Superman had choked on, and quite frankly, Dylan didn't want to talk about it. As a matter of fact, he wasn't going to talk about it, especially in front of Skeeter.

With a softly muttered curse, Hawkins shifted his attention back to the fax and continued reading.

"Sumba," he said after a moment, speaking the word in a voice so cold, Dylan felt the hair rise on the back of his neck.

He took a careful breath, told himself to calm down. He wasn't surprised the island of Sumba was mentioned in the report. He just didn't like being reminded of the damn place, not that he wasn't thinking about Sumba and Hamzah Negara, the bastard who owned it, twenty-five out of every twenty-four hours in the day right now.

Hawkins didn't say another word, just stood there, staring at the fax, until finally, after an endless, tension-filled minute, he folded the piece of paper and put it in his pocket.

"Shouldn't I, uh, make a copy of that for the files?" Skeeter asked. "Maybe scan it into a documents folder?"

"No," both Dylan and Hawkins said at the same time, then looked at each other.

"No," Hawkins repeated, shifting his attention back to the plans.

Dylan hazarded a quick glance in Skeeter's direction. She was poised like a cat on the edge of her chair, doughnut paused in midair, curiosity damn near perking up her ears, and her gaze locked on Superman's pocket.

"But it's a commendation," she said. "General Grant likes to stockpile those things, use them for budget fodder."

"Not this commendation," Dylan said in a tone that would brook no argument. He wasn't too worried. The girl was nothing but trouble, but she was hell and gone out of luck if she thought she could lift that fax off Superman without him knowing it. Nobody was that good. His secret was safe, at least from her. Hawkins was another story, and Dylan could tell by the grim expression on Superman's face that he was going to want to talk about the Jakarta mission—a lot.

Too bad.

"I know just where to put it," Skeeter said, interrupting his train of thought.

He slanted her another glance. He obviously needed to work on his brook-no-argument tone.

"No."

"We have half a dozen folders on him, including the black ones, the ones that need top-secret clearance. If you don't want to see the commendation again, we could deep-six it into one of those, but it should be archived."

Deep-sixing into black files? Since when had she had access to SDF's top-secret documents?

He no sooner thought the question than he knew the answer: since she'd damn well figured out how to access them herself, that's since when. The girl ran wild at Steele Street.

And who in the hell "him" was she talking about? "Half a dozen files on who?"

"Negara," she said. "Hamzah Negara, the Indonesian warlord whose fortress is on the island of Sumba in the Sabu Sea."

If she'd meant to freeze him into place, she'd done a damn good job, and suddenly he regretted every ounce of Scotch. It was churning in his stomach, and if he got sick, he was going to feel like a royal fool.

"He's billing himself as an Islamic jihadist these days," she continued. "But he's cut more than a few deals with the CIA when it was to his advantage.

His legitimate businesses include controlling interest in the Java Resorts Group, and he's big into vice, with high stakes in prostitution and gambling. A lot of people think he's the power behind the Jai Traon pirates harassing the shipping lanes in the South China Sea, but his major source of income is still China White—Southeast Asian heroin."

And who in the hell, he wondered, had been briefing Skeeter on his missions?

He angled his gaze at Hawkins, who gave him a slow shake of his head.

Good God. Just how deeply had the girl gotten herself into the secrets of Steele Street and SDF? The potential answer to that question unnerved him. There were things she really shouldn't know—including what she'd just said.

"The commendation stays where it is." Non-existent, nothing but a piece of paper in a pocket.

Jakarta was behind him, and Washington, D.C., was here and now. They had the Godwin file to deal with, and after he stole the Godwin file, there'd be another mission, another job, and then another, until Negara was nothing but old business, best forgotten, and that's the way he wanted it. He did not want the damn Jakarta thing hanging over his head like a friggin' guillotine—but it was, ready to drop without a moment's notice.

But that was just him, and a little residual paranoia, which, really, was to be expected, considering where he'd been last week—at least where he thought he'd been, mostly.

Shit.

He brought his hand up and wiped it across his mouth. The cramped cell on the hillside was clear in his mind, the filth, the smell, the shackles, and his neighbor—the guy hanging next to him, dying. He'd been thrown into that cell, and he'd made his escape from that cell, but in between those two events, sometime between the dark days and darker nights, there had been someplace white, and clean, and excruciatingly bright.

It hurt even to think about it, how bright the place had been, the light almost blue, searing into his brain, making time stop. There had been nothing to hold on to in that place, no handhold for reality, and maybe there hadn't been any reality at all. Maybe the white place had been a drug-induced hallucination.

Because there had been drugs. God only knew what. God and the doctors on the U.S.S. *Jefferson,* he hoped.

After his escape, a Navy medical team had checked him over, inside and out, and told him he was fine—probably just fine. If the injections Negara had given him had been lethal, he would have already dropped over dead, probably. That had been five days ago, plenty of time for their antidotes to counteract the warlord's chemical soup—probably.

A week would be the true test.

Probably.

Shit.

He didn't have to look to know the bruises were still there, two of them up the inside of his right forearm, each with a tiny pinprick in the center where Negara's needles had gone in, three more where the Navy had run their counterattack. As an added—but probably unnecessary—precaution, the doctors had given him a series of backup antidotes, three injectable Syrettes safely nested in a square of foam rubber inside a small stainless steel case—red if his body temperature started to rise over the hundred-degree mark and/or he started hallucinating; blue if his temperature dropped below normal and/or his guts started turning inside out; and yellow if his heart stopped. So it was red—hot and whacked; blue—cold and puking; and yellow—dead. He felt like freaking Alice in Wonderland.

And, yeah, injecting himself with the yellow Syrette if his heart stopped was *probably* going to be a real good trick. He'd meant to tell Hawkins about the potential necessity for that particular procedure as soon as he'd walked into Steele Street last night—but he'd gotten distracted.

His gaze strayed back to Skeeter. Hell, he was still distracted, which made him wonder if instead of harboring a time-delay component, Negara's chemicals hadn't already taken full effect, simply making him stupid—because it was nothing but stupid to be so wound up about things, especially being so wound up about her. He had no business taking her anywhere. Stealing things was his business, his real business. Beautiful punk-rock girls and delayed-reaction toxic chemicals with names like NG4, XT7, and XXG2 were new fields for him—fields he wanted to get the hell out of as quickly as possible, preferably with all his parts still in working order.

Two more days.

That's all he needed.

He did not need Skeeter Bang driving him crazy and Hawkins giving him the evil eye. The commendation was a done deal, no matter what the two of them wanted.

"So how's Kat?" he asked, changing the subject to Superman's wife and hopefully taking the heat off himself.

And it worked. Something damn close to a smile actually came across Hawkins's face.

"Still pregnant," his friend said, the almost-smile broadening into the real thing.

"*Very* pregnant," Skeeter added. "She could go any minute."

"Not any minute," Hawkins disagreed, glancing over at the girl. "Kat's cervix is softening, but she's only dilated to two."

O-kay. So much for that subject. The last thing

Dylan wanted to talk about was Katya Hawkins's cervix—ever.

"So what are we dealing with at Whitfield's?" he asked, moving things along.

"A Halloran-Jenks security system for the estate," Hawkins said, returning his attention to the plans and running his finger over a scale drawing of the mansion. "Including video surveillance, with banks of cameras here, here, and here, a two-story office with keypad entry, and a biometric wall vault hidden behind a bank of bookcases on the second-floor loft."

"Biometric? Hell." That was going to take some preparation. It was going to take time. Something they didn't have.

"Yeah, I know, but Grant said he had Whitfield's fingerprints. He'll have them sent to your hotel," Hawkins said.

And that was the advantage of having a renegade general for a commanding officer. Grant knew how to get things like a senator's fingerprints. Hell, he'd probably lifted them himself last night, off of something in Whitfield's office.

"Wasn't that a Halloran-Jenks system we breached in Montreal?"

"The same, but Whitfield doesn't have the T-21 upgrades."

"Even better."

"The loft is semicircular," Hawkins continued. "It

rings half the upper floor and overlooks the main-floor office below. Access is via an open-cage elevator or a circular staircase. There are floor-to-ceiling windows on each end of the loft, looking out over the back of the estate. Access to the small room containing the vault is through Chaucer."

At Dylan's inquiring glance, Hawkins shrugged.

"Whitfield is old school, and he's hosting a reception for the British ambassador tonight. You'll be going as Michael Deakins, a State Department aide. The invitation for you and your wife, Jeanette, will be waiting for you at the hotel, along with—"

Whoa. Dylan held up his hand.

Whoa. Whoa. Whoa.

"—the appropriate identification, and a—" Hawkins's voice ground to a halt. "What?"

Wife?

He couldn't even get the word out. He pushed his sunglasses down on his nose, his gaze zeroing in on Hawkins. Superman couldn't possibly be thinking what Dylan thought he was thinking.

"Jeanette?" he finally managed to say. "There is no Jeanette." Because there was only one possible Jeanette, and she had sugar on her nose.

"Yes," Hawkins said. "There is a Jeanette. She's part of your cover."

No. No, she wasn't.

"No wife." No way in hell. *Good God.* Skeeter Jeanne Bang undercover as the wife of a State

Department aide at a Washington, D.C., black-tie reception for the British ambassador; the underage street Goth princess with a flute of champagne in her hand and a lightning-bolt tattoo streaking up her leg, with the Chinese symbols for Honor, Duty, and Loyalty inked into her upper arm, and lo and behold, even more of the damn lightning bolt snaking up over her shoulder.

It made his head spin.

He sent the "street princess" a quick glance, the whole ball-capped, mirror-sunglassed wonder of her, expecting confirmation of the complete idiocy of Superman's plan—and immediately realized his mistake.

She'd seen it all, every ounce of disbelief, panic, and denial that had swept over his face, and she'd taken every one of his knee-jerk reactions very, very personally. *Dammit*. He hadn't known a mouth that soft could set itself into such a hard line.

Tough. He was the boss, and this was his call.

Wife. *Jesus*. The last thing he needed was an excuse to treat her like a wife. That was asking for trouble.

"Driving," he said succinctly. "That was the deal we cut."

She didn't say a word, just sat there looking mutinous, her arms crossed over her breasts.

After a couple of long seconds, Hawkins broke the silence. "Okay, then. Let's finish going over the setup at Whitfield's, and the two of you can work out the details later."

Details?

There weren't going to be any details.

And there wasn't going to be any "wife." He didn't care how much cover Superman thought he needed.

FISH.
Net.
Combat.
Boots.
Lightning.
Bolt.

From where Dylan was sitting in the plane seat next to her, he could see Skeeter's tattoo zipping up her leg and the zigzag just above the hip-hugging waistband of her skirt. The highly stylized line of ink appeared again higher up, zooming out from under her tank top with another zigzag on her shoulder blade, following the curve of a tiny pink bra strap down to the kind of curves that made it impossible for him to sleep at night.

All of it was mesmerizing, but he'd gotten stuck on one small spot less than two inches in width, a break in the bolt, a small spot on her upper thigh where there was no ink.

Black.

Ops.

Afghanistan.

Mission.

Skeeter.

Skinned.

He took another slow sip of coffee.

There it was, staring him in the face, the perfect example of everything he'd been trying to say last night, of every reason he'd had for not bringing her with him, which didn't exactly explain why she was within touching distance at 30,000 feet, working on her laptop and smelling like the sugar she'd long since licked off her lips—sweet.

Very sweet.

Edible—and he knew right where he wanted to start, a little fantasy of his he probably wasn't going to get a chance to indulge, not in a 747, not even in first-class. If he was down to his last few hours on earth, it might be nice to check out with one shred of integrity still intact.

Or not.

The tank top was stretchy white lace. Her

shoulders were bare, the right one practically touching him—a silky soft, creamy smooth shoulder with that slinky little pink bra strap running over the top curve.

He was trying not to think about it.

He shifted in his seat to get an extra quarter inch of distance between them and looked at his watch. Thirty-six hours left before his week was up.

Thirty-six hours.

That really wasn't much. Not in the broad scheme of things. He should probably make love to her. So what if he lost his last shred of integrity? He at least would have had her, and there wasn't a doubt in his mind that she was worth more than anything he had in his bag of tricks—including his last shred of integrity.

Also on the upside, making love with her was probably as close to heaven as he was ever going to get, and that bore some thinking about, given his current condition, and if he keeled over dead afterward, well, then he didn't have to worry about breaking her heart.

Great. He'd convinced himself. It was a win/win situation.

So what was that odd sense of unease, that little sizzle of panic he felt?

He let out a heavy breath, ran his hand back through his hair, and tried not to think about it.

That seemed to be his standard operating procedure this week—don't think.

"Ms. Bang?" The flight attendant, an attractive brunette in her thirties, leaned down over Skeeter's aisle seat with a notebook and pen in hand, a conspiratorial smile on her lips. "The man in 4B wondered if he could have your autograph. He told me his daughter is a huge fan."

Fan? What the hell? Dylan lifted himself up and looked over the back of his seat. *Since when did covert operators have fans?*

Never. That was when.

He spotted the guy, and just as he'd suspected, 4B was checking her out—checking out her hot pink bra and endlessly long, fishnet-covered legs. *Christ.* He was even checking out her combat boots. Somebody ought to tell 4B she could take his face off with one of those boots.

The man glanced at Dylan then and caught the cold, hard stare Dylan was giving him, and yeah, it took him a second, but he got the friggin' message.

That's right, dude. Your face.

Satisfied, Dylan dropped back down in his seat and looked over to see Skeeter scrawling the word "Pink" across the paper.

Pink. Hell. The rock star. "You're prettier than Pink."

A set of mirrored sunglasses shifted in his direction, but only for a heartbeat, before she was smiling at the flight attendant and handing back the note-book and pen.

Prettier than Pink? He let out another breath and tried to remember the last time he'd said something that dumb to a woman.

Okay, nothing was coming to him, because he'd never said anything that dumb to a woman.

God, it was going to be a long flight.

"You need to stop staring at my leg," she said.

A *really* long flight.

"I'm not staring at your leg."

"You have been, ever since takeoff, right at the spot where I got hit in Afghanistan."

Caught. Red-handed.

He cleared his throat.

"I was just thinking how perfectly the scar illus-trates my point about you staying with the car at Whitfield's." It was the only detail they'd worked out after Hawkins had finished the briefing, and as far as Dylan was concerned, it was the only detail they'd needed to work out, except for a new one that had just come to him. He pulled a pen and a small notepad out of the inside pocket of his suit jacket and jotted down a number. "If there's a prob-lem—*any* kind of a problem—tonight, I expect you to leave the area and call this number as soon as you're clear. Let it ring twice and hang up. You'll get a call back in less than five minutes."

He ripped off the page and handed it to her.

She just stared at it.

"Run away," she finally said, "is not in my vocabulary. I have been trained to fight, not retreat."

"You were shot." And that was pretty much his bottom line.

"Skinned. Kid gets shot. He gets shot all the time, and you don't tell him to run away."

"Kid is—" He stopped abruptly, seeing "quagmire" written all over anything he said.

"A man?"

"No. Well, yes, but that wasn't my point."

"So what is your point?"

Good question.

"My point is that Kid is, uh . . . not you."

Geezus. Two stupid statements in less than three minutes. He was going for a record.

"You're being unreasonable."

Probably.

"And you're too young to be involved in this or any other operation." And that was the truth, and that was the end of it. He put the phone number in her hand, then reached for the *Wall Street Journal* stuck in the seatback in front of him and snapped it open.

"We send eighteen-year-olds into combat," she said. "I'm twenty-one, and the nation's capital is not a combat zone."

"You're not twenty-one." How interesting, the DOW was up a few points.

"I will be tomorrow."

And the NASDAQ was down. And twenty-one or not, he still wouldn't want her anywhere near one of his missions. *Christ.* Look what had happened to him in Indonesia.

Or not.

It had all been a bit gruesome, even by his standards.

Letting the corner of the newspaper drop, he signaled the flight attendant.

"Scotch," he said. "Two." To start.

The sunglasses turned toward him again. "I've never seen you drink before a mission."

She'd never seen him chained to a wall, either.

He turned the page and straightened the newspaper back out.

"I'll be watching you tonight, to see how well you perform, how well you follow orders. Make no mistake, this is a test, a trial, and I *am* the one who will set the course of your career at SDF, or decide if you will even have a career on the team." And that should have her eating out of the palm of his hand, snapping to attention every time he entered a room and asking "how high" every time he said "jump." He knew how much SDF and Steele Street meant to her—the world and then some.

"You could watch me better if I was working next to you instead of sitting on my butt out in the car."

The Standard & Poor's Index was holding steady—like her capital A attitude and the pair of brass balls she had hidden under her skirt.

"Actually, I'll work better if I know you're sitting on your butt out in the car, watching the house."

The Scotch arrived, and he wasted no time twisting the lid off the first bottle and pouring it over ice. Scotch on the rocks, that's what he needed, not five feet eight inches of unadulterated insanity.

He had a brain. He needed to be using it, and by God, he was going to start right after he finished his drink.

"What the hell," she said, sitting up straighter in her seat and whipping off her sunglasses, an unusual enough occurrence to rivet his attention. "What's that?"

"What's what?" God, her eyes were blue, a pale, silvery blue, and they were narrowed on him like a laser, honed in on his drink—but not quite on the drink.

"That," she said, and suddenly he knew exactly what "that" she meant.

He shifted his attention back to his hand and noted how far up his arm he'd let his shirt cuff ride, far enough to reveal the bruised, raw skin around his wrist and the line of stitches just above the bruises. The shackle on his right side had been a snug fit to begin with, then Negara's goons had added a razor component to help get his attention.

It had definitely worked, almost down to the bone.

"Well, yes." That.

He'd been more careful with his clothing last night and this morning, but there was something about the whole "countdown" aspect of his run-in with Hamzah Negara that was starting to push him to the edge. He had no business trying to steal anything tonight, let alone from a U.S. senator. It was asking for trouble and a permanent address change to Leavenworth.

"That's where I, uh, got tangled up in a small accident in Jakarta, a car accident."

"Liar."

Often, he could have told her, and usually damn good at it, or at least better than he'd just been.

"The report is on file with the Jakarta police—a Land Rover and a Mercedes at the corner of Ananta and Lubis, last Wednesday about five P.M. You're pretty good with that thing"—he gestured at her laptop—"go ahead and check it out."

He went back to his newspaper, giving it a small snap, and hopefully signaling to her that the conversation was over.

He should have known better.

"Those contusions are more than three days old."

Yes, they were.

"The Wednesday before three days ago. *That* last Wednesday."

"Except your stitches aren't ten days old."

Right again.

He was obviously not on his game, so he ignored her, not bothering to look up from his paper.

"And your wrist has a distinctly mangled look."

Distinctly.

"Overall, you look like hell."

Thank you.

Thank you very much.

"I think we should talk about Sumba."

"I don't." The Fidelity Fund was up.

"Okay. Then let's talk about the commendation." She reached down and pulled a single sheet of paper out of her backpack.

He gave it a brief, wary glance.

Impossible.

"You didn't lift that off Superman."

Yet there it seemed to be, the fax transmission, with all its gory details.

She closed her laptop and smoothed the paper out over the top of it. "I could have. Don't doubt it for a second," she said. "But in this instance, it wasn't necessary. Hawkins gave it to me when you went upstairs to pack. He wants some answers. I agreed to get them."

Jesus H. Christ.

"Let's start with the word 'escape,' which I

believe will explain what I'm seeing on your wrist a little better than the car accident theory."

Theory? God, she did have balls.

"Let's *not* start with 'escape,' " he said. Ever. Period.

"Okay," she agreed after a long moment, her voice tight. "How about your capture?"

Clean, he could have told her. Professional. Off-limits.

He kept reading.

"Silence isn't going to work here, sir. You have an obligation to me, as your partner tonight, to disclose any current circumstances that may affect our mission."

The hell he did.

"If you've been hurt, and you obviously have, or are suffering from any mental or emotional trauma—"

"My current circumstances," he said, cutting her off, "are strictly on a need-to-know basis."

Letting out a heavy sigh, she crossed her legs and turned more fully toward him in her seat. "Look, sir, my butt is on the line here. Hawkins made that very clear to me before I left. Whatever 'test' you want to dish out tonight, I'm up for, one hundred percent, but if I don't bring you back alive and in one piece, he's going to fillet me with my own knife, the seven-inch one I carry on my tactical vest. In addition to the whole Lone Ranger act you've been playing since last winter, this"—she lifted the commendation— "has him on edge. So help me out here. Don't make me have to get physical with you."

He looked up, not believing what he'd heard.

Physical? What did she think she was going to do? Wrestle him down and torture the answers out of him? Not very damn likely.

"You're out of line."

"Mr. Hart . . . Dylan." She leaned in closer, sliding her hand up the side of his neck and pretty much freezing him to his seat, one of those hot freezes, where the sensation of touch, no matter where it was initiated, somehow ended up galvanizing your balls. *Fuck.*

He didn't need this.

"I think you better stick with calling me 'sir.' " And put on a parka, or something, anything to cover up all that hot-pink, white-lace, and soft-skin fashion statement she had working from the waist up.

Her fingers slid a little higher.

"This isn't about lines, *sir.* This is about getting the job done. It's about coming home safe. It's about finding out exactly how much valorous action it took to get you a freaking commendation from the secretary of defense." A smile curved her mouth, slowly, sweetly, and just as slowly, it dawned on him where her fingers were, how much pressure she was starting to exert, and how dangerous she might actually turn out to be.

"You wouldn't dare," he said, his gaze narrowing

on those silvery blue eyes, the ones with the devil dancing in them.

"Superman calls this the Vulcan Death Grip." The pressure on his neck increased ever so slightly, and her smile broadened, still so deadly sweet.

"In Bangkok, it's called the Butterfly Sting," he said. "Unexpected, lethal."

"Or merely temporarily paralyzing."

"And I repeat—you wouldn't dare."

She gave him a lift of her eyebrows, except the one with the scar cutting through it only went partway, giving her a slightly quizzical expression, and in the odd way of things between them, it broke his heart, right then, right there.

Twenty stitches. That's what it had taken to put her back together. She'd lost so much blood that night, Hawkins had given her a unit of his own in the ER.

Dylan let his gaze follow the path of the scar up to where it disappeared under a swath of platinum blond bangs.

He'd put her father in his sights once.

Okay, he'd done it twice.

But he hadn't pulled the trigger either time. Anders Bang, a godforsaken, brutally twisted, alcoholic meth freak, was still alive on the streets of Denver, which was more than he deserved for breaking a whiskey bottle on his daughter's face. It hadn't been the first time her father had hurt her, but it had been the last. Hawkins had seen to it.

Dylan, of course, had been someplace else when it all happened. *Christ.* He was always someplace else.

Except today.

Today, he was sitting next to her, and she wanted something from him badly enough to threaten him.

"I'm the one who taught Hawkins the Butterfly Sting," he said. "I'm also the one who taught him the countermove."

"You're not going to counter me," she said, sounding awfully sure of herself.

With good reason, he had to admit.

"No. I'm not." The countermove was a vicious strike, and the last thing in the world he wanted was to hurt her, ever, in any way.

"So you're at my mercy." The devilish light in her eyes tipped the corners of her mouth, and he started to get that whole "galvanized" feeling in his balls again.

Geezus. He really needed to deal with this.

"Yes," he answered, lifting his hips off the seat enough to reach into his pocket. He had to give her something, and it might as well be something useful.

He pulled out the stainless steel case and popped it open, revealing the line of Syrettes nested inside.

Her smile instantly disappeared.

Removing her hand from his neck, she sat back in her seat.

"Superman isn't going to like this," she said.

"No," he agreed. He didn't like it, either, but that didn't change the facts. "I ran into a few pharmaceuticals in Indonesia, or rather, they ran into me. There might be delayed reactions attached to a couple of them. What I'll need from you, if I need anything, will be help with the yellow Syrette. If I go down, mainline it. Hit a vein."

She reached out and touched the case, then pulled her hand back, her gaze locking on to his.

"You should be in a hospital."

"I was, on the U.S.S. *Jefferson*."

"And you left? With this hanging over your head?" she asked incredulously. "Why?"

You.

Sitting next to her, looking at her, being close enough to breathe her in, the answer was suddenly so stark and clear in his head. With time running out and the future looking so goddamn unreliable, he'd left the *Jefferson* for only one reason—to get home to her.

To see her again.

Fuck. He was in so far over his head here. She didn't make sense, in any way, in any part of his life, but it was no accident she was on the plane to Washington, D.C., with him. For all his bitching and moaning and the crap he'd dished out last night, he wouldn't have left Denver without her—not on a bet. No way. He hadn't come halfway around the world to spend what might be the last two days of his life without her. He could have stayed in Indonesia for that.

So here he was, running at about half speed, his head a little fucked up, his nerves shredding, dragging her with him into what should be a cakewalk but, given the way his luck had been running lately, probably wasn't going to be.

"Did you requisition a sidearm for each of us before we left?" he asked, putting the case back in his pocket and ignoring her question. Wanting to be with her, taking her with him, and keeping her by his side did not require a full-out confession of his ulterior motives. They were together. It was enough. He'd save the declaration of undying love until the last—if it came to that.

"Yes," she said after a long moment, during which he could tell she was deciding just how far to push him. Fortunately, she chose the not-very-far route, at least for now. "I personally called in an equipment list to General Grant's office. Our gear will be at the hotel when we get there, along with a car."

"Good." He went back to his newspaper.

"What is the red Syrette for?" she asked after another long moment of silence.

"Increase in temperature and hallucinations."

"And the blue?"

"Decrease in temperature and losing my lunch." He gave her a quick glance.

She had her fingers steepled in front of her face and was staring straight ahead, thinking. He could almost hear the wheels turning inside her head—and that wasn't such a bad thing.

She was a very smart girl—brilliant, actually. If the heist at Whitfield's didn't go well, for any reason, it wouldn't be such a bad thing to have a smart girl on his side, figuring things out.

"It's not like you to get caught," she said after a minute, so quietly he wasn't sure if she was talking to him or not.

Regardless, she was right. In seventeen years of nonstop, out-and-out thievery, he'd only been caught three times. The bust for grand theft auto, at sixteen, had been an inside job, with a guy they'd picked up as a stringer turning them in to the cops. His arrest in Moscow six years later had been a bit more complicated, a setup where he'd fallen for the bait, a choreographed attempt by the CIA to get to his boss, a man even General Grant knew only as White Rook.

And ten days ago had been his third strike.

After months of planning and six weeks in Indonesia to actually put together and pull off the job, he'd been caught with his foot halfway out of the country, on his way to the airport in Jakarta.

Negara's timing couldn't have been better. His

associates couldn't have been more professional or the execution of the kidnapping smoother. Dylan had been snatched off the street like a cherry girl hooker.

"Who knew where you were?" she asked, and yeah, he knew what she was getting at. He'd thought it himself a thousand times, but hadn't been able to come up with anyone who could have set him up—not yet. Broadening his investigation along those avenues was at the top of his list, right after Godwin, right after thirty-six more hours of waiting to see if he was going to have a chance to broaden anything—like his relationship with her.

"Grant, Hawkins, Bill Davies, and probably you," he said, casting her another glance. Bill Davies was the assistant secretary of defense for special operations, and Grant's liaison at the Pentagon.

Pale blue eyes met his without a flicker of guilt. "I get paid to know where you are, where all of you are, but even I didn't have access to your itinerary in Indonesia."

"Nobody did. I flew low, under the radar all the way."

"What about the secretary of defense?"

"The mission came from him, but like every mission we take, the method and means of accomplishing it were left to us. The less he knows, the happier he is."

"Us?" she asked skeptically.

"Me," he admitted.

"So are you getting sloppy?"

It was a legitimate question, and he'd asked himself the same thing dozens of times over the last ten days. Every time, he'd come up with the same answer.

"No." He hadn't left a trail—physical, paper, or in cyberspace. His covers were bulletproof. Dylan Hart hadn't stepped foot in Indonesia for over five years. John Barr, a banker from Philadelphia, had been there doing business with the Indonesian government and been snatched off the street.

"Then we have a break in SDF's security, in the chain of command," she said.

"It's a damn short chain, and we've already listed everyone on it."

She just looked at him, tapping her fingers together.

"There's another list," she finally said.

Yeah. He knew it.

"The Everybody Who Wants to Wax My Ass list."

She nodded.

"That one's a bit longer," he said.

"No kidding." She flipped up the top of her computer. "Should I open a new document? Or are we going to need a spreadsheet?"

A grin curved his mouth, the first one in over a week.

"Spreadsheet."

CHAPTER
7

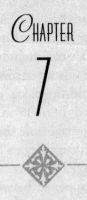

FROM THE living room of an expansive Tudor-style house in Prince William County, Virginia, twenty miles outside Washington, D.C., Tony Royce looked out over a small lake and the green expanse of the heavily wooded grounds beyond. Not so much as a finger twitch betrayed his impatience. He was calm, steady, his anger curbed on a tight leash. He was a pro, a seasoned veteran of twenty years of CIA operations, and hell would have to freeze over twice before he'd let Hamzah Negara rattle his cage.

Especially when their whole goddamn problem was Negara's fault. Royce had fulfilled his part of their bargain. He'd delivered Dylan Hart's head on a platter, and Negara had lost him, allowed him to escape from a damn-near inescapable island. Royce had been at Negara's compound on Sumba a week ago, and the place was a fortress, complete with a garrison and around-the-clock guards. Given the condition Hart had been in at the time, Royce found it doubly unimaginable that the man had escaped. The kind of drugs Negara had been pumping into him should have left him comatose.

So what had happened between the interrogation Royce had witnessed Sunday night and Monday morning when Hart had vanished from the island? Two guards had been found dead, one with his throat slit, the razor still in it, a deed well within Hart's capabilities under normal circumstances, but the circumstances shouldn't have been normal. The man should have been down for the count, not overcoming his guards and escaping.

And Negara had the balls to keep him cooling his heels, after a fuckup like that?

Royce discreetly checked his watch again. Forty minutes, that's how long he'd been waiting for Negara to get out of his bath, or off the phone, or finish his lunch, or whatever it was he was doing behind the set of closed doors at the end of the living room.

"Mr. Royce."

Tony turned at the sound of the voice. A slight man in a dark shirt and slacks, one of Negara's "enforcers," gestured toward the now-open door. There were two more men of a similar demeanor in the room, both of them armed, both of them lethal, even without the pistols he knew they each carried concealed in shoulder holsters beneath their black suit coats.

Royce didn't trust either one of them, any more than he trusted Negara. The only thing keeping his ass in one piece in this den of murderers and thieves was his ability to deliver Dylan Hart—again.

"Mr. Negara," he said, entering the office. Two more guards were inside. All of the men he'd seen in the house had tattoos on the backs of their hands, a circle with three long lines running through it—Jai Traon pirates.

"To-nee," a small, white-haired man said with a big smile, pushing out of the chair from where he'd been sitting behind a mahogany desk. Hamzah Negara, Butcher of the Sabu Sea, weighed in at one-thirty on a good day, one hundred and thirty pounds of seventy-year-old sinew and bone wrapped around the heart of a despot.

"It's good to see you," Royce said. It wasn't, but the lie came easily enough. They always did.

"And you, To-nee."

"I trust your flight went well?"

"Yes, yes, very well." Negara gestured at a chair in front of the desk, part of a group of three, and Royce moved to sit down.

"I see you brought your house guards."

"Yes, most of them," the old man said, taking the closest chair and signaling one of his men. "There are more arriving this afternoon, to help with security a little, here and there." He gave a slight shrug. "As you know, I am an international businessman. Besides my property holdings, I have many current investments and commitments in your country."

Bullshit.

Negara had seventeen million dollars' worth of current commitments in the United States and not a penny more, not this week. That's how much of the warlord's China White cash Hart had gotten away with, under orders. Somewhere, some Foreign Affairs experts in the upper echelons of Washington's more hallowed halls had decided the Indonesian government's goodwill was more important to the United States than Hamzah Negara's in the prevailing world climate, and they'd put forth a clandestine policy change to reflect the new view. Hart had simply been the messenger. Royce knew how the game was played.

So did Negara. The old barbarian had contributed his "expertise" to more than a few CIA operations over the years, and Royce had seen no reason to let the relationship end on a sour note—not when Negara was willing to pay six figures for him to deliver his enemy into the warlord's hands.

"And yet it is important to me to see Mr. Hart again," Negara continued. "He is here, correct?"

"Correct." Or he would be by the time Whitfield's party started. Royce had made damn sure of it. "He'll be at Senator Arthur Whitfield's mansion tonight, for a reception the senator is giving for the visiting British delegation."

"And where will he be staying?" the old warlord asked.

Negara hadn't exactly paid for that information, but Royce could be generous, especially when he was getting what he wanted.

"I would post men at the Four Seasons and the Lafayette." He'd studied his enemy for years, and nine times out of ten, Hart stayed at one of the two most expensive hotels in the city. With this trip having come up so suddenly, Royce figured Hart would be more inclined to fall back on habit, especially considering the shape he must be in—not so good, even after almost a week of recovery time.

"Thank you, To-nee." Negara glanced at his nearest guard and made a hand gesture. The man immediately left the room.

Royce hid a smile. Hart was never going to know what hit him. Royce hadn't had a doubt when Ambassador Godwin had been assassinated all those years ago that making himself a copy of the files would someday come in handy. Negara's mistake had created that someday, and twenty years of moving through the shark-infested backwaters of congressional Washington had given Royce the means to deliver the bait to draw out Dylan Hart with precision accuracy. The Godwin affair had been dirty, the dirtiest, just the sort of dirt that sank to the bottom of the Potomac but never went away. All Royce had done was help it resurface in the most likely place to get him what he wanted, in the hands of Arthur Whitfield, chairman of the Senate Armed Services Committee. The names on the bottom of the Godwin orders guaranteed a phone call to the Pentagon, and it would have taken only one to stir up a hornet's nest, the kind nobody wanted to touch with a ten-foot pole.

Enter General Richard "Buck" Grant, the Department of Defense's dirty dog of dirty deeds, and his band of renegade operators, known as SDF. His orders would have been cut and dried—get the file back or get another line of work. Either outcome worked for Royce. He didn't care what happened to the Godwin file, the people who'd signed it, or Buck Grant. He didn't care what happened to Hamzah Negara's seventeen million dollars.

He did care about Dylan Hart.

The man had been a thorn in his side for years, and their last go-around had cost Royce his reputation and his career. For that, Royce had handed him a one-way ticket to hell—except he'd escaped.

Hart was going to wish he hadn't. The second

trip Royce had been forced to cobble together made the one he'd spent weeks planning look like a fucking garden party. He was pretty damn proud of it and his ability to produce work of such high quality on such short notice, if he did say so himself.

"There will be a woman with him this time, a girl, actually. I think you'll find her very useful in getting Mr. Hart's cooperation. As a matter of fact, if you can get the girl, I doubt any more drugs will be necessary. Hart will tell you everything, and then he'll go get your money back himself."

Negara's sharp-eyed gaze narrowed slightly at the mention of a woman.

"Who is this woman?"

"No one of any official importance, a punk, a mechanic who hangs around Hart's office."

"Mechanic?"

"Car mechanic," he explained further. "She works on automobiles, on the engines. But she is important to Hart." When Royce's man in Denver had told him a girl with a long blond ponytail and Chinese tattoos had gotten on the plane with Hart, he had hardly believed his luck. He remembered how protective of her Hart had been the last time they'd met—the night the Dominika Starkova case had blown up in his face. Royce had been the one to actually handcuff Starkova and bring her in, but he'd still ended up looking like a fool, a fact that had been reflected in the grinding halt of his career.

The fucking CIA. Royce was making ten times more money as a freelance contractor than he ever would have made sticking with an agency that no longer appreciated his talents.

"Her name is Skeeter Bang," he said, reaching inside his jacket.

Two pistols were instantly drawn, both of them leveled at his head.

He froze, his hand half inside his coat.

"A photograph," he explained, willing his heart rate back to a bearable speed. "Just a photograph, so you'll recognize her. She'll be easy to identify."

At a nod from Negara, he finished pulling the photo free and handed it to the old man.

"Tell your men at the hotels to ask about her. She'll be the one people remember, not Hart. If she's there, he will be, too."

Negara looked at the picture for a long time. Royce understood his interest. The girl was custom-made to appeal to a man of varied tastes, and Negara was still that, even at seventy.

When he'd looked his fill, the warlord gave the photograph to the nearest guard, along with a stream of instructions delivered in Indonesian. Even if Royce hadn't spoken Negara's native tongue, he would have understood the tone of voice and the gleam in the old man's eyes.

Bring her to me. Untouched.

It was the same in any language, the wielding of

power over lesser men for the spoils of war. Unlike Hart, Skeeter Bang's usefulness might last out the month. But in the end, no matter what she did, her time would come. Or perhaps, given what Royce remembered of her, she would prove so unyielding that a few drugged encounters would be enough to dull her charms and she wouldn't make it to Monday morning.

Either way, her fate was sealed and could be summed up in two simple but profound words— "collateral damage."

"Do you have the transcripts?" he asked Negara, nodding his thanks as tea was brought out and set on the table between him and the old man.

"Yes, yes," Negara said, lifting his hand to one side.

One of the guards stepped forward and gave him a sheaf of papers. Negara handed them over.

Royce flipped through the pages, one by one. They'd been heavily edited, with lots of blank spaces, but he'd expected as much. Whatever information Negara's medical staff had wrung out of Dylan Hart would have been subject to Negara's censorship, especially anything concerning his banking practices and the movement of his drug money into his more legitimate investments, which is what Negara had been looking for—how Hart had diverted seventeen million of his dollars, and how the process could be reversed.

Royce wanted another type of information, and finally, on page five, he found it, for all the good it did him.

He lifted his gaze to Negara's. "This is all he said? White Rook?"

Negara nodded. "Dr. Souk asked the question many times, in many ways—'Who at the State Department gives you orders? Who saved you from prison after you were caught in Moscow? Who chose General Grant as your commanding officer?'—many ways. Always, as you will see, he only said 'White Rook.' "

Disgusted, Royce shifted his attention back to the papers. He needed a real name, not a fucking code name. He wanted to know who to go after next, when he was finished with Hart.

But he could use "White Rook," put it out there, let it slide around, see what came up, or if anyone came after him.

"Ask him again, after you have the girl," he said. Hart would give up the name then, especially if Negara held true to form and added a few creative twists to his torture. Hart was tough, no doubt about it, but he didn't have what it took to watch someone work over a teenage girl.

On page seven, something else caught his eye. The same words had been circled in red ink four separate times.

He couldn't help himself—he grinned.

"Special Defense Force, 738 Steele Street, Denver, Colorado, U.S.A." He glanced at Negara, his grin broadening. "You'll never get inside. The place is sealed tighter than a vault. Without the codes, all you'll be able to do is stand out in the street and look at the building."

Royce had been inside, but he'd been let in, authorized by the CIA and routed through SDF's chain of command at the Defense Department. Last year, rumor had it that Senator Marilyn Decker had gotten in with a squad of Marines, but she was one of the Defense Department's favorite politicos. She pushed their budgets and their agendas hard, fast, and usually through the opposition. There wasn't a person at the DOD who wouldn't give her whatever she wanted, including access to the bad boys at Steele Street at a moment's notice.

Hamzah Negara was a different story. Nobody was going to give him anything.

The old man nodded, but didn't look perturbed. His words proved why. "Mr. Hart revealed the codes, and my men will be in place tonight. If I do not have my money back by then, they will take Steele Street apart brick by brick, and kill anyone they find inside. It will be a slaughter, my friend."

They weren't friends, and the rhetoric was typical warlord, but Royce knew Negara could and would deliver on his threat. Still, he had to wonder if anyone had ever told Hamzah Negara about

Superman, or Creed Rivera, the SDF operator who had not only snatched Dominika Starkova out from under Royce's nose last January, but married her. Cody Rivera was the woman's name now.

Those boys knew slaughter. Royce could guarantee it. He'd seen Creed's handiwork. He'd never met Peter "Kid Chaos" Chronopolous, another SDF operator, but his reputation was the stuff legends were made out of—legends and bad guys' nightmares.

None of which was Royce's concern. If Negara wanted to sacrifice a few of his guys going up against SDF on their home turf, that was his business. Royce's business was Hart, and it was personal. He didn't need to kill the guy himself. He just wanted him dead.

CHAPTER

8

***

GIVE THEM *an inch*.

Dylan couldn't believe what he was seeing, or how much of it there was to see.

And they'll take a mile.

The invitation to the reception, all the necessary identification, and the gel prints of Whitfield's fingertips had been waiting for him in their hotel suite when he and Skeeter had arrived. But there was more, ever so much more.

"What"—he made a flailing gesture at all the gear piled and stacked in the living area between the suite's two bedrooms —"what *is* all this stuff?"

He turned to look at Skeeter, who was standing

protectively in front of a small tower of high-impact equipment cases, her arms crossed in front of her chest, looking mutinous.

"It's our kit for the mission."

Kit?

She'd turned an elegant three-room suite at the Hotel Lafayette into a freaking armory.

He walked over and opened the top case in the stack behind her.

"A submachine gun?" *Geezus.*

"It's an HK UMP45."

Obviously.

He cocked an eyebrow in her direction.

"A Heckler and Koch Universal Machine Pistol in .45 caliber," she explained.

Fine. Great. He didn't care what she called it, the weapon he was looking at was a submachine gun—in .45 ACP, with a folding stock.

Okay. That was pretty cool. He wasn't the shoot-out artist Kid was, but when he did shoot somebody, he preferred to do it with a .45 rather than a 9mm. He liked his terminal ballistics to be as terminal as possible.

"I requested two from Grant's office, one for each of us," she added, "and fourteen 25-round magazines."

Two subguns and enough ammo to stage a Third World coup—he squelched a sigh and refrained from shaking his head. She had never worked with him before, not really, not on one of his missions, so she couldn't have been expected to know how he operated, which was very, very low profile. A laptop, a brain, a cell phone, a concealed sidearm, a pair of gloves, and a few tools for breaking and entering—that was usually enough to get him through a heist.

He moved the UMP onto the bed and opened the larger case underneath.

"A sniper rifle?"

"A Knight Match SR-25 in .308 with a PVS-10 day/night scope and infrared light source."

He did let out a breath at that, kind of a heavy breath.

"And a laser range finder," she added.

Of course.

"You are going to be on the ground, in the car, in Whitfield's driveway, not on a rooftop somewhere, doing overwatch with a badass long rifle trained on the senator's historic mansion."

The thought made his head spin. He'd *known* he shouldn't have brought her into this. God only knew what the concierge had thought when Grant's staff had delivered the stuff.

He pointed toward two large rucksacks leaning against the couch. "What's in those?"

"Tactical gear," she said, still with that mutinous look on her face. "And a couple of assault vests for carrying our equipment."

Just what he needed to go with his tuxedo, a fully rigged-out assault vest.

"Including threat level II soft body armor," she continued. "In case we get in a situation where people are shooting at us."

That was *not* going to happen.

"I have been to dozens of receptions for foreign dignitaries in Washington, D.C., and have *never* needed soft body armor." This is what happened when a guy brought a kick-ass girl to a party. She wanted to kick ass.

"Flex cuffs," she said, undeterred. "Four each."

He looked her square in the eye. "We will not be handcuffing anyone tonight. Guaranteed." Unless it was each other—but his luck didn't seem to be headed in that direction.

"A three-cell blue diode flashlight."

Finally, something he could use.

"Thank you. That will come in handy."

"Tac II combat knife."

"No." There would be no mano a mano knife fighting at the senator's tonight.

"AN/PVS-7 night vision devices."

"Unnecessary."

"Ground/air locator strobe with IR hood."

"Unnecessary."

"Fifty feet of five-fifty cord and ten feet of hundred-mile-per-hour tape—each."

"Always handy, but in this instance, unnecessary," he said firmly.

"Fragmentation grenades."

Sweet freaking sonuvabitch.

"Fragmentation grenades," he said calmly, trying not to imagine just exactly how much damage a well-thrown frag could do to the Whitfield ballroom and the three hundred or so guests who would be in attendance.

Enough to get him the electric chair, he decided.

And Skeeter, too.

The look he was giving her must have said as much.

"I've got a feeling about tonight. That's all," she said, still standing stoically in front of her outrageous stacks of gear.

Yeah, he had a feeling, too, and it was spelled D-I-S-A-S-T-E-R—unless he kept a lid on things, unless he kept a lid on her, a screw-on, lock-top lid.

"Sidearms?" he asked. She'd confirmed the request on the plane. The guns had to be here somewhere in all this stuff.

"A Glock 21 for you and a Para-Ordnance LTC for me, both in .45 caliber."

"Thank you." That was all he needed, a loaded .45 and a spare magazine.

"Five magazines for the Glock. Thirteen rounds each."

Okay, fine. Four extra magazines. He'd only be taking one with him.

"I'm going to grab a quick shower," he said, "and shave, then we'll head over to Whitfield's and make sure everything is laid out the way it is on the plans we've been looking at all day. I don't suppose you've got a pair of binoculars in there?" He gestured at the rucksacks.

She nodded. "Steiner Predator, 8×42."

Of course she had binoculars, he thought. They'd be packed next to the kitchen sink.

THEY were the perfect Georgetown couple, Dylan thought two hours later, him in his button-down shirt and conservative dark suit, and her in fishnet and combat boots, looking stunningly beautiful.

He'd put his foot down about the ball cap. The damn thing was not to be seen again for as long as they were in Washington, no argument. So she'd put her hair up, piled it every which way on top of her head, and just let it fan out all over the place and trail down the sides of her face, with a few loose strands drifting down her back, all white blond and silky against white lace and hot pink. It made her look older, sophisticated, like she knew her way around.

It made her look old enough for anything, and everything about her looking old enough for anything put him on overload, every hip-rolling stride, every dangling tendril, every breath she took.

They'd had their late-afternoon lattes, and re-conned Whitfield's from the café's streetside patio. Grant's intel had been impeccable, as usual. The plan Dylan and Hawkins had put together should work without a hitch, *would* work without a hitch. There wasn't room for failure. There wasn't time.

Any time, for anything, least of all indecision.

He checked his watch. They had four hours before they planned to arrive at the party. A lot of anything could happen in four hours, especially if two people had finished their recon work, felt good about their plan, and were alone in a three-room suite at the Hotel Lafayette—naked.

He let his gaze drift over her. She'd stopped in front of a shop with bins of merchandise set up on the sidewalk. It was all very colorful, piles of small, embroidered purses with bits of mirror, leather wallets, belts, and scarves, all very high-end. One belt in particular had caught her eye. Black leather, of course, with silver conchas, it was exquisite, with a price tag to match.

He pulled out his wallet and peeled off two hundred and fifty dollars to pay the clerk.

"Happy birthday," he said when Skeeter looked up at him, her eyebrow quirked in that slightly off-kilter way.

Another woman might have demurred, put up a

fuss, played coy. Not Skeeter Bang. She had enough of the street rat left in her to know a good deal when she was handed one.

"Thanks." She grinned and looked down to buckle it over the chain-mail belt already hanging on her denim miniskirt. The buckle was a bit complicated, though, and after a few moments of watching her not quite get it right, he took the two ends of the belt and slipped them together himself.

Big mistake.

He had to stand way too close to get the job done. The backs of his fingers brushed against the soft, bare skin of her midriff, and she still had that sweet, sugar smell on her. It wasn't cheap perfume. Cheap perfume made him sneeze. This made him crazy.

"What's your perfume?" he asked. It wasn't doughnut sugar, not after all day.

"Cookies."

"Cookies?" He slipped the buckle tang into a hole.

"There's a fragrance designer out of L.A. that Katya knows, and Cookies is his newest perfume," she said.

Katya Hawkins, of course. Superman's wife would know the newest designers and their newest perfumes.

He finished sliding the tail end of the belt through the restraining loop and should have let go of her then. He should have stepped back. Those were the reasonable things to do, but suddenly he wasn't feeling very reasonable, and instead of moving away, he looked into those damned mirrored sunglasses of hers.

"It's not on the, uh, market yet," she said, suddenly sounding a little unsure, but not moving away any more than he was. "Kat got me a sample. She said it reminded her of me."

No kidding—sugar, sweet, cookies, Skeeter. It reminded him of her, too.

"It's very nice," he managed.

This was it. The moment he'd been waiting for—seven months of waiting, seven months of wanting, seven months of running to avoid the inevitable. He was going to kiss her. Now. Before his time ran out. The sun was shining down. A soft wind was blowing, and the wall of heat they were generating between the two of them was damn near electrifying him. Take one step forward, that's all he needed to do. He'd done it hundreds of times with dozens of women—taken the step, taken the kiss.

He took a breath, nearly moved his foot—but froze instead, his body held in place by the image flickering across the surface of her sunglasses.

Jesus!

Every instinct he had said, *Turn! Face the enemy!* Dylan didn't flinch.

"What?" she asked, instantly on alert.

"Across the street. Ten o'clock," he said, giving her the position of the man who'd walked across the mirrors of her sunglasses.

He saw the shift of her gaze behind the lenses.

"Seven, eight, ten people moving at ten o'clock. A family, two women, three men—Asians, mid-twenties to thirties, five feet five to eight, dark shirts, dark pants."

Three. *Fuck.*

"Back of their hands. Tattoos?"

"Minivan, minivan . . . Sorry, boss, they're gone."

"Get back to the hotel." He turned her around and gave her a little push—but she didn't budge, at least not in the right direction. With an incredibly smooth move he hadn't seen coming, she slipped out of his grip and was stepping off the curb, heading across the street.

He reached for her, missed, nearly had a heart attack, and lunged after her, but sonuvabitch, she was already on the move.

Christ. He'd seen her PT charts. If it came down to a foot race, he was frickin' toast.

He started after her, dodging traffic. She wasn't dodging anything. She was sliding, moving with the cars, making every break work for her, and leaving him in the dust. To anyone else watching, she was a leggy blonde crossing the street. He was the only one who would have noticed her hand slide into the leather tote she had bandoliered across her torso, the only one noticing how she'd read the traffic, calculated her moves, and implemented a flawless plan to gain a few seconds' advantage.

Maybe the Asians were just Japanese tourists, or Bangkok Bobs visiting the U.S. capital. Because what were the chances, really, of them working for Hamzah Negara?

Slim to none to absolutely no-fucking-way none.

It was just that, for a second there, he'd thought he'd recognized the guy he'd seen in her sunglasses. Of course, he was still a little jumpy about the whole awful ordeal on Sumba; so conceivably, the sight of any Asian man reversed in a pair of slightly dusty mirrored sunglasses would be enough to jump-start his adrenal gland.

Jesus, he thought, stepping back out of the way of a taxi. He needed a vacation, and if he lived past the weekend, he was going to take one, a really long one, the kind of vacation where all he needed was a toothbrush, a towel, and a lover—*her.*

CHAPTER

9

DAMMIT. She'd lost them.

Skeeter stopped at the corner and looked all four ways of the intersection. There were no Asians anywhere in sight.

Dammit. She reached up to pull her ball cap lower over her face—an automatic action—then remembered Dylan had made her take it off. She swore again under her breath. She felt naked without her cap, exposed, not that anyone around her seemed to be noticing the scar that angled across her forehead. No one in the café seemed to have noticed, either, which was probably something she needed to think about, but not now. Dylan was right behind her.

"The hotel is in the other direction," he growled, taking hold of her arm.

He was absolutely right, but he didn't sound any too happy about it.

Well, he could join the club. She wasn't any too happy, either.

"We're not going to do this," she said, checking behind her one more time. Damn minivan caravan, cutting across her line of sight like that and making her lose the Asians.

"Not do what?"

She turned and faced him square on. "Not do the 'you run and hide like a good little girl while I take on the bad boys' routine." As far as she was concerned, the whole damn mission had just taken a sharp turn into a PSD, Personal Security Detail, with Dylan being the Personal part and her being the Security Detail.

Back in front of the belt shop, she'd felt a flash of fear come off him, and nothing could have surprised her more. For three years, she'd been hearing the stories of Hart and Hawkins, and fear wasn't part of them, ever. What she'd felt hadn't taken any ESP, either. It had been in his eyes, in the sudden draining of color from his face. He'd been scared, which just begged the question—what in the hell had happened to him on Sumba? Besides, of course, getting drugged with God only knew what kind of chemical crap and being chained to a wall.

She wasn't a fool. She knew what the bloody mess around his wrist meant. He'd been shackled, and those stitches weren't there for decoration. He'd been cut, tortured.

"We'll do any routine I order," he said, either missing her point entirely or underestimating her, again.

"Okay," she said, stepping closer to him, her hand still on the pistol inside her tote. "You're right. We should be back at the hotel." Anywhere but on this damn corner, out in the open. They'd walked all over Georgetown, especially the area around Whitfield's mansion. It was tourist season, and they'd seen dozens of Asians—but these men had set something off in him, and that set her off.

She all but tripped the next taxi that came down the street, and in under twenty minutes had him back in their suite, under lock and key, with enough ammo between her and the door to hold off a small army.

"You're not being very subtle," he said when she went to the windows and pulled the drapes closed.

"I'm not trying to be."

"I don't need a bodyguard, Skeeter."

"You were damned nervous for a moment back there on the street," she said, putting it kindly.

"Damned scared," he corrected her.

She stopped cold in the living room, set back on her heels. The last thing she'd ever expected from Dylan Hart was a confession of fear. It was just one step more likely than a confession of love.

"I've got your back, Dylan. I swear." She wouldn't let anything happen to him. At least not anything she could prevent. Yet she knew the possible worst of what could hurt him was completely out of her control—the damn drugs Negara had given him. She'd done some research while he'd been in the shower earlier, and nothing she'd learned had eased her mind. He was in danger just standing there.

"It's not my back I'm worried about, babe, and it wasn't me I was scared for back on the street." He held her gaze for a long moment, long enough for her to get the message and know what was coming next. "You're done, as of right now. You can stay here in this room tonight, or you can go home, but you're not going to Whitfield's, not even Whitfield's driveway."

Skeeter didn't blink. She was a smart woman, smart enough to let him think what he wanted, but actually, she *was* going to Whitfield's, all over Whitfield's, any place and anywhere she thought she needed to be. What she wasn't going to do was argue with him about it. Arguing would only complicate an already complicated situation.

"Jai Traon pirates have tattoos on the backs of their hands," she said. "Their left hands."

"I know."

Of course he knew, and now he knew that she knew, too. Whatever he thought he'd seen, what he'd expected to see was Hamzah Negara's men, dogging him.

"Do you want to tell me about Sumba?"

"No." The word was concise, clear. "What I want is for you to stow this gear or, better yet, get Grant's guys to come back and pick it up. What I want is to get a couple hours of sleep before I hit Whitfield's tonight, and what I want is room service and a blood-rare steak before I go."

"Carnivore." It wasn't a judgment, it was a fact.

"In every way." He held her gaze for another second before nodding at all the gear. "Make it so, Skeeter."

She watched him turn and walk away. He didn't completely close the door to his bedroom, which she knew was more for her benefit than his. Although, who he thought could possibly get into their suite with her on guard was beyond her. Nobody was getting in—and the equipment she'd requisitioned wasn't going anywhere.

Make it so?

She was going to make it so, all right.

Pulling out her cell phone, she speed-dialed General Grant's assistant.

"Red Dog" came a perky voice on the other end.

"Red Dog, it's Skeeter. Where's the Mercedes I ordered this morning?"

"I'll be pulling into the hotel's parking garage in about fifteen minutes."

"Good. Come to the room when you get here. We've got gear to load up."

"Roger that."

She hung up the phone. That's what Skeeter loved about Red Dog. The woman didn't need to roll out a mile of red tape in order to cut to the chase. Since Red Dog had been assigned to Grant's staff a month ago, the whole organization had been running a lot smoother.

The way Skeeter was going to make sure things ran smooth tonight, and there was nothing better to smooth out any rough edges that might crop up than a suppressed .45 semiautomatic pistol, or an HK UMP45, in case any of those rough edges had Jai Traon tattoos on them. She wasn't taking chances, and she wasn't traveling light.

She looked around at the gear and made a command decision: It was all going with her.

But Dylan was right. There was a lot of it, and after another minute of standing there looking at the weapons she'd chosen, and not doubting for a second the instincts that had made her order so much gear in the first place, she made another command decision: She needed backup, somebody besides the guy she was protecting, somebody she wouldn't have to set aside her weapon for in the middle of a gunfight so she could mainline him a yellow Syrette.

Yeah, that's the guy she needed, and she knew right where to find him.

CHAPTER

10

KID CHAOS Chronopolous was a genius. So was Skeeter Bang, and their brilliance didn't show to a better advantage anywhere in Steele Street than up on the eighth-floor firing range.

Travis James finished reloading the spare magazines for his Glock 21 and keyed a shooting drill into the computer.

A lot of the folks at SDF would disagree with him, citing instead the awesome race-quality tune-ups Skeeter did on the brute-powered muscle cars in Steele Street's garages, or her uncanny clairvoyance that Hawkins swore she used to anticipate the lead on a moving target. Kid, they would say, was one of the most elite snipers to ever come out of the U.S. Marine Corps, an institution known for breeding and birthing some of the greatest snipers the world had ever known, like the legendary Carlos Hathcock—and they'd be right.

But for Travis's money, one of the coolest benefits of all that technical, mechanical hoodoo voodoo and marksmanship skill was the firing range on the eighth floor and the computer program Skeeter and Kid had designed to run it.

He loaded a magazine into the Glock, chambered a round, then released the magazine and topped it off with another cartridge before loading it back into the pistol. With the spare magazines on his belt and the Glock in his holster, he was ready to go. Forty shots for ten targets, some stationary, some moving, and he was going to blow the hell out of all of them in record time.

Yeah, it was good to be home, especially in one piece, even if one of those pieces was being held together with ten stitches. He and Creed had gotten fucked in Colombia. Two of their guys had been wounded, one seriously, and both he and Creed could just as easily have been whacked. The mission had been to hook up with a patrol from the Colombian Marine Corps and go with them to set up some highly classified surveillance equipment at an airstrip hidden in the jungle on the Colombian/Venezuelan border. Creed had cut his teeth on similar missions.

Travis had been with him on the last two. But this time they'd walked into an ambush. A band of Colombian rebels had been waiting for them, and there was nothing the narco-terrorists would have loved better than to have caught a couple of gringos in with the Colombian Marines.

Well, none of the narco-bastards were going to catch anything ever again.

Creed had been ruthless.

Travis flipped the pistol's safety on and put it in the holster strapped to his thigh. He'd been pretty fucking ruthless himself.

He'd known what the job was when he'd first started coming to Steele Street to work out with Skeeter, not just in the weight room and on the mats, but in here, on the firing range, shooting thousands of rounds of ammo. Every time he'd pulled the trigger, he'd known exactly what the real-life goal had been: to trade paper targets for flesh and bone. No one knew better than he did what a bullet did when it hit a chest cavity. He'd been an EMT long enough to have been called out on a few shootings. He'd seen death. He'd picked it up off the street and scraped it off the highway.

But to become an instrument of death—he hadn't seen that in his future a year ago, and he sure as hell hadn't seen himself doing what he'd just done in Colombia, not what he'd done with a knife.

Fuck.

He stretched out his right arm and rolled his shoulder, trying to release the kinks he'd gotten during the long plane ride home without moving his left side too much—and he waited.

Hawkins had trained Skeeter so she could protect herself. But Travis had come to Steele Street with a different goal in mind—to protect others. He was no Kenshi the Avenger like Skeeter drew him in her comic books, but if some badass wanted to go mano a mano with someone, especially someone Travis loved, like a Colombian drug lord had done last year with his friend Nikki McKinney Chronopolous, they were going to have to go through him first—and he'd made himself damn hard to go through.

The screen color changed on the computer, and he stepped up to the firing line.

He took a breath, relaxed, and let the anger leave him. Shooting was both a science and a skill, and both were best practiced with cool, calm deliberation. *Slow is smooth, and smooth is fast.*

It wasn't the deaths in Colombia that bothered him, not most of them. When he shot at somebody, he damn well expected them to die. That was the whole plan. He was no one-shot, one-kill, thousand-yard, cold-zero sniper, but he spent a helluva lot of time making damn sure he could hit what he aimed at with a handgun.

Without warning, the lights snapped on at the other end of the range, starting the timer and revealing the random pattern of targets he'd asked the computer to position. With smooth, gunfighter-fast precision, he drew his pistol and started unloading his first magazine. When it was empty, a smooth, tactical reload gave him another thirteen cartridges to run through his Glock—*Bam! Bam! Bam!* The .45 caliber bullets smacked through the targets, one shot after another. His second reload found him cleaning up on the moving targets, trying for at least three shots on each. Four on every target was the goal, as tightly grouped as he could get them, but he hadn't done it yet, not with moving targets in the drill.

When he'd run through his ammo, he released the pistol's slide, flipped on the safety, holstered the gun, and walked down the range to get his targets.

He'd never pulled a trigger in anger, not even in combat. It was the main reason Creed put up with him, the FNG, the Fucking New Guy, on his missions, Travis's Zen-like imperturbability.

Still, he didn't think Creed wanted to know his Psych-major partner had minored in Mediation and Conflict Resolution, not when Creed's idea of conflict resolution more often than not involved a seven-inch, military issue, combat knife—just like Travis's.

Fuck.

He reached in his pocket for a handful of extra

cartridges and began methodically reloading one of his magazines.

There was nothing cool and calm about a knife fight.

He slid the last cartridge into the magazine and then reloaded his pistol, performing the same procedure as last time, as every time—racking one into battery, then releasing the magazine and sliding in an extra cartridge.

His sidearm was always loaded plus one—always. And he was never without it.

He stepped over to the computer to restart the drill, when his phone rang. A quick look at the screen brought a smile to his mouth.

"Hey, Baby Bang. How's tricks?" It *was* good to be home, with Skeeter being one of the main reasons. "And where are you?" He'd really been looking forward to seeing her when he'd gotten to Steele Street. But the only people in the building had been Hawkins and Katya, a very, very pregnant Katya, and Cody Rivera, Creed's wife.

"Am I roaming at twenty gazillion bucks a minute," she asked, "or are you back in Denver yet?"

"Denver."

"Then tricks are good, even if you didn't tell me that Dylan had authorized you for active duty."

"I was going to," he said, feeling a pang of guilt, but not much of one. "Eventually."

"Have you been with Creed in Colombia?"

"Yes." And Baby Bang would have had no business being there.

There was a short pause, while she digested his answer. She'd never been on one of Creed's jungle trips. She'd always gone with Superman, which typically was a different kind of mission, but she'd know what it had been like up there on the border. She'd been around Steele Street long enough to know. She knew the history better than he did.

"You okay?" she asked, her voice making the question so much more than the obvious.

"I will be," he said honestly. Experience was what he lacked, not courage or the commitment to get the job done. With experience, he'd have more resources for putting things in perspective. He knew how it worked. It was just tonight that was rough, coming home to the real world and being alone.

"Then how fast can you get on a plane to Washington, D.C.?"

A welcome sense of relief washed through him. That's what he needed, to get the hell out of Dodge.

"Half an hour, if there's a flight. What's going on?" His bags were by the eighth-floor elevator, still packed. Creed had gone upstairs to his jungle loft and his wife, but Travis had headed straight for the firing range. Nobody needed a third wheel for their postmission reunion with their sweetheart, which was always a guy's first priority. It would have been

Travis's, too, if he'd had a sweetheart, but he was batting a big zero in that department. He seemed to be on the most amazing streak of bad-luck love, never wanting the women who wanted him and never being able to hold on to, or even get his hands on, the women he wanted. The last "love of his life" he'd fallen for, a wild girl with a lot of issues she hadn't been able to give up yet, had moved to the coast, the West Coast. She went to school during the day, worked in Katya's Los Angeles art gallery at night, and always answered his e-mails—but that was as far as he'd gotten in five months, which looked like a strike-out to him.

So he was giving it a rest, swearing off love, working hard instead, and trying not to think too much about sex—because he wasn't getting much, and he sure wasn't getting any tonight, which broke his heart. He could use sex tonight, something to take the edge off. Colombia had been such a fucking mess.

"There's a flight," Skeeter assured him. "And I need backup. Log on to a computer and download the Whitfield/Godwin file and all the Hamzah Negara files. You'll find the access codes to the black files on Negara engraved on Babycakes's headers. That'll get you up to speed. The problem we've run into here is the possibility that Negara's Indonesian pirates were less than a block from Senator Whitfield's mansion in Georgetown this afternoon. I'll make your reservation from this end, pull some strings if I have to. You just get your butt out to DIA. Red Dog will pick you up at Dulles."

"Red Dog?"

"General Grant's new assistant. She's damned efficient, a real go-getter. Wants to get into State."

Travis knew Skeeter meant the State Department. He also knew that General Grant's office in a hell-and-gone annex about a thousand light-years from the Pentagon was a place people hit on their way down, not on their way up. Somebody should probably fill Red Dog the Go-getter in on the facts—somebody other than him. He was done with being the nicest guy on the block.

"So what does Red Dog look like? Who will I be looking for?"

Skeeter let out a short laugh at the questions, and yeah, he understood.

"She'll find you," Skeeter confirmed. "But just in case she goes temporarily blind, you'll be looking for five feet five inches of bright-eyed serious in sensible shoes, with—you guessed it—red hair. Have a good flight, and I'll see you tonight."

Red hair, of course, and Travis figured she probably looked like a dog. That's just the way his life had been going.

IT was going to be a long night, Tony Royce thought, looking at the rows of surgical tools neatly laid out on a gleaming, stainless steel table in the center of the room—a long, endless night for Dylan Hart.

The table was set up next to a dental chair bolted to the white-tiled floor. The walls were also tiled in white. Even the ceiling was covered in white ceramic tiles. Everything, everywhere was tiled and white, for easy washdowns and quick cleanups.

He was quite impressed. The room was an exact copy of one in Negara's medical building on Sumba, right down to the drain in the floor. This building was so well hidden in the trees on Negara's Virginia estate, Royce hadn't even seen it when he'd arrived.

"You will stay for the festivities?" Negara asked.

It wasn't a question, and Royce didn't assume for a second that it was.

"Of course. I wouldn't miss them." Not often, but every now and then he felt a small pang of remorse for the turn his life had taken, but it never lasted long enough to make much of an impression, and it was never these situations that generated the emotion. He'd been in rooms like this many times over the years, officially, under orders, and righteously assured that he was one of the good guys— one of the good guys strong enough to stomach what it sometimes took to keep the world safe for democracy.

Then, somewhere along the road, he'd started thinking he was keeping the world safe for capitalism, and from there it had been a very short jump to keeping the world safe for current political expediency. It hadn't been too much of a leap from there into independent contractor status and keeping the world safe for his own financial gain.

None of it ever made him lose sleep. Tonight's "festivities" wouldn't, either.

"You were right about the girl," Negara said. "She is quite memorable, and for a small fee, she was remembered checking into room four eighteen at the Hotel Lafayette."

God, he was good.

Royce smiled. "I'm pleased the information was useful."

"Quite." Negara also smiled. "And perhaps you can be of further use to me."

He didn't like the sound of that, but was very casual in his reply.

"Perhaps. What do you need?"

Negara's smile broadened, which was sometimes a deceptive expression. Royce had a feeling this was one of those times.

"Room four eighteen was empty when my men got there, and though there were still items of a personal nature present, I am not inclined to leave any holes in my net."

Of course not, Royce thought.

"So you're still planning on posting men at Whitfield's," he said. "I think that's a good idea."

"Yes, yes," Negara said. "I knew you would understand a multipronged approach."

Royce inadvertently reacted to Negara's statement, allowing a quick, skeptical lift of his brow. Almost as quickly, he schooled his features back into a bland mask.

"You do not approve?" the old man asked. He didn't miss much.

"Actually, I do," Royce said, though in truth, it had been the multipronged approach to the Dominika Starkova case that had contributed to his career's demise. Too many agencies with their fingers in the pie, and his own boss putting other agents in the field without telling him, had all helped make him look like a fool by the end of the day. "I would keep two men at the hotel and deploy the others at Whitfield's. With men at both places, you'll greatly increase your chances of success."

"Yes, yes." The old man looked happy again. "This is my plan, but now I feel I am—how do you say?—short-handed at the senator's, especially since I am also covering Hart's base of operations in Denver tonight. Attacking on three fronts at the same time, I believe, will surely gain us some advantage, and at least one hostage. If you could be at Senator Whitfield's, strictly in the background, of course, to add your expertise, it would be deeply appreciated."

Or you can kill me now and be done with it—or so

you think. Royce knew the difference between a request and an ultimatum. He also knew how exposed Negara was by being in the United States, away from his lair on Sumba. It wasn't just the money that had drawn him out, it was the need to save face as well. If agents of the U.S. government could get away with seventeen million, they could just as easily get away with seventy million. Negara needed to send a message, and if the agent who had done the deed disappeared and was never seen again—so be it. Having Royce help coordinate the hands-on part of the operation, as he'd done in Jakarta, greatly increased its chances of success.

And for that, no thinly veiled threats were necessary. Royce wanted Hart taken out, and he was willing to ally himself with Negara in the heart of America to get the job done.

"I would be honored to help," he said, and later tonight, when Dylan Hart was strapped into the dental chair, any risks he'd taken would pale in comparison to the satisfaction he'd feel at having overcome his enemy.

CHAPTER

11

Look for *an angel*.

Those were her orders, and Gillian "Red Dog" Pentycote was good at following orders—even crazy ones, like "look for an angel."

Roger that, she thought, looking for all she was worth. But the only thing she was seeing was hundreds of very unangelic, crabby people trying to find their luggage in the baggage claim area of Dulles International Airport. Everyone arriving on the flight from Denver looked frazzled—businessmen wearing rumpled suits, families who needed their hotel rooms and room service, people at the end of their day who were getting home late to their wives, children, girlfriends, boyfriends, pets, whatever.

But no angels.

She pushed her glasses back up on her nose. She'd give it a couple more minutes, then call Mr. James at the cell phone number Skeeter had given her.

Angel, she thought again, giving her head a little shake. It wasn't like Skeeter to be so vague.

A small smile curved her mouth. There sure as heck wasn't anything vague about Skeeter Bang in the flesh. Gillian had never met anyone more "there," more colorful, distinct, and utterly unique. The voice Gillian had been dealing with over the phone for the last month had not prepared her for someone so young and with ten times her muscle tone. The head-shot photo in Grant's files showed little beyond a black ball cap with a dragon embroidered on it and a pair of mirrored sunglasses. There was the button nose, but the photograph on whole had been remarkably lacking in information. There had been no clue about the hair, or the tattoos, or the scar across her forehead . . . or that body.

Gillian instinctively stood a little straighter. She'd had some training, self-defense and weapons, since she'd started at SDF. General Grant had insisted on it, but she was a long way from looking like she could kick somebody's butt, and even further from actually being able to do it. Skeeter looked like she did it in her sleep.

This "angel" named Travis James probably looked the same way, the way all the guys at Steele Street looked—Hart, Hawkins, Rivera, Younger, and Chronopolous. The file photos she had of the operators were pretty good—well lit, no hats, no sunglasses—and not a one of them looked anything like an angel, except maybe Creed Rivera, if there had been a way to get the feral look out of his eyes. That boy was wild and definitely no angel. They didn't even have a photograph of Mr. James on file, or even a file on the guy, which just highlighted the reason she'd been hired to tidy up General Grant's loose ends. He had about a million of them hanging out of his filing cabinets and stashed around his small suite of offices next to the boiler room in an annex nobody else in Washington, D.C., even knew existed. With the boss out of town, she'd planned on working a little overtime to see if she could get ahead of all the general's junk, especially his top-secret junk, which, inexperienced as she was, she knew was supposed to be secured somewhere, inside something with locks and codes on it. Some of the documents she'd run across in the last month she shouldn't have seen dead.

Besides, it was the weekend, when her life slowed down to somewhere between a crawl and a full-out stop. No, sirree. Not much happened in Gillian

Pentycote's life between five P.M. on Friday and nine o'clock Monday morning, other than dinner with her parents and a full dose of relatives on Sunday after church, including her two sisters, two brothers, and various wives, husbands, children, aunts, cousins, and uncles. Not even Skeeter almost instantly hanging her with the really cool handle "Red Dog" when Grant had first hired her changed the basic facts of her social life, but this weekend, fate had stepped in and handed her a mission, at least as close to a mission as she'd gotten. After only a month on the job, she'd spent the afternoon doing a weapons check.

A weapons check—God, she could still hardly believe it, loading submachine guns, checking batteries in equipment, and testing communications devices. It sure beat the hell out of her last job, buried in the Environmental Sciences labs at the University of Arizona, running errands and scurrying around after her VIP—Very Important Professor—husband.

Ex-husband, she reminded herself, and it wasn't as if her name wasn't also on the book they'd written, detailing the ecology of the Paleocene Eocene Thermal Maximum. It was, right after his, in smaller print—*dammit*.

She would be damned surprised, though, if Dr. Kenneth Pentycote ever managed to see his name on another book. Her organizational skills aside, without her insightful brilliance discerning the

underlying correlations between all those facts
Ken was so enamored of unearthing and flaunting,
there'd be damn little of actual academic signifi-
cance to make a book of his worth publishing, and
he could take that to the bank. Or rather, he
couldn't take it to the bank.

But her past was behind her, the disaster of it,
the pain of it. She only hoped the best for Ken and
his new wife, and the child they had on the way.
Divorce happened. People moved on, and she, for
one, had finally stopped moving in circles.

A boy—that's what Ken and Kimberly were
having, a baby boy.

Gillian blinked, then blinked again. She'd stopped
crying, too. Oh, man, she'd *way* stopped crying, given
it up months ago. Thank God.

She blinked one more time, pushed her glasses
up again, and went back to doing what she was getting paid to do tonight—find an angel.

It didn't take much looking around at this crowd
of washed-out, run-down travelers to realize there
wasn't an angel anywhere in the—

Holy Mother of God. Her heart caught in her
throat, and she tightened her hand on her bag.

*Angel at two o'clock, coming around the baggage
carrel, coming out of the crowd*—and moving in slow
motion, she swore it. Everything suddenly seemed
to have slowed down, except her pulse. Her skin
flashed hot, then cold, and she gripped her messen-

ger bag tighter. An edge of dizziness threatened to take hold. Then she realized she was holding her breath.

Breathe, Gillian Pentycote, she admonished herself. *Breathe.*

But so help her God, it was Travis James. She didn't have a doubt in her mind. Six feet of power and grace and blond hair pulled back in a ponytail at the nape of his neck. Gray pants, white T-shirt, black jacket, and incredibly blue eyes—Caribbean blue. And the face, so help her God, chiseled, beautiful, the shadow of a beard across an elegant jaw.

Skeeter should have warned her, should have said something—something more than "angel." "Angel" could mean anything: kind, warmhearted, a comfort in a time of need, somebody with wings. There was nothing about the word that implicitly implied drop-freaking-dead gorgeous.

But he was, completely gorgeous, completely unexpected, and he most definitely looked like a comfort, one of those seriously dangerous and dangerously addicting comforts she hadn't had in a very long time.

God help her.

He stopped and leaned over to lift a large backpack off the conveyor belt. A woman bumped into him, turned to excuse herself, and instead all but melted into a puddle at his feet. Gillian saw the whole thing, the cool apology ready on the woman's lips, the stunning moment of awareness, and the complete and total capitulation of her common sense.

Then the angel smiled back, and every synapse Gillian had blew—like fuses.

Sex. That's what his smile said. *Hot sex. All over you sex. Inside you sex.*

Her mind was suddenly so utterly blank, she was lost. She couldn't remember her own name. One breath passed, then another, and she was still riveted in place, trying, frantically, to reboot her brain.

TRAVIS hadn't been in Washington, D.C., for a few months, but nothing had changed, not in Dulles. It was still crowded, still hectic, still exactly like dozens of other airports he'd been in and out of lately. He looked around the baggage area, looking for five feet five inches of bright-eyed serious in sensible shoes, with red hair.

He almost instantly spotted a likely candidate, but the woman didn't look particularly bright-eyed or serious. Her wire-rimmed glasses were slightly askew, and she looked a little shell-shocked behind them. He dropped his gaze to her feet and reconsidered. The shoes were right, athletic wear, very sensible, except one of them was coming untied—and the legs were nice, what he could see of them peeking out from under her sensible just-above-the-knee khaki skirt, which matched her sensible tucked-in-at-the-waist khaki shirt, except the shirt was coming untucked, and both items of clothing had a number of cargo pockets stuffed to the gills with pens, pencils, scraps of paper, small notebooks, and even smaller electronics, which gave her kind of a loose-around-the-edges look. Wires snaked from a couple of the pockets to a few others, which gave her kind of a miniature-suicide-bomber look and made him wonder how in the hell she'd gotten into the airport, and made him hope she wasn't Red Dog.

Starting forward anyway, just in case she was his ride, he sidestepped a couple of young boys wrestling their way through the unclaimed luggage. When he looked up again, the woman's gaze was clearing and was definitely focused on him.

Well, hell. Just his luck. She was Red Dog, even though her hair wasn't red, not in a carrot-top way. It was auburn, chin length, and more than a little tousled, like it had gotten away from her during the fixing stage, the same way her sensible clothes were getting away from her. Or maybe there was a gale-force wind outside the terminal.

She looked to be in her early thirties, which even at twenty-four, he normally considered a very nice age for a woman—*very* nice, for all the right reasons. But Red Dog wasn't quite fitting into his very-nice-thirty-year-old-woman category. She was fitting into his probably-perfectly-nice-thirty-year-old-urchin category—and she had the lock on it, even with those legs.

But he was here, with Skeeter to hang out with, and he had a driver, and he got to work with the boss, Dylan Hart, which beat the hell out of being home alone and thinking way too much, so things were good.

He'd done his homework on the plane, and the Whitfield/Godwin part of the mission didn't look too risky or difficult, not with Hart pulling the heist. But the Hamzah Negara crap was nothing but bad. If Skeeter was right, and the Negara boys had followed Dylan to Washington, D.C., this thing could be a goatfuck waiting to happen.

And she'd called him to help out, not Creed, not Kid, who, admittedly, was in Paris, or Quinn, who wasn't, and not Hawkins, who was still in a cast, but him, the FNG. He liked that, and he wasn't going to let her down. It didn't matter that he'd been put on active duty ahead of her, he knew who had the maddest skills.

The urchin was moving toward him now, too, and at about forty feet and closing, he started reevaluating his first impression. She was a bit of a mess, sure, but she was a bit of a cute mess, and very bright-eyed behind her caddywampus glasses, just like Skeeter had said. At thirty feet, he admitted that he liked the way she moved. For someone who wasn't very big, she had a strong, purposeful stride.

At twenty feet, he could tell her eyes were a warm, amber brown. At ten feet, he noticed how sweet her mouth was, very expressive and curving into an unsure smile. At five feet, he could see that she'd missed a buttonhole on her shirt. There was a small gap where the extra buttonhole curved out, and another gap where she hadn't quite gotten the zipper on her skirt completely closed, and during her short walk, her left shoe had come completely untied.

He liked women, loved them, especially when they were coming undone—and she was, one little loose edge at a time. He smiled, which made her cheeks turn pink, which he loved even more, and at three feet, at a standstill with his hand out, he found himself smiling down at her and wondering what it would take to get a perfectly nice thirty-year-old urchin into bed. He didn't consider himself a player. He *wasn't* a player—but he wanted to play with her.

Nothing could have surprised him more. Not only wasn't she his type, but with her pockets full of papers and wires, and with—no kidding—a small piece of white first-aid tape holding the corner of her glasses together, all of it making her look like Gadget Girl, she was the complete opposite of his type.

"Red Dog?"

"Mr. James."

"Travis." He took her hand when she extended it.

He also especially liked smart women, gravitated toward them, but he'd never been sexually attracted to the goddess geeks and nerdettes of the world.

Never.

"Thanks for coming down to pick me up," he finished.

Except once. Regan McKinney, the love of his life, who had married another SDF operator, definitely qualified for royal geekdom. She'd recently finished her doctorate in Geology and spent her days scraping away at dinosaur bones for a natural history museum in Denver, and he knew for a fact that she liked all things that had to do with science, all kinds of science, but especially dinosaur science. The thing with Regan, though, was that she looked like every guy's favorite sex fantasy, blond and built, with elegant cheekbones, long bangs, and a soft, full mouth. She did not look like anybody's idea of a dinosaur doctor.

"It's my job, Mr. James . . . um, Travis, and I'm very happy to be doing it," Red Dog said, looking very serious behind her crooked glasses, and still shaking his hand.

And Regan had underwear, a whole wardrobe of it, sheer silk and lace, in every color of the rainbow. He'd never actually seen Regan in any of her underwear, except in one notable photograph her sister, Nikki, had taken, but he'd seen the underwear. In fact, he'd spent some of the most formative years of his life ogling Regan McKinney's underwear while it dried on the towel bar in the upstairs bathroom of the McKinney house in Boulder, Colorado. Old Doc McKinney should have charged him rent for all the time he'd spent up there.

"Skeeter left some things for you at the hotel," Red Dog continued. "We'll stop there first, and then I'll take you over to Senator Whitfield's. So, if you have all your luggage . . . ?"

But this woman, even with wanting to take her to bed, he wanted, somehow, also to straighten her up, had a real urge to tap a few pocketfuls of paper into a tidy stack, to clean the smudges off her glasses, to redo the buttons on her shirt, correctly, to zip her and tie her, and get her back into her clothes, before someone else noticed she was coming undone.

"This is everything, just the pack," he said, finally releasing her hand, and not so absently wondering what kind of underwear a girl named Red Dog would be wearing underneath all that sensible, serviceable, and practically falling-off khaki.

CHAPTER

12

LEANING BACK against an empty Town Car parked in Whitfield's driveway, Skeeter took one long, last drag off her cigarette before dropping it on the concrete and grinding it out with the toe of her boot. That was her last one. She swore it.

She popped a couple of cinnamon mints in her mouth and went back to doing what she'd been doing—watching and waiting, and biding her time. She'd already done everything else, including taking it a little too personally that Travis still hadn't gotten to Whitfield's. She didn't need the extra aggravation. Dylan had been giving her plenty. Between him getting up, and getting his steak, and finally get-

ting in the Mercedes, it had just been one argument
after another tonight. But by God, she was right
where she'd planned on being, or close enough,
right here in the freaking senator's freaking parking
lot of a driveway, with dozens of other drivers and
what seemed to be about forty frat boy valets.

Okay, it was a compromise, like wearing the
cheesy chauffeur uniform Dylan had gotten her, instead of her very cool Versace gown, but at least
she wasn't sitting on her butt back at the Hotel
Lafayette, or on her way back to Denver, and even
though she was the one dressed like a nutcracker in
a black suit with black satin piping, gold braid, and
epaufreakinglets with red fringe, she had the satisfaction of knowing that Dylan, the world's biggest
Mr. Know-It-All, didn't know nearly as much as he
thought he did.

He didn't know what was in the trunk of their
car, which she'd parked on the street, down a ways
from the mansion for a better getaway. He hadn't
taken the time or even suspected for a moment that
he should look in the trunk, because he'd *ass-umed*
that she'd followed orders instead of thinking on
her feet, which is what she got paid to do.

Just as well. Mr. Know-It-All had enough on his
mind without the burden of knowing she'd brought
all her toys to the party—and then some.

A small smile curved her lips. She hadn't con-
fessed to half of the equipment she had stuffed in

her rucksacks. She had flash-bangs and flashlights, tactical, high intensity—the kind where a girl could blind the bad guys and shoot them at her quick-fingered leisure. Dylan didn't like her Tac II combat knife? Well, maybe if the going got tough, he'd prefer one of her razor-sharp, five-inch folding knives, or her "MacGyver" knife and gizmo tool. She had sling ropes, carabiners, pressure dressings—which she hoped to God she wouldn't need—and a weatherproof notebook with plastic-laminated pages. In case she fell into a lake or had to ford a river. Here. In the middle of Senator Whitfield's driveway.

Geez. Maybe she was overprepared.

Nah, she decided after a moment's considera-tion. She'd nailed this gig.

The sudden vibration in her pocket was a good sign, something she'd been waiting for since before they'd left the hotel.

Pulling out her phone, she flipped it open and brought it to her ear. "Skeeter."

"Hey, Skeet. Travis. I'm with Red Dog. *Whoa* . . . watch out for that . . . uh, truck. . . . Uh, Skeet, we're heading to the hotel now. We're still at least—*oh, geez* . . ."

There was a short pause.

"Half an hour out," Travis said, sounding a little breathless.

"You okay?"

"Yeah, I'm . . ." There was a long, pregnant pause, during which she could sense him holding his breath again. ". . . fine, just fine. Uh, maybe you should . . ."

"Should what?" she asked, when he didn't continue.

"Uh, not you. Red Dog. Uh, Red Dog, why don't you let me take that and . . . uh, put it over here. . . . No, honestly, there's plenty of room."

"Are you sure you're okay?"

"Fine," he answered, a little too quickly, she thought. "Just fine. Half an hour to the hotel, or less, and Red Dog says the Lafayette is just a few minutes from Senator Whitfield's, so hopefully . . . *damn* . . . I can be there in under an hour."

An hour. "Damn" was right. She hoped to be headed back to the hotel herself by then.

"We'll stick to the plan," she said. "With you coming to Whitfield's ASAP. If Dylan and I get ahead of schedule on this end, I'll call."

"So how does it look?"

"Like a very big party. Nothing unusual . . . yet." She wasn't looking for trouble that wasn't there, but she still had the same uneasy feeling she'd had this morning when she'd called in her equipment list to Red Dog, and that feeling said trouble was looking for her, or Dylan.

"Let's hope it stays that way. I'll be there as soon as I . . . *whoa* . . . can."

Whoa can? What the hell was *whoa* can?

"Thanks. I rented you a tuxedo, the best I could get on short notice. It'll be in the closet in my room at the suite. I'd like you to work the party from the inside."

"How bad is the best you could get?" For a couple of seconds, he sounded skeptical, instead of breathless.

"You'll be fine. You won't stand out. I promise." Skeeter wasn't worried about the quality of the tuxedo. Travis James made everything look good. He even made nothing look good. Some people would say he *especially* made nothing look good, being the favorite nude model for one of the hottest rising stars on the American art scene—Nikki McKinney Chronopolous, a name that was a mouthful by anyone's definition.

"Then I'll see you as soon as I get suited up."

She could almost see the smile she heard in his voice, and the unusual nervous edge that went with it—damned unusual. Nothing made Travis James nervous. He was the personification of the laid-back, Boulder slacker dude, imperturbable. Of course, he'd just gotten back from Colombia with Creed, and those missions sometimes slid toward a wild, dark side. She'd know just how wild when she saw him. None of the guys could hide anything from her—except Dylan. He was the boss, the loner, the brick wall she could never get around, which was damned inconvenient for a lot of reasons, especially tonight.

"Thanks. I'll see you when you get here." She hung up the phone and stuck it back in her pocket. Then she checked her watch.

She and Dylan had hammered out a schedule. Actually, Dylan had hammered out a schedule, while she'd held her tongue and silently fumed. She'd won the war, she told herself, she was at Whitfield's, but she'd definitely lost the schedule skirmish.

The plan, according to Dylan, was that he would mingle and schmooze for an hour or two on his own and discreetly check out the lay of the land, including spotting any added guards on duty for the party, or cameras that hadn't shown up on the plans of Whitfield's security system. Then once he'd made himself perfectly at home in the posh palace and practically invisible in the posh crowd, he would mosey on back to Whitfield's office, jimmy open the door, use Whitfield's fingerprints to open the safe, then grab the file and mosey back out to the party, and from there, back out to the Mercedes, while she stood around and stayed out of trouble.

Well, they were well into the mission, and she'd done plenty of standing around. She'd also mingled with the chauffeurs, schmoozed with the valets, discreetly checked the lay of the land, and located the outside door into Whitfield's office, and she was ready to make her move, which was not leaning her butt against somebody's Town Car and shining the side panels all night with her black satin piping. The Godwin file was as good as hers, and once she got it, she was calling Dylan on his phone and telling him to ditch the party, they were going home.

Then she was going after Negara. The research she'd done this afternoon on the drugs used in interrogations had scared the hell out of her. Dylan should have stayed on the U.S.S. *Jefferson*. He'd had no business coming home, and no business whatsoever in taking the Godwin mission tonight.

She didn't want to think about the injuries she'd seen on his wrist, but she had been, a lot.

Yeah, Negara was hers, but it was going to take time. She'd need months of intel gathering and preparation for the mission, and she'd need Kid Chaos to make the hit.

She popped another couple of cinnamon mints in her mouth. She didn't need anybody's help to get the damn Godwin file. After Dylan had gone upstairs to pack this morning at Steele Street, she'd done a little packing of her own. For the most part, both hers and Dylan's rucksacks—whether he'd claim his or not—were identically equipped, but she'd brought a few extra pieces to put in hers: a small biometric fingerprint pad no bigger than a compact, which it resembled, and her own version of a decoder ring—the DRSB303. The only biometric lock in Steele Street belonged to Creed, and she'd taken the damn thing apart and recoded it so many times, it was a wonder it still worked. Except, of course, she'd made damn sure it worked, even after the time she'd programmed it to open only when reading the print off her left butt cheek.

Creed had thought that was a hoot.

His wife, Cody, hadn't thought it was quite so funny. "*Kids,*" she'd said.

Old married people, Skeeter had thought.

She didn't have anything quite so creative in mind for Whitfield's safe. Using her own fingerprints was out of the question, of course, but she had the vice president's, a little souvenir Grant had sent her a few months back, and since Whitfield and the veep were in the same political party, she figured the deed would create a lot of private conversation but not much press, which was just the way they liked things at SDF—media free.

Cripes. She wished Travis were already here. Her "spidey sense" was humming.

She wanted him on the inside, watching out for Dylan, since she'd been banned from the party and told in no uncertain terms not to budge her butt from the car.

Screw uncertain terms. She'd budged big-time, and she was ready to budge again. She couldn't afford to wait for backup. She wanted to wrap this thing up and get the hell out of there—and the time to start was now. She'd "cased the joint," and the party looked exactly the way it was supposed to look, like well-controlled chaos. Everybody was moving in the right direction, everybody doing their job, including the guests she'd been checking out since she and Dylan had first pulled up.

So this was it.

Pushing off the Town Car, she did a quick check of her pockets to make sure she had her B&E— breaking and entering—tools, and her handy-dandy interference remote for messing with the camera honed in on Whitfield's office door.

Her suppressed Para .45 was concealed in a shoulder holster under her uniform jacket, her Tac II combat knife was in a sheath on her belt, and she knew for a fact that she wasn't the only chauffeur in Whitfield's driveway packing heat and a seven-inch blade. Some of these "drivers" had necks as big as her thighs.

She could think of a lot of ways she would have preferred to cross the huge expanse of open lawn from the driveway to Whitfield's office, like invisibly, on her belly, in camo cream and a balaclava, but given that there was damn little hope of stealth in her cheesy outfit and amid the crowd of chauffeurs, valets, and caterers milling around the grounds, she was sticking with a full-out frontal approach. She'd just walk past all of them and then blend into the scenery at the back of the house. Yes, sir, she'd take all the gold braid and black satin piping Dylan had stuffed her into and pretend to be a tree—like maybe a Christmas tree. She wasn't even going to mention the red fringe.

He'd done it on purpose. She knew it. There was no way to get a uniform this gaudy by accident. But if he thought it was going to clip her wings, he was wrong. Her biggest problem was the guard patrolling the back of the mansion, but even dressed like a Christmas tree, she had enough skill to make sure he didn't see her.

DYLAN had a bad feeling.

It wasn't new.

He'd gotten this bad feeling ten days ago at the exact instant that he'd been snatched off the street in Jakarta, and though it had alternately gotten much, much worse and somewhat better, it had never gotten close to going away. It was clinging to him, like a giant leech with its sucker locked onto his skin.

Interestingly enough, there had been actual leeches attached to him on Sumba. Not torturously, just naturally, a few dozen hugely fat, free-range leeches that had made him their home for a few days, and since he'd been shackled to the wall, they'd pretty much had their way with him.

Fuck.

He hated leeches, and there was absolutely no reason for him to be thinking about them while he was going through the contents of Arthur Whitfield's safe, looking for the Godwin file and breaking out in a sweat while he did it. The air-conditioning in the rest of the mansion didn't seem to reach back into this cubbyhole of a vault room behind Whitfield's bookcases—and he wasn't out of there yet.

Dammit.

That was the thing about going through a lot of papers—trying to find the right one, and Whitfield had a boatload of documents in his safe. Shelves of them, and the likelihood of a clearly stamped name on the envelope containing the file he needed was damn slim, especially in the case of something like Godwin, where even the best of it would be couched in acronyms and double-speak. Ordering the assassination of two fellow countrymen had a way of making people obscurant.

That had been the rumor—assassination of a legally appointed ambassador from within, decided by a secret committee who had answered to no one except themselves and a member of the president's cabinet. The orders had been processed through the most clandestine channels. The hits planned and executed by a group of shadow warriors whose names had never been revealed, not even to the men who had signed the orders.

Shadow warriors like him, Dylan realized, not taking much comfort in the fact.

Finally, a date at the top of the next folder caught his eye. Twelve years ago was about right.

He broke the seal on the envelope inside the folder and ran the blue light from his diode flashlight over the top page. By page three, he knew he'd hit pay dirt. He quickly flipped to the last page and checked the signatures on the orders. In spite of himself, he was impressed and, in one instance, downright amazed. He hadn't thought the guy whose signature he was looking at had those kind of balls. Grant had been right. The Godwin file was a political dirty bomb, well worth the effort of getting it. Satisfied, he packaged the papers back into their envelope and slid the folder inside his jacket.

He'd been inside the vault room for five minutes—five overheated, get-your-ass-busted minutes. When everything was put back in place, he closed the full-length door on the vault and ran his flashlight over the inside of the small room housing it, assuring himself that nothing had fallen off the shelves or been inadvertently left outside the actual safe.

One quick check and he was good to go.

He flipped off his flashlight before easing out of the closet-sized room and around the swing-open bookcase, where "Chaucer" held the key—or rather, in this instance, the keypad. With the miracle of impeccable engineering, the whole section of the bookcase swung closed without so much as a snick of sound, but he'd barely put his foot on the first step of the circular staircase when something set off his internal alarm system.

He went instant mannequin, all his senses on alert. He couldn't see or hear anyone, but he knew without a doubt that there was another intruder in the room—someone who smelled like cinnamon. The spicy scent of it was faintly, but indelibly, in the air.

Stepping back into the shadows of the loft, he angled himself to watch the staircase and the bookcase, and he waited. This was not the first time he'd run into another thief during a heist. It was actually the third time, and like the other two times, this guy was too late. The deed was done. Godwin was his. Unless they were after something else, and considering all that he'd seen in Whitfield's vault, that was a distinct possibility, especially if the thief was looking for cash, jewelry, or one or more of the art pieces Dylan had been surprised as hell to see in the senator's possession. He'd been tempted by the small Picasso himself.

If it hadn't been for the cinnamon, the intruder would have been nearly undetectable. His moves were silent, like a wraith's, yet Dylan could feel his presence and sense his movement up the stairs. As soon as the other guy was inside the vault room,

Dylan would descend to the main floor and let himself out of the office. The other man would never know he'd been there.

No one would . . .

Except for her.

The thief suddenly came into view, and Dylan's jaw clenched, like a vise.

Unfuckingbelievable.

She slid up the last few stairs and into the loft, no more than a shadow, nearly imperceptible except as an eddy of darkness—with the glint of a gold epaulet.

He couldn't believe it. He'd been absolutely unequivocal in his orders, so what part of "stay in the car" hadn't she understood?

Four lousy words, and she couldn't do as she'd been told?

That was it. Her career was toast. She was a rogue, a renegade, and she'd just bought herself a one-way ticket to the Commerce City garage and Johnny Ramos's broom. He wouldn't tolerate this kind of insurrection. SDF had been built on teamwork. He needed team players. Not someone he couldn't count on to hold her position, and her position had been the two square feet of Cordovan leather that made up the driver's seat in the Mercedes. Automotive leather plus her butt. It was all so simple.

And she'd blown it.

Why?

What could possibly have compelled her to disobey a direct order?

She was past him now, looking for Chaucer on the shelves of books, and he reached up and wiped the back of his hand across his upper lip. Even outside the vault room, the loft was still hot, typical August in the nation's capital.

He could have moved then, gone over and cut her party real short in a damn hurry, but something held him where he stood—good, old-fashioned curiosity.

Professional curiosity.

He'd automatically started a clock in his head the instant she'd reached the loft, and the seconds were ticking down. How long to breach the bookcase? And could she possibly open the safe?

He couldn't imagine her coming this far without a plan in mind, and he was damned curious to see what it was. He'd put Whitfield's fingerprints back in the case in his pocket. She was on her own there. Grant had only sent one set.

The bookcase opened, and she moved inside.

Okay. Ten seconds to find the book, key the code, and disappear behind the shelves. That was A+ work by anybody's standards. But the cinnamon, damn, that was flunk-your-ass dangerous. He'd have to tell her to forgo the mints on a heist, before he let her out of his sight again.

Which, of course, was a moot point. Not only was she not going to be in his sight for him to let her out of it, but she wasn't going to be out of the sight of whoever's sight she was in, like Johnny Ramos's, or Superman's—or something like that. Suddenly, it wasn't very damn clear in his head, because it was getting just a little too damn hot in the loft to think.

And the leeches.

He looked down at the big one that had just dropped from out of nowhere onto his shoe.

Jesus.

Another one almost instantly landed next to the first, splatting onto his laces.

Double Jesus.

This wasn't right. Pink phosphorescent leeches should not be falling from out of nowhere, or the ceiling, or wherever, and landing on his shoe.

He shook them both off, and they disappeared, which was not necessarily a good sign. As a matter of fact, as far as signs went, that one sucked. He lifted his gaze and refocused on the bookcase.

He was in trouble.

There wasn't a heat wave in the loft. There were no leeches dropping off the ceiling, and even if there had been, they would not have been Day-Glo pink, like the image of Skeeter's bra, which suddenly seemed to be indelibly inked on his brain in the shape of a butterfly, like the one floating a few inches in front of his face, gently flapping its wings—*dammit*. His wires were crossed—the hard way, with the XTNWO, whatzit 7, 8, 9, 10 crap Negara had injected him with back on Sumba.

He took a breath, steadied himself. He knew what to do here. He had a plan.

He reached into his pocket, pulled out a silver case, took one look inside, and told himself not to panic—but his Syrettes had melted. There was nothing left of them except a thin gel sheet.

Then it hit him—*wrong case.*

Checking his other pocket, he pulled out the second case and popped it open.

Still in trouble, he thought.

He was supposed to have three Syrettes: red, blue, and yellow. And he did have three, but they were all Day-Glo pink and wiggling around in the case like leeches.

Fuck.

Everything was starting to wiggle around, including the floor, where he was standing in a small but growing pile of Day-Glo leeches.

God, he hated leeches, and if they started inching their way up his pants legs, imaginary or not, he was going to freak.

He looked back at the case in his hand and knew the odds were not in his favor. He couldn't just grab one of the slippery things and try to inject himself, hoping he'd picked the red Syrette.

He needed help.

He needed Skeeter.

He slowly lifted his gaze to the far end of the loft, peering across a small sea of pink phosphene leeches and pink flapping butterflies, and goddamn, it suddenly looked like a very long way to the vault room.

CHAPTER

13

———◆———

DYLAN HART was here. The sense of satisfaction Royce felt was almost overwhelming. He knew his enemy and had predicted his moves with commendable accuracy.

From the backseat of a black Land Rover, he watched the girl, Skeeter Bang, make her way across the grounds of Whitfield's estate, and if she was here, Hart was here. The party was complete. There were people everywhere, inside and outside the mansion: the hundreds who had been invited; the dozens it took to serve them; plus one thief, one mechanic in a chauffeur's uniform, and five pirates, including him.

Yes, tonight he counted himself among the Jai Traon, at Negara's request and by his own choice, and so he would remain, until Dylan Hart was dead. He was hoping the commitment didn't last much beyond noon tomorrow. Of course, if the retrieval of Negara's money required Hart's physical presence at any stage, the man would not be killed tonight. Dr. Souk would take him to the edge of life, the very edge, but would be careful not to take him so far that he couldn't be brought back.

It was a fascinating thing to watch—Dr. Souk manipulating scalpels and syringes like a maestro of destruction. It never failed to amaze Royce just how much damage could be done to a man's body before a fatal level was reached. He'd never watched a woman being tortured, but if pressed, he would put his money on a man lasting longer. With luck, he'd know the truth of that within the week.

Negara had made it clear that he wanted Skeeter Bang alive and untouched to begin with, and Royce couldn't imagine that his interest in the girl wouldn't last at least a few days before he gave her to Dr. Souk. If nothing else, she would make a fine gift to the pirates—not including him. He thought the girl was disgusting, a piece of street trash who should have stayed in the alleys of Denver where Christian Hawkins had found her. SB303—that was her tag, and it summed up what he hated most about SDF, Special Defense Force. They were a bunch of misfits, psychos, ex-cons, and juvenile delinquents who ran wild on Uncle Sam's dollar. They didn't play by the rules. They didn't follow protocol. Rumor had it that they'd stolen half a million dollars' worth of rough-cut diamonds out of a shipment of dinosaur bones a year or so ago and used the money to supplement their budget and top off their slush fund.

It was no way to run a government operation, and the government who sanctioned them was no place for Tony Royce. They wanted rogues? Well, he'd made himself one of the best, or one of the worst, depending on a person's point of view. All he had to do was look at the men with him in the Land Rover and see the company he was keeping. Fucking pirates, every one. He knew two of them from Sumba, the men named Kota and Garin. Kota was the only one who spoke English in the group, and he was obviously the leader. Royce hadn't seen the other two men before this afternoon at Negara's Virginia estate. He didn't know their names and wasn't interested in finding out. In his mind they were Jai One and Jai Two, and both of them looked capable of delivering whatever mayhem the night required. Royce didn't have a doubt in his mind that every pirate Negara had deployed for the evening's activities was similarly skilled, though he had serious doubts about how much good any of that skill was going to do the Jai Traon assigned to the attack on Steele Street.

He let out a small dismissive sigh, still watching Skeeter Bang. The men in Denver were doomed, but that wasn't his problem. His problem was Hart and the girl, and neither one of them should be too difficult to handle. Hart must still feel about half dead. He'd been used and abused on Sumba, and if Royce wasn't mistaken, some of the drugs Dr. Souk had injected him with should still be causing him problems. Once he had them restrained and in the Land Rover, he'd call Negara and have him call off the men waiting at the Hotel Lafayette. Then everything on his end would be cleaned up. They could all go over the border into Virginia and, as Negara had put it, let "the festivities" begin.

"It is her?" Kota asked, pointing out the window at the long-legged blonde in the dark suit making her way toward the back of the house.

"Yes," Royce said. "Once you have her, Hart shouldn't be too hard to capture. He'll come for her. Remember, she's just a girl, and your boss wants her unharmed, so don't get any rougher than necessary. Negara won't appreciate you making a mess out of her." It was always a good idea to reinforce mission priorities with this group. Jai Traon pirates had a tendency to get carried away once they were set loose. "As far as Hart goes, the only limit is death. Don't kill him. If you do, don't bother coming back." And that just about covered the night's rules of engagement—keep the girl in one piece, keep Hart breathing.

Kota relayed the instructions in Indonesian, along with the plan of attack he and Garin had worked out between them. Royce listened carefully, but felt no need to add anything. These boys had been kidnapping people since they'd all been in short pants. It was second nature, along with violence of action. They always hit hard and fast, as the girl would find out soon enough, much to her dismay.

A smile curved Royce's mouth. He wasn't really a psychotic, score-keeping bastard, but it would be his second triumph of the night, when he had the cocky little bitch sniveling at his feet and begging for mercy.

TRAVIS had never ridden in a Honda Civic before, and given half a chance, he would never ride in another one, especially one driven by a slightly deranged, homicidal maniac who couldn't keep more than one hand on the wheel because she needed the other to shift and to keep from getting crushed, overwhelmed, and/or buried by the ungodly amount of crap stacked, packed, piled, and/or sliding around inside the car.

"Skeeter had me get you a pistol," Red Dog said. "You'll find a Springfield 1911 and four mags in the case behind your seat."

Count on Skeeter to take care of all the right details, not that a semiautomatic pistol was going to help him survive his current death-defying crisis.

"W-watch—" *Out.*

Geezus. That had been close. They were on the freeway headed into the city, moving at light speed with no fear.

Against his better judgment, he shifted in his seat, turning his back on the road, and reached around to search through a few dozen piles of crap for the gun case. Amazingly, he found it pretty damn quickly. She'd set it on top of a box.

"Did you . . . uh, recently move?" he asked, sitting back in his seat and facing forward into the thrill-a-minute zone. There was too much variety of stuff in her car for this to have been an accidental pileup. There were kitchen supplies in a small box at his feet, and he was sitting on a sock.

"Yes, about a month ago." She flipped on her blinker to change lanes at God-knows-how-many-miles-per-hour, and he braced himself. She hadn't killed them yet, and he was praying their luck held all the way to the hotel.

"New to the D.C. area?" he asked, gripping the door handle.

Yeah, right, like that was going to save him.

"I grew up here," she said, giving the steering wheel a little spin and jacking up his pulse in the process, "but was gone for about ten years."

When she straightened out and settled into the new lane, with everything and everyone still in one piece, he let out the breath he'd accidentally been holding and hazarded another quick glance around the inside of the car. Yes, this had "major move" written all over it, not a cross-town hop. The U.S. map stuck in the passenger's visor with the big red line drawn across it was another pretty good clue. From the part he could see, it looked like she'd started in Arizona.

"It's changed a lot since I was a kid," she continued, then flipped her blinker back on to go for the fast lane.

Oh, crap.

"Divorce?" In his experience, and he had quite a bit of it listening to women pour out their hearts, divorce was a prime mover of the fairer sex, especially if they went back to the nest.

"Yes," she said, sounding completely taken by surprise and whipping her head around to look at him—right in the middle of her freaking lane change.

Shit!

He made some ridiculous flapping motion, momentarily struck dumb by fear, trying to direct her attention back to the freeway they were screaming down.

"How did you know?" she asked.

Because my life is flashing before my eyes, and in it,

*my obituary says I was killed in a freaking Honda
Civic driven by a divorced woman.*

"The road." He gritted the words out, and she
went back to watching it, still cruising along at the
speed of light, whipping here and there.

"No, really, how did you know?" She gave him a
quick glance, but thankfully went right back to
watching where she was going. "I mean, it's not like
written on my face or anything, is it?"

Rough divorce, he decided.

"No. I have a counseling business in Boulder. I
see a lot of divorced women."

"*You're* a therapist?" Another turn of her head
had his heart in his throat again.

"The road."

"I thought, well, I didn't think SDF operators
had other jobs."

"They don't. I'm the new guy, and I'm still in the
process of—*ho-lee* . . ." Words failed him, even his
usually reliable four-letter words. Nothing could
adequately express the sheer terror of streaking
back across four lanes of traffic, to the right this
time, trying to make an exit she should have been
preparing for three miles back.

They hit the damn thing at hyperspeed, and she
immediately went for the brakes.

It was chaos—utter, freaking chaos.

Everything inside the car shifted position—eight

fucking times—during her slow-down for the traffic light waiting for them at the end of the exit.

Just his luck, the thing turned green just before they got to it, so she kept right on going, effectively destroying any opportunity he might have had to catch his breath.

Skeeter would never believe this. She would never believe anyone would drive a Honda Civic like it was Angelina, or Roxanne, or Babycakes, or, God forbid, Mercy—muscle cars all, the heaviest, the toughest, the baddest badass cars in Denver.

Now there was Red Dog's stick-shift Civic in Washington, D.C.

And God save him, they were still miles from the hotel.

CHAPTER 14

INSIDE THE vault room at Whitfield's, things were moving along at a good clip. Skeeter had her DRSB303 connected to the guts of the biometric reader, and her own biometric compact connected to the DRSB303. It took her all of another thirty seconds to lay Vice President Hallaway's fingerprints on the reader and encode them into Whitfield's system, and *voilà*, she was in.

She swung the vault door open—and stood there for a full five seconds, just staring at the contents.

Holy cripes. The vault was deep, like a walk-in closet, and it was absolutely stuffed with filing cabinets and boxes of documents; a few trays of jewelry, the really good stuff; a few bundles of cash; a couple of small sculptures; and even a few paintings.

Including one Picasso—*holy freaking cripes.*

For another couple of seconds, she was stymied, not sure where to begin. The Godwin file was here, right in front of her somewhere—but where?

If Whitfield was planning on taking it to a meeting Monday morning, it was probably close to the front of the safe, she decided, going for the first filing cabinet.

She was less than halfway through the top drawer, and coming up empty-handed, when she suddenly knew she wasn't alone. Someone had entered the closet behind the bookcase.

In one move, she melted back into the shadow of the vault door, swinging around to face the opening, her Para .45 drawn and cocked—and pointing right at Dylan's chest.

Body shot, that had been her plan, and her finger was on the trigger, taking up slack, ready to execute in a heartbeat or less.

"How's it going?" he asked.

Geezus holy freaking kee-rist. A tremor went up the length of her arm as she backed off the trigger. *How's it going? Was he freaking nuts? Sneaking up on her like that?*

"Good. How about for you?" *Geezus. And oh, crap, it's Dylan, and I've been caught, and how much trouble am I in?*

He shrugged.

For another full three seconds, she was completely stymied again.

Dylan Hart? Shrugging?

She'd never seen the boss do anything other than make well-thought-out and deliberate moves. So what was with the shrug, when he should be carving her up into little pieces and threatening her with total annihilation?

"Here, I'll get that," he said, stepping forward and brushing his hand across her shoulder.

All-righty then.

She glanced at her shoulder, wondering what in the world he'd just done.

"Oh. Just a sec." He did it again, taking another step forward and brushing his hand across her other shoulder, but this time, he didn't step back, not an inch, not a millimeter. "We've got a problem," he said, breathing down on her.

Uh, no kidding. Mr. Don't-Go-There was acting strange, had her backed up against the filing cabinets, and was practically plastered against her—chest, thighs, *geezus*. There was no way to get some distance between them, not without pushing him away, which—no big surprise—she wasn't inclined to do. But man, oh, man, she could feel the heat coming off his body. He was that friggin' close—and that friggin' hot.

Hot. Oh, shit.

Understanding dawned on her in one blinding flash.

"Dylan, do we need—"

"Mints," he interrupted, leaning in even closer and sliding his hands up under her uniform jacket, until they rested on her bare waist. "Cinnamon. Don't. Ever again. I knew you were in the office before your foot hit the first stair."

Point taken, and under any other circumstances, she would have been appropriately chagrined, probably even mortified to have made such a stupid mistake—but she was slightly electrified by the whole hands-on-the-waist thing, and she had a feeling they had a bigger problem than her smelling like cinnamon, like possibly a red Syrette situation.

"Are you hallucinating?" That's what she needed to know.

"Maybe." He grinned. "Do you have a butterfly on your nose?"

Cripes.

"Dylan, listen to me. I need the silver case with the Syrettes."

"Sure." He nodded.

But he didn't give her the case.

"Dylan. I think you're having a relapse, a reaction to the drugs Negara gave you during your capture." She flipped the safety on the Para and holstered the gun.

"Yeah, the NG4," he said, still nodding. "It's a bitch. Sorry about the leeches. I may have—"

He stopped abruptly, swore under his breath, then reached in his front pants pocket and pulled out a silver case.

Leeches? That's what he was seeing? *Holy crap.* She happened to know the man hated leeches. It was in his phobia file, which admittedly was pretty damn short. Leeches and his mother pretty much covered it. She took the case, popped it open, and refused to panic.

"I need the other case, Dylan." The one with the Syrettes, not the one with Whitfield's fingerprints.

They'd never actually talked about his mother, but she'd picked up a few bits and pieces here and there, mostly from Superman, about Dylan's supposed childhood, which hadn't had much "child" in it. And then, of course, she'd gone digging on her own, and yeah, she thought she knew his real name, where he'd gone to prep school, why he'd left home, and how old he'd been when he'd done it. She did not know what had happened to the five million dollars that had disappeared out of his father's company the day before his dad had died.

Nobody did, and a whole helluva lot of people had spent the last seventeen years looking for it. A whole helluva lot of people had spent the last seventeen years looking for him, including his mother and the man she'd married less than a month after his father's death. As far as Skeeter could tell, though, only one person had found him—White Rook, whoever the hell that was. Not even she had been able to unearth White Rook's real name or his connection to Dylan, other than the creation of SDF.

"Yeah. Sure." He patted his pants down again. "The NG4, it's, uh . . . bad, something new, a new class of . . . of . . ."

He looked up, catching her gaze, his brows furrowed.

"A new class of designer drug used in interrogations," she quoted from her research, trying to help him out, to help him focus.

"Yeah. That's it. Bad stuff. I may have fucked up on Sumba." He still looked confused. "I told the doctors on the *Jefferson*, but they might not have acted, might not have, well, you know how it is with us."

Yes, she did. Not even the Department of Defense acknowledged SDF's existence. They were Grant's bad boys, not anybody else's. They were expendable. Dylan was damn lucky the brass on the *Jefferson* had even let him on their ship. Which made her wonder what kind of care he'd really gotten.

"The NG4, the place where they gave it to me, it was white."

"White?"

"Yeah, white, all white, everywhere, and it hurt to be there. The whole thing hurt."

Skeeter just bet it had. Tight-jawed, she quickly slid down his body, frisking him. They were running out of time, and she was running out of patience with herself. She should never have let him come here tonight. Screw the Godwin file. She'd known about the pain. She'd read about it on the freaking Internet. She didn't know what he meant by "white," but the pain of being injected with the NG and XT classes of drugs had been mentioned numerous times. The U.S. government had banned the use of all NG and XT drugs in their detention facilities for humane reasons and because of the potential danger of their time-delayed side effects, including a whole lot more than what Dylan had told her on the plane. There could be worse in store for him than getting sick or hallucinating, which she knew was one reason the Navy doctors had given him the yellow Syrette. For some of the other possibilities, no Syrette in the world was going to do him a damn bit of good.

She started back up his body, checking every pocket, searching for the other case. She'd made damn sure he'd had it with him before they'd left the Lafayette.

"I'm getting really hot, Skeeter."

No shit. He was burning up. Standing next to him was like standing next to a radiator, and if they didn't get out of the vault pretty damn quick,

she was afraid one of them was going to faint—
probably him.

Definitely him—*dammit.*

She didn't faint, ever.

So here they were, in Whitfield's vault, searching
for a Syrette, with him melting down and her trying
not to freak out, just the two of them.

Jammed together, up close and personal.

Dylan Hart.

And her.

Hot and scared.

" 'NG' stands for Next Generation," he said.

Yes, she knew that.

"Our government banned them. Too dangerous,
they said."

Yes, she knew that, too.

"Not that we ever admitted to having a psy-
chopharmacological arsenal."

Actually, in one of the articles she'd read, one
senator had mentioned what a good trick it had been
to ban something the U.S. government had suppos-
edly never used, but nobody had paid him too much
mind.

"The NG4," he said, "it's next-generation sodium
pentobarbital, with some latent admixtures to
really get inside a guy's brain—that's where I
screwed up with Negara and Souk. Uh, hold on a
minute, hold still. I've got it." He brushed off her
shoulder again.

More leeches. *Cripes.*

"What screwup? And who is Souk?" That was the second time he'd mentioned a mistake.

She ran her hands up under his jacket and over his chest—and hit pay dirt, a whole lot of pay dirt.

"You've already got the Godwin file." She was flabbergasted, and impressed as hell.

"Yeah." He didn't sound nearly as impressed with himself as she was. "Skeeter, you know about sodium pentobarbital, right?"

Yeah, she knew. "Truth serum."

What she really needed was in his shirt pocket, and she pulled it out, the silver case with the Syrettes. She started to open it, but he stopped her, moving his hands to her arms and holding her.

"Skeeter, I tried, but it's all such a fucking mess in my head. Sometimes, this last week, I've thought I had it all sorted out, but then it all goes to hell again. Like now. I'm just a little fucked up."

"I know. I'm going to help you."

He shook his head, like he didn't quite believe anything was going to help.

"I don't know, Skeet. I don't know what I gave them. It could have been everything. I could have answered every question they asked. I warned Hawkins before we left this morning, but what I need you to know is . . . is . . ." His voice trailed off.

What? she wondered. He was looking at her so intently, his gaze so confused, like he couldn't quite get her into focus, but whatever he was trying to say, it was damned important to him, important enough for her to give him another couple of seconds, even though the sand in their hourglass had run out. They had Godwin. They needed to get the hell out of Whitfield's.

"What?" she whispered when he didn't continue.

A frustrated sigh left him, followed by a muttered curse.

"You," he said. He swore again, tightening his hold on her and lowering his head into the curve of her neck. "I never would have given them you. Never. No one knows what you mean to me. No one. I swear it."

She opened her mouth to say something, then closed it, struck completely dumb. He couldn't possibly mean that no one knew he thought she was a royal pain in the butt.

Everybody knew that.

No, this was something else.

"God, Skeeter Jeanne, I've got you buried so deep inside me." A short laugh escaped him. "So deep, wrapped around my guts. No matter what Souk shot me up with, he couldn't go that deep. Not as deep as I want to be inside you . . ." His voice trailed off again, and he let out another sigh, a soft breath she felt all the way down to her toes.

And that did it. The whole freaking insane

night had just taken a sharp left into the Twilight Zone. She couldn't have been more shocked if he'd kissed her.

Then he did—simply opened his mouth on her neck and ran his tongue over her.

Her knees almost buckled from the shock and the heat.

"You are so damn sweet." He breathed the words on her neck, and began unbuttoning her jacket. Another wave of heat poured down her body.

Oh, geez. Oh, God. Oh, no.

No, no, no.

Not like this. Not because of some freaking hallucinogenic drug racing through his system.

"Dylan," she said. "Dylan, stop."

He didn't, not even close. His mouth was on her. He finished with the buttons and his hands were sliding back under her jacket, sliding over her skin.

"Dylan—" she started again, then pulled her thoughts up short.

Wait a minute.

This was it, the moment she'd been dreaming about for three long years, the moment when Dylan Hart revealed his undying love for her, and good God, he was on truth serum.

And good God, they were in the middle of a heist.

"Dylan." She grabbed his hands.

And good God, she was supposed to be saving him.

"Dylan, I need to give you the medicine in the Syrette."

"Later." His voice was a low growl in her ear, and his mouth was hot on her skin. Then his hands slid up over her bra, cupping her breasts, and for a second she could hardly breathe.

This couldn't possibly be happening, Dylan touching her—intimately. She'd dreamed about it so many times, how it would feel to have his hands on her, but oh, my, God, her imagination had fallen far short of the mark.

"*Jesus*, Skeeter. You smell so good, taste so good. Like candy, baby. So beautiful," he murmured, caressing her, his hands all over her, his mouth all over her, teasing her, kissing her, driving her crazy. "The most beautiful woman I have ever seen, I swear to God. Sometimes, I . . . hell, most of the time, I feel like I'm going to fall apart if I can't have you naked and wrapped around me."

Naked and wrapped around Dylan—oh, yeah, she'd imagined that, too many times to count, and there was nothing she wanted more than to give in to what he was making her feel, but she couldn't. Not like this. Not here, not now, for crying out loud.

Get a freaking grip, girl.

"Dylan." She took hold of his hands and very firmly pulled them out from under her shirt. Good Lord. Her head was reeling, which was *not* what they needed right now. "Dylan, I need you to pay attention to me. I'm going to take off your jacket."

"Good idea. Let's take everything off." He started shrugging out of his tuxedo, and she let him, just because he was moving in the right direction, mostly. He was still pressing her up against the filing cabinets, still had his mouth on her—on her cheek, and her brow, and the side of her nose, heading for her mouth, which was going to be the end of both of them.

"Oh, no," she said, ducking aside when he got too close, trying to get a couple of inches of safe zone. She was about half successful.

"Are you going to take your clothes off, too?" he whispered between kisses on her face. "I'd love that, Skeeter, really love that. I can't tell you how many hours, days, weeks I've spent fantasizing about taking off your clothes."

He got stuck about halfway out of his jacket, and she helped him get it the rest of the way off.

She just ignored what he was saying. She had to. She couldn't possibly think straight if she was thinking about Dylan thinking about her taking off her clothes. That was *her* fantasy, stripping for him, stripping him, the two of them naked and all over each other. *Geezus*, she had sketchbooks full of that little daydream, and having to rely purely on her imagination for some of his more interesting parts hadn't slowed her down a bit.

When his jacket hit the floor, she opened the box of Syrettes and got damned serious.

So did he, coming to a complete standstill when he saw what she was holding.

"Uh, Skeeter, there's a problem."

Yes, there was. Like how pale he'd suddenly become, and the sweat breaking out on his brow.

"What problem?" she asked.

"I, uh . . . can't do that." His gaze was riveted to the box of Syrettes.

Simple enough.

"You don't have to, I'll do it for you." That was the plan. It had been the plan all along, that she would do the deed.

"No."

"No?" "No" was not acceptable.

He took a step back, started to take another, but she grabbed on to him, recognizing an escape in the making. Screw that. He wasn't going anywhere.

"What's wrong? Tell me."

DYLAN stared at the Syrettes, seeing them absolutely clearly—red, yellow, and blue—and he felt his gut churn.

Tell her?

How did he tell her he was scared shitless? It had all seemed so perfectly logical on the *Jefferson*, and this morning on the plane, but the truth was that the Syrettes were a one-way ticket to hell, just like everything else connected to Sumba. And not just regular old going-to-hell hell. Bad hell. Tear-out-your-guts-and-fuck-you hell, all of it couched and cocooned in pain.

"The Syrettes, those drugs . . ." he started, then couldn't finish.

"What?" she insisted.

He looked up from the box, into her eyes, the pale, silvery blue of them, her golden lashes, her golden eyebrows—and the jagged pink scar cutting across her forehead.

She knew about pain. No one who looked at her would ever doubt it.

"They aren't easy," he said. "They don't go down easy. They don't go in easy."

"Are you still seeing leeches and butterflies?"

He nodded. They were everywhere, phosphorescent, moving, multiplying. He hadn't wanted to tell her, but another leech had landed on her shoulder. He was trying to ignore it, trying not to prove how fucked up he was by reaching out and brushing it off.

But *shit*, they were crawling up under his pants legs now, had been for the last couple of minutes, and it was taking everything he had not to just go berserk.

He kept telling himself it wasn't real, to stay calm. The only real thing in the room was her—and he'd wanted to kiss her. That was all. Having his mouth on her, his tongue on her, tasting her, feeling her breasts in his hands, it had all been so good. Something he could count on.

But he was feeling sick to his stomach and getting so hot it was starting to hurt. Everything was starting to hurt.

"Then we're going to do this," she said, taking out her knife and cutting up his sleeve. "Together."

"I want to kiss you." That was the truth. The only truth. The rest of it—he didn't want to think about the rest of it. He didn't want to think about what she was going to do.

He remembered what it had been like in the white room, and . . . and he hadn't been able to think, hadn't been able to breathe, or even feel. Everything had been disconnected, his body from his brain, his hands in one place, his heart beating in another, far away, across the white room, in a corner—so cold.

Fuck. He didn't want to go there again. He didn't want any part of it.

He closed his eyes, squeezed them shut, and tried to think, tried to clear his head. There had to be a way, another way to do this.

"Sex," he said, opening his eyes, the word and the deed coming to him in a flash of brilliance. It was the only thing that could save him, the promise of something beyond the pain. "You and me, afterward, and I have never been more goddamn serious in my life, Skeeter. No sex, no Syrette. I'll just take my fucking chances."

Okay. He'd done it. Shocked the street rat with the combat knife on her hip and the .45 holstered under her arm, the bad girl—bad, bad Baby Bang. She was staring at him, her mouth a perfect little "O" of surprise.

"Sex?"

"Sex." No compromise. "Hot and wet, sweet and dirty. Sex, no holds barred."

Hell. She didn't know the half of being bad, but he could teach her. Oh, yeah, he could teach her how to be bad all over him.

And that would almost make what was going to happen next bearable. All she had to say was yes.

"Ah, sure."

Good enough.

He nodded, and she got back to business, twisting the shirtsleeve around his biceps, tight, then tighter. Then she twisted it some more and held it in place. "Take hold of this. Don't let go. Make a fist."

He took the twisted ends of shirt with one hand and made a fist with his other and pumped it, getting his veins up. "Goddammit, Skeeter, you promise? Right? About the sex?" *Goddamn*, he was going to hate this.

"I promise. Red, right?"

Red. That's right. Pay attention, man.

Or don't pay attention. Maybe that was the better call.

"Red," he said.

"Okay, I've got it."

"Wait . . . *wait* . . . I can't breathe," he said, feeling the black edge of panic creeping into his head. Oh, man, this was all going downhill so fucking fast, and really, she shouldn't be hitting him up when he couldn't breathe.

Right?

Or was it just the opposite?

"I'm going to help you with that," she said, so very calm, so very sure.

Geezus. He was glad somebody thought they knew what they were doing.

Her hands were on him—strong, sure hands, supporting his forearm, readying the Syrette.

"Tighten more. We only get one shot at this, so let's do it right."

He pumped his hand again, watched her run her fingers over the inside of his elbow and a little lower, feeling for the vein.

"Hold a fist for me."

He did.

"And keep breathing."

Yeah. Right. His heart was starting to pound like a jackhammer. He *knew* what was coming.

Then the stab of pain, fierce and sweet and so

cold, he gasped. It was like being injected with dry ice, searingly cold, and so fucking, mind-bendingly sharp, like a razor slicing up his arm through his vein. A primal, animal sound left his mouth, and for one awful second, his whole body went rigid.

Then there was nothing.

CHAPTER

15

G EEZUS H. *Freaking Cripes.* She'd killed him.

Complete and utter shock froze the moment in time.

She'd killed Dylan.

She'd injected him with the Syrette, killed him with the damn thing, and barely caught him as he'd fallen to the floor.

Within the frozen fractions of the passing seconds, as she slid with him to the bottom of the vault, a thousand emotions tore through her. Then training took over. Coming up on her knees, she pressed her fingers to his carotid artery.

The breath that had been stuck in her throat released in relief. There was a pulse, weak, but there.

But, *freaking cripes*, something god-awful had just happened.

Keeping one hand on him, on his chest to monitor his breathing—that it didn't falter—she smoothed the hair off his face and leaned in close.

"Dylan." She spoke his name and smoothed his hair back again. "Dylan, can you hear me?"

God, they needed to get the hell out of Whitfield's, especially out of Whitfield's safe.

This was all so insane.

"Dylan," she said again, and slowly, his eyes opened.

WOW.

This was just exactly the way Dylan liked waking up, with a sultry, exotic woman leaning over him, her hand on his chest, her breasts practically spilling out of her bra, her hair all silvery blond and mussed and falling down around a face he'd seen in his dreams thousands of times.

She was so beautiful, it broke his heart. His gaze went over the scar running in a line across her forehead. She'd been hurt, and it made him feel so bad—and yet . . . and yet he felt so good.

His arm hurt like hell, living, fire-breathing hell, but somehow he didn't really mind.

He closed his eyes again just to feel the cool, streaming rush of whatever she'd hit him up with run through the rest of his body. Normally, he didn't do drugs. He was the guy who busted people who did drugs, especially the people who sold drugs—millions of dollars' worth of drugs. He was one of the good guys.

But this rush, *geezus*. Who wouldn't dig it?

"Are you okay? Are you with me?" she asked, and her voice was so smooth, he closed his eyes again, just to savor it. "Dylan, talk to me."

Yeah. Dylan. That was him. Dylan Hart, good guy, and she was Skeeter Jeanne Bang, his baby, baby, Baby Bang. . . .

"Look at me, okay? Stay with me," she said.

He opened his eyes again and took another look. Oh, he was staying with her, all right. He was staying with her all night, one way or another.

Sex. He'd asked, and she'd said yes. She'd promised. It was a dream come true, a hot dream, the hottest, and he wasn't letting it get away from him.

"Talk to me. How do you feel?"

He felt great. Better than great. So great, in fact, he decided to drift off again and just feel the rush.

"Oh, no, you don't. Come on. Look at me, Dylan." She sounded kind of worried, like she was losing that cool, calm edge he liked so much about her, so he opened his eyes, and she was even closer than she'd been before, almost on top of him, leaning over him, one of her hands sliding up to his brow, like she was feeling for a fever, the other slipping inside his shirt, over his heart—which sent that rush he was feeling in a whole new direction.

God, this is so good.

"I saw you naked once," he said.

"No you didn't." She looked truly startled. Almost half of her hair had fallen out of her fancy, upswept hairdo, and it made her look undone, like she was coming undone for him.

"It was just your ponytail, and your back, part of your leg, and your ass. You were swaying across some pages, and I just kept flipping through them, over, and over, and over, and over. . . ." *And over, and over.* His eyes drifted closed again.

"Dylan?" She sounded more than worried, like she was edging toward panic. That was no good. "Dylan, open your eyes."

"Hey," he said, obliging her with a smile.

"Hey, yourself," she said. "Don't leave me. Okay?"

"Never . . . ever. Ever," he promised. Nobody in his right mind would leave her. Hell, he wasn't in his right mind and he wasn't going to leave her.

"Good. Stay focused. Stay here." She was looking at him so intently, her ice-blond eyebrows bunching together over her silvery, swirling blue eyes. It was so cool. Her lashes were golden, her lips pink, the whole of her so pale and lovely, his heart broke again, right there on the spot.

God, she has beautiful breasts.

"Can you sit up?"

Sit? Who needed to sit?

"I don't need to sit. I'm floating. Can't you tell?"

"Freaking H. Cripes," she muttered like she couldn't believe it.

Letting out a heavy sigh, he reached up and put his hand over hers, where her palm was so warm on his chest.

"I love you." That should make her feel better. It made him feel better. It was such a relief to finally get the words out. They'd been trapped inside him for so long. "I think we should sleep together. Just the two of us. Together." It was too good of an idea not to share. "And probably we should do it now, while we're floating around, waiting."

Waiting for what, he didn't have a clue, but it was still a good idea.

Entwining his fingers with hers, he reached down with his other hand to undo his pants. This was going to be great. He'd wanted her for so long.

But she stopped him before he could even get his pants unbuttoned, let alone unzipped.

"Dylan." She had a definite edge in her voice now. "The antidote for the NG4, do you know what—" She stopped, her head turning. A soft curse left her mouth.

He didn't hear anything—except the next curse that came out of her mouth.

Her hands tightened on him. "Don't you move," she said under her breath, her voice taking on an unexpected fierceness. "Not even if this crap wears off and you can. Not. One. Inch."

"Sure." No problem. As long as she was on top of him, he wasn't going anywhere—guaranteed.

But suddenly there was a problem, a giant problem. She was leaving, moving away from him and sliding out of the vault, low to the ground, drawing her pistol.

He reached for her, but it was too late. She'd slipped through his fingers, slipped through the bookcase, and closed it behind her.

Damn.

HAWKINS was nesting.

That's what all the pregnancy books called it when parents-to-be puttered around their home, preparing for the new arrival, and he loved it, nesting with Katya, waiting for the baby to come. Except for the "false" labor part. He just didn't think there was anything "false" about it.

Creed was calling the night's activities "hanging out at home on a Saturday night baby-proofing Superman's apartment and going without sex." Sex that he needed, because he'd been in freaking Colombia for the last ten days with the FNG, who had done a helluva job, even if they had gotten their asses ambushed and pushed around a little bit.

It was all in the report, and as soon as the two of them went over it again and deleted any incriminating evidence and all the really good stuff about who "did" who and how they'd done it, Hawkins would fax a copy to General Grant's office for him to send to the secretary of defense and to Bill Davies at the Pentagon. Privately, he'd fax an unedited copy to General Grant himself.

That's the way things worked at Steele Street. Only clean bills of health ever went to the Pentagon or to anyone over at the Department of Defense. No matter what happened, what they did, or who they did it to, nobody wanted to know the truth about Special Defense Force. Officially, and even unofficially, they didn't exist. That one simple fact made everything they did possible.

"You know, Cristo, that back room has to go," Creed said, returning from the kitchen to the living room area with a couple of cold sodas and two bottles of organic strawberry cream smoothie for the girls. Creed's wife, Cody, had come upstairs with him to hold Katya's hand through the "false" labor.

Kat loved organic strawberry cream smoothies. She'd been loving them for months now, and every little organic cream smoothie she'd drunk had just added to the wonder of her pregnancy—added pounds of wonder. She was so fulsomely round, he sometimes looked at her and was struck dumb with guilt.

He'd done this to her. Taken his more-curves-than-a-cyclone, green-eyed blonde and turned her into a dumpling, a lush and lovely dumpling who was almost as big around as she was tall. Even at five feet two inches, that was quite a feat.

"What do you mean, go?"

"The guns, all of them," Creed said, setting the sodas and smoothies down on the coffee table and settling in next to his wife. "We can haul it all down to the armory tomorrow. Nobody, and I mean *nobody*, needs a .50 caliber M107 semiautomatic long-range sniper rifle in their guest bedroom."

"We don't have guests." Not at Steele Street.

"You still don't need that thing—or half those H&Ks you've got up here—after tonight, not with a baby in the house."

A baby, the sodas, the smoothies, the wives—God, the whole scene was so domestic, it made Hawkins grin. Life was good—until the lights suddenly went out.

Nobody panicked. He and Creed waited out the next few seconds, waited for the lights to come back on. When they didn't, they waited another few seconds for the backup generator to come on, and Hawkins got a flashlight off the mantel. Of course, while they were waiting, Creed had gotten up and was walking back toward the guest bedroom.

"Christian," Kat said. "None of the other buildings' lights went out."

Their sophisticated and elegantly furnished loft had thirty feet of fifteen-foot-high windows overlooking the rest of the city, and Denver was still lit.

"I know, honey." He wasn't panicked. He was pissed off. Without giving him nearly the information Hawkins was going to get out of him, Dylan had warned him about a potential security breach at Steele Street because of a situation he'd encountered on Sumba.

Hawkins guessed that was one way to put it. The words "torture" and "interrogation" were a little more blunt and probably a whole helluva lot more accurate, and they were the ones he'd used with Creed to explain why he wanted the four of them to spend a little "quality time" together tonight. Dylan had escaped from a notorious warlord who had probably all but killed him trying to get information about the seventeen million dollars Dylan had hijacked out of Negara's heroin profits, and in the melee, the boss had probably spilled his guts about a lot of things.

And now Steele Street's lights were out.

But not for fucking long.

Creed came back and handed his wife a Remington 870P tactical shotgun. A Skeeter special the girl had built herself, it was guaranteed to rock and roll.

He also gave Cody an MP5 subgun.

"You know the drill, babe," Creed said, handing the second weapon over to her. "Kick ass."

There had been a time, not too long ago, when Cody's life had been threatened by a lot of dangerous men willing to go to great lengths to hurt her. "Never again" had been Creed's wedding vow, and he'd made good on his promise. Cody not only had the shooting skills to protect herself, she had the mind-set to use them.

Armed women were safe women—that was Creed's bottom line, and Hawkins agreed. But he was counting on Cody tonight. A little dumpling retaining water in her fingers and her toes, who could barely waddle from here to there, had no business trying to fire a weapon. Even with the training he'd given her, Hawkins was afraid Kat might hurt herself.

As for himself, he was definitely out to hurt somebody, a whole lot of somebodies, if they'd invaded his home.

"I'm going to be damned disappointed if this turns out to be an electrical problem," the jungle boy said with a grin, heading with him toward the door.

Hawkins smiled back. They'd spent the afternoon preparing a few welcoming surprises for their potential callers, baiting the trap. Hawkins had already decided that Hamzah Negara was going down. The warlord had been at the top of General Grant's hit list for years, and now the gloves were coming off. The message SDF was sending him tonight was just the beginning.

CHAPTER 16

MOVING QUICKLY and silently across the loft, Skeeter pulled a black Nomex hood out of her uniform pocket and pulled it on over her head, covering her hair and most of her face. At the balcony, she carefully looked over the side.

Sonuvabitch.

She'd heard them from inside the vault, and now she could see them—dark shapes, four of them, entering the office from the lawn, using the same entrance she had, and spreading out from the door.

They were either here for Dylan or they were here for Godwin—and she'd left both of those things lying in the vault, pretty much in the same damn position—helplessly exposed. *Cripes.*

She looked back over her shoulder, checking. The bookcase was securely closed, but that wasn't going to keep him safe for long. Chances were, anyone who had bothered to break into Whitfield's office knew where Whitfield's vault was hidden.

One of the first things Superman had ever told her—and he'd only told her once, in a tone that had said he didn't ever want to have to tell her again—was to never, ever, ever think the other guys didn't know what they were doing. Their lives were as much on the line as hers, and like her, they weren't in the game to fail.

That wasn't to say there weren't guys in the game who weren't a few French fries short of a Happy Meal. Amateurs abounded among the thugs of the world. She tilted her head to better peer around a spindle.

Two of the men were sliding through the office, moving with the stealth and silence of real pros, which told her plenty about the kind of trouble she was in. One of the other two men hadn't gotten much past the door, though, and the last guy had gone back outside, and neither of them, inside guy or outside guy, was holding his weapon at the ready. The guy outside had his subgun pointed at the ground, just letting it hang from his hand, like he either didn't know how to use it or didn't think he was going to need it.

All the better for her.

She checked the first two men again. They'd both carted a subgun to the party, too, the perfect weapon for close-quarters combat, hostage rescue, and hostage taking.

She didn't doubt for a second which end of the kidnapping scale these boys were on, both the pros and the amateurs. Anybody dressed in black and sneaking around a senator's private office in the middle of the night with a submachine gun slung over their shoulder and a semiautomatic pistol holstered on their body was up to no good—herself included.

A brief, hissed exchanged of words at the door proved it. She didn't know the Indonesian language from shinola, but she knew an Asian dialect and an Asian accent when she heard it, and she suddenly knew with absolute certainty that she and Dylan were in desperate danger.

She also knew they'd been set up. There wasn't a coincidence in the world big enough to bring Skeeter Bang, Dylan Hart, and four Jai Traon pirates together inside Arthur Whitfield's office.

Hamzah Negara was still after Dylan, and someone had arranged the Godwin file to be the bait that brought them all together.

Holy freaking cripes. They needed to go over

Dylan's Everybody Who Wants to Wax My Ass spreadsheet again.

Rising to a half crouch, she slipped back into the shadows along the bookcase and moved to intercept. Just as she'd expected, one of the men had headed directly for the stairs. He knew where the safe was located, and whether he was after Godwin or Dylan, that was the place to start.

She pulled her combat knife out of her sheath. Her plan was to take him out as silently as possible and buy herself a few seconds to come up with the next part of her plan, the one where she got three more of these guys before they got her.

Geezus, she wished Kid was here, or that Dylan was in his right mind, or that they'd waited at the hotel until Travis had arrived, anything to give her more of a tactical advantage.

The squawking of a comm unit blew that possibility all to hell.

Everyone in the office froze.

Then the squawking came again—from outside.

These bad boys had not slipped by the grounds guard, she realized. They'd brought him with them, right on their heels, and he was calling for backup.

Okay, she thought. That could work for her or against her.

"Halt! Drop your weapon! Move away from the door!" the guard's voice came from outside.

Against her, she decided. The guard had called

for backup, but he wasn't waiting for it—and he should have. Oh, yeah, she had a flash of insight that said he should have waited.

This was bad, bad, bad. She saw it all in an instant: The guy was working his last shift. Even as she saw it, she was drawing her Para and leveling it at the fourth intruder's head, the guy outside who had swung his submachine gun up and was—

Blam-blam-blam.

Kerr-ack. *Krack*. Her .45 took the fourth pirate down, but it was too late for the guard. He'd been hit, maybe not mortally wounded, though. She could hear him swearing and gasping outside the door.

She'd delivered killing shots. She always did. Every single time. The pirate was gone, flat on the ground with a double-tap through the heart.

And all hell was breaking loose.

Out on the lawn, waiters and caterers were running, the backup guards were arriving, their weapons drawn and comm units giving off static. People were talking, yelling, some woman screamed.

It was all background noise, background commotion, and had nothing to do with what Skeeter was doing for this second, and the next, and the one after that, ad infinitum, until her immediate threats were neutralized.

Two pirates were coming up the stairs now, the first man and the guy from inside the door. She'd lost sight of the second man—*dammit*.

She covered the top of the stairs with her muzzle, looking for the flash of movement that would give her opponent away. She'd resheathed her knife. Silence was no longer on the menu. Survival was. Her shots had revealed her position, and even though she'd moved and hadn't stopped moving, the Jai Traon knew they had an enemy in the loft.

The sudden, instantaneous rising of the hair on the back of her neck had her twisting to the right. Something grazed her cheek. A foot, she realized, a foot trying to take her head off. It hit her hand instead, with terrible force, and knocked her pistol away, and she knew that could be the last mistake she was ever going to make, losing her weapon in the middle of a fight. The second man had made it to the loft without using the stairs, and he was in ninja mode. She didn't have time to wonder why he hadn't just shot her. He had a subgun slung across his back, but he was coming at her like Bruce Lee in *Fists of Fury*. She ducked, and kicked, and struck out with the side of her hand, a stunning blow if she could have landed it, but it slid off the man.

Then her hand was caught from behind. She went with the hold, turning into it and bringing her leg up and out in a stunning roundhouse kick that went straight to her new opponent's solar plexus. He went down, hard, doubled over, but the first guy was still on her, and she could see pirate number three launching himself in her direction.

Any one of them could have shot her, or tried to cut her with a knife—or at least given it their best effort—but no, they were hand-to-hand fighting, and even leaving the killing blows out of that.

They wanted her alive, which was not a comfort. Far from it. The realization only spurred her on to fight harder, faster against the two pirates still standing. Then the guy she'd put down started getting back to his feet.

She was good, but the pirates were well trained, and two of them were damn good—too good. She'd gotten in a couple of powerful hits, even heard something crack, but she wasn't going to hold off three Jai Traon. She was drenched in sweat, her head was ringing from some blow she hadn't been able to completely block. When the third man finally stood up, she knew the end was near.

Lights were coming on all over the grounds, floodlights. She could hear people running down the hall, heading toward the office. Someone was shouting orders. All the sounds and sights of crisis and response were happening, quickly, all around her, and the fists and feet kept coming.

Block. Parry. Strike.

They were all running out of time.

Then one pirate ran completely out of time, suddenly, irrevocably. The suppressed shot was a clean hit, and coming out of the barrel of a .45, it all but blew his head off.

Dylan.

He stepped out from behind the bookcase just as the office door flew open on the main floor—and it was an exodus. One of the pirates let loose with his subgun, blowing out the second-floor windows from the loft to the manicured lawns below, and both men went through the hole, leaping to the ground.

She and Dylan weren't too far behind. He'd grabbed her arm almost instantly and dragged her with him to the opening.

Two shots came from the main floor and buried themselves into what was left of the molding around the broken glass—but by then, she and Dylan were in midair. Again, training took over, and Skeeter landed as softly as possible, keeping her body loose and flexed, letting her legs take up the shock. Then they were off and running.

STILL HOLDING on to the Honda's door handle as if his life depended on it, which he was damn sure it did, Travis looked down at the book that had ended up in his lap after Red Dog's last wild lane change.

Her picture was on it, along with some guy's.

He tilted his head to one side, reading the type down the spine, and realized it wasn't just any guy's picture. It was her ex-husband's—Kenneth and Gillian Pentycote, and they'd written a book Regan McKinney would love, something about the Paleocene Eocene Thermal Maximum.

He looked over at the woman driving.

Gillian was a pretty name, much prettier than

Red Dog, and writing a book about anything concerned with Paleocene Eocene Thermal situations was over-the-edge academic.

And she'd left all that behind to work as a glorified secretary for General Grant in the hell-and-gone annex?

Not just a rough divorce, he decided, but one of those cataclysmic divorces.

"Still in the process of what?" she asked, and it took him a moment to remember what they'd been talking about.

"Cutting back on my client list in both my traditional therapy and sexual imprinting practices." Might as well get that out there, he thought. A full sixty-five percent of his sexual imprinting clients were recovering from divorce. It was possible that Red Dog could benefit from his professional services. Not that he was going to offer. He wasn't. He'd listen to her talk out her troubles all night long, if the gods smiled on him and gave him half a chance, but he didn't want to be her therapist, with all the ensuing legal restrictions and responsibilities. Hell, no.

"S-sexual imprinting?" She cast him a quick, wary glance, which pretty much told him all he needed to know. "What in the world is . . . s-sexual imprinting?"

Wow. She could hardly say the word. Old Ken

must have done a number on her—not that sexual deconstruction didn't work both ways. It did.

"Not necessarily what it sounds like," he assured her. "It's a combination of traditional talk therapy combined with massage and other types of bodywork designed to help people overcome . . . *geezus* . . . sexual dysfunction."

She'd just gone through a red light. *Red*, as in *Stop*. Traffic was slowing down all around them, but not her. She just kept going, finding every open space and using it to keep going, and going, and going. For a second, it crossed his mind that she might have had some kind of tactical driving training.

"I . . . I have a small counseling clinic in Boulder, where I see clients and do research for a paper I'm—"

She hit the brakes to keep from plowing into the back end of a truck that had rumbled out in front of them from a side street, and he had heart failure.

That was it, the last straw, the bottom line. He was driving. He wasn't the kind of guy to get heavy-handed with a woman, but she'd just—double-clutched her Civic into first, dodged the truck, and was power-shifting her way back up the gears.

It occurred to him then that, despite the absolute chaos of the ride, they were making record time and he didn't have a scratch on him.

"Who taught you to drive?"

"My brother. He used to be a terror on the

streets and the track. Now he's an Army Ranger in Afghanistan."

Yes, he could see potential Ranger tactics in her driving, a lot of effectively directed aggression and equally effective evasion combined in a strategy to never give up ground.

Hoo-yah.

He took another look around the inside of the car, and discovered there was a sort of order in the chaos. Clothes—jeans, shirts, a couple of sweaters, but no underwear—were mostly stacked on one side of the backseat. Papers and files were mostly stacked on the other side, though her driving tactics had made a jumble of them in the middle. Books, magazines, and CDs were everywhere. All the gadgety stuff was in a box behind the driver's seat, spilling out a little, but mostly in the box, all things with wires and buttons and dials, including an expensive-looking alarm clock.

"You didn't move your alarm clock into your new place?" That seemed curious.

She let out a short laugh. "If I'm lucky enough to fall asleep, I don't want anything waking me up."

The tsunami of divorces.

"I have a yoga sequence I could—*geezus* . . ."

She whipped a left-hand turn into the underground parking garage of the Lafayette—barely avoiding getting sideswiped by a limo—plunging them into a dark labyrinth of concrete pillars and silent cars.

And finally, *finally*, she slowed down to a reasonable speed—but it was too damn late for him. He felt rode hard. That last bit of "life flashing before his eyes" had done him in.

It had been a black limo, with a grille and a hood ornament, both of which had been bearing down on him at eye level, just inches from the passenger side of the Civic.

Goddamn. He slid down in his seat and closed his eyes, still clutching the door handle—*goddamn*.

He'd barely gotten out of Colombia with his ass intact, only to have it put back on the line on the streets of Washington, D.C.?

He rested his other hand low on his abdomen, a few inches from the stitches that went down his left side. His injury hadn't been bothering him all day, but it did now—*dammit*. The next time Nikki painted him, there was going to be one less wound she had to imagine. The narco-bastard's knife hadn't caught him deep, just deep enough that stitches had been a good idea.

Travis had caught the narco-bastard deeper, though, buried his blade to the hilt in the guy's neck and jerked it hard. It was amazing, really, how much strength it took, even with a razor-sharp blade, to cut a guy's throat, almost as amazing as how much blood there had been.

He'd been covered in it.

Drenched.

At the end, when it was finished, Creed had come over, taken one look, and helped him to his feet. "Good work" was all he'd said.

No questions. No doubts.

With Creed, like with Kid and Hawkins and Quinn, it always came down to one simple thing— winning the fight. It was a good lesson to learn, to win at all cost, at any cost, no compromise, and the thing that amazed Travis the most was how easy the lesson had been to learn, even for a guy who had taught graduate-level courses in the art of compromise.

The two things were not mutually exclusive, the art of killing and the art of compromise, but there were situations that simply could not be mediated, not in the real world. There was no negotiating with evil. Until the night Nikki had been kidnapped, he hadn't realized how closely evil could linger, undetected, or how quickly it could strike.

Still, he'd killed three men in Colombia, which brought him up to six, and yeah, he had a feeling he was the only guy at SDF counting bodies, and typically, for a goddamn philosophy major, there was no way for him not to have to think and work his way through the facts of his last mission—something he wouldn't have had time to do if he'd gotten killed in a freaking Honda Civic on his way to the hotel from the airport.

Geezus. Red Dog needed to come with a warning label.

He let out his breath and took another, trying to ease his way into a calmer state, to ease himself away from the sharp pain in his side. She'd jacked him up with that last blast of near-death experience, and it was going to take a moment or two for him to come down and find his balance, a moment for the underlying dull ache in his stitches to dissipate. He knew what had happened. He'd gotten whacked by her book, and now he hurt like hell— *dammit.*

"Mr. James?"

He took another breath.

He wasn't answering to "Mr. James." Someone who had almost gotten him greased could at least call him by his first name.

"Travis?"

That was better, but he still wasn't inclined to break his concentration enough to reply. He needed to breathe himself through this. The car had stopped moving, though, and that was a good thing, very helpful.

She turned off the engine, and that helped even more.

"Sir?"

Oh, hell, no. He wasn't going to answer to "sir," not this side of the grave she'd almost put him in. His heart was actually racing, and that pissed him off a little. He'd already been fried before he'd gotten on the plane, let alone in her car. He'd had a helluva week. His resources were low, and he needed to get back up to speed. He had a job to do tonight.

He heard her shift her position on her side of the car, felt her move closer.

"Oh, my God," she whispered—and that didn't sound good. "You're bleeding."

That sounded even worse.

He opened his eyes and found her looming over him, her gaze riveted to the left side of his chest.

"Oh, my God," she repeated.

He glanced down and blanched.

Fuck. He was bleeding, all right.

"I need to get you to a hospital." She started to slide back behind the steering wheel, but he grabbed her before she could get too far.

"No." He wasn't doing it. He wasn't letting her start the damn car again and take another shot at doing him in. "It's fine. Really."

"No, it's not, you're—"

"Bleeding. I know. I had a couple of stitches put in last night, or this morning, actually, and I just got hit by the book you wrote, that's all, during the last turn, into the parking garage."

While he was in the middle of explaining his version of events, a version borne out by the book still in his lap, the corner of it angled toward the bloody smear on his T-shirt, his phone rang.

It could only be one person.

"Travis," he said, answering.

"Stay put." Skeeter cut right to the chase. She sounded breathless as hell. "We're done here. Whitfield's is one big amazing mess right now, and we're getting out of it ASAP."

"Are you okay?" He could hear all sorts of commotion going on in the background, sirens and, if he wasn't mistaken, maybe even gunshots.

"We're good. I'll explain more when we get there. Just stay put at the hotel. We'll come to you." She hung up, and he did the same.

Then he glanced at Gillian, and she looked guilty as hell.

"I am so sorry," she said when he'd finished slipping his phone back in his jacket pocket.

"Don't be. I'll live." As long as she didn't restart the car and go careening off again.

"I know, but I—oh, I have a first-aid kit," she said, her voice brightening, which suited him a whole helluva lot better than her feeling guilty.

"Great idea." First-aid kit, sure, he could do it, let her patch him up a little. "If you've got some gauze pads or something."

"I do. I know I do." She leaned back between the seats and started digging around through her stuff, one knee on the console, her tush in the air—and suddenly he felt better. A lot better.

She had *very* nice legs.

And the shoe that had come untied? He was very tempted to push it off her foot and let it fall to the floorboards, just sort of help her come a little more undone. That's what he needed more than another gauze bandage—somebody soft and warm and supple wrapping her legs around him. It's what he'd wanted all day.

Okay. For weeks.

And weeks.

Geezus, he had such a one-track mind.

But, my God.

She leaned farther into the backseat, and a sigh lifted his chest. This was great. This was amazing—the lovely curve of her thigh just inches from his face, the hem of her skirt barely keeping her modest. He knew if he leaned forward even the slightest bit, he could probably see her underwear, but he didn't do it. The whole underwear thing, and how much of it he ever got to see, was strictly her call—and he knew it was the last thing on her mind right now, even if it had just become the first thing on his.

"Here it is," she said, a note of triumph in her voice.

She moved into her seat, the kit on her lap, and he slipped out of his jacket, tossing it over the back of the seat. Then he reached for the bottom of his T-shirt.

"Oh. Oh, my goodness," she said, as he carefully

pulled the T-shirt off over his head, revealing the extent of his bandages. "Wh-what happened to you?"

"Classified." He really couldn't tell her, and working for General Grant, he knew she would understand. But the knife cut started on his left side, under his arm, and curved around toward the front.

There was blood on the bandages, not a lot, but enough to have soaked through in spots and stained his T-shirt.

"If you'll just put another piece of gauze over this, I think that'll be good enough for tonight," he said, looking the situation over. He'd see Doc Blake tomorrow, back in Denver. Tonight, he had a job to do.

When she just sat there, the first-aid kit clutched in her hands, he glanced up.

Okay, he thought. *This is good.*

She had that shell-shocked look on her face again. It wasn't the first time the sight of him half-naked, or completely naked, had put that expression on a woman's face. It happened all the time. It was why Nikki painted him, and why those paintings sold for tens of thousands of dollars. Mostly he liked it. Sometimes, rarely, it annoyed him. And sometimes, every now and then, it really worked for him.

This was one of those times.

Red Dog was damn cute in a tousled, repressed, coming undone sort of way, and up close, in the shadows and the half-light of the parking garage, with the little piece of tape on her glasses barely discernible, she looked damned cute in a very exotic way. She had an elegant nose, and one of those mouths where the upper lip was only slightly less full than the lower, a sensual mouth—and her shirt was gaping open where she'd buttoned it wrong, and she couldn't seem to tear her gaze away from his naked chest.

Still, he knew better than to kiss her. So he took the first-aid kit out of her hands, and that broke the moment, and between the two of them they decided to just go ahead and change the whole bandage, and put on another layer of antibiotic, and put on a double layer of gauze, and extra tape, and why they hadn't just gone up to the hotel room to do it all, he didn't know, except it was very quiet and very private in the garage, inside her Honda, where they had to work in very close quarters.

Very close.

She was practically on top of him the whole time, and he was loving it just a little too much— the whole thing, with her hands on him, and her voice close, and her fingers smoothing down the edges of the tape and sliding over his skin. Her elbow would brush against his forearm. Her knee touched his. Every now and then, he would feel her breath on his shoulder. With every moment of contact, the heat in the front seat rose another degree.

It was wonderful, and fascinating, and absolutely riveted his attention.

"So how does a woman named Gillian Pentycote end up with a handle like Red Dog?"

A brief smile curved that sensuous mouth. "You'll have to ask Skeeter. She's the one who started calling me Red Dog, and my name is going to be Gillian Shore as soon as I get it changed back."

"Pentycote was your married name?"

"Was," she confirmed, tucking her hair behind her ear before she tore off a new piece of tape. Her smile had disappeared.

Interesting, and very self-explanatory, but he went ahead and did the dance, mostly out of true curiosity, but also out of habit. People liked to talk about their problems, and he liked listening.

"How long have you been divorced?" It was an easy question to ask, the obvious question, but he'd never had anybody give him anything but a hard answer.

"The final papers were signed four months ago." She laid the last piece of tape across his bandage and very gently pressed it to his skin. "And Ken, my ex, is . . . uh, having his first child with his new wife any minute now."

Another hard answer to the question—one of the hardest.

"I'm hoping I can sleep better once the baby

comes," she continued, running her fingers over the tape again. "That must sound pretty odd."

"Actually, it makes perfect sense." And it did. "Considering the timing, and the infidelity, and the pregnancy making the whole thing incredibly public, it will probably be a huge relief when that part of it is finally over."

Her smile returned in a fleeting curve, and she gave a slight shrug of her shoulders.

"Do you have any children of your own?" he asked her.

She shook her head. "Ken always said the timing wasn't right, and for the most part, I agreed. We were busy doing research and trying to get our first book published."

And then old Ken had gone and gotten some other woman pregnant. No wonder she couldn't sleep and could hardly say the word "sex."

"Not much of a deal. She gets the baby, and you get a book."

A short laugh escaped her. "You're the only guy who's ever said that to me." She glanced up and met his gaze. "My women friends say it, especially my sisters-in-law, but a lot of my colleagues at the university seemed to think I did get the better part of the deal, getting published instead of getting pregnant."

Then a lot of her colleagues at the university didn't understand women.

"What university?"

"Arizona."

Bingo. The map in the visor was marked with her escape route.

"So you drove all the way out here from Arizona a month ago, but never quite finished unpacking the car?"

Her smile came back, and he realized it was something he was really starting to enjoy—making her smile.

"I guess I'm waiting to see if it's going to work out."

He reached down and lifted an item out of the box at his feet. "And until you commit, the egg beater stays in the Civic?"

That got him another laugh, a better laugh, and if he wasn't mistaken, a slight blush.

"You know a lot for someone who's so young."

Yes, he did. He knew she hadn't moved back to her seat, even though they'd finished playing doctor, and he knew her blush was deepening, and that she was having a hard time holding his gaze. He knew that despite her best attempts, her attention kept straying to his chest and his abs, and down the length of his arms.

He knew she looked like a woman who had not been held in a long time.

"I'm not that young." Not when it came to soft blushes, soft mouths, and sweet women who were coming undone—but not quite undone enough.

Not when it came to what he had in mind.

"You missed a button on your shirt."

"Oh." She reached for it, paused with her fingers almost doing the deed—unbuttoning and rebuttoning her shirt in front of him—then reconsidered.

He should have reconsidered, too, but he didn't. He reached for her instead.

It was crazy.

He was crazy, but there she was, with her glasses resting a little crookedly on her nose, with her cloud of tangled hair and her pockets spilling over with notes and pencils, and he was going to kiss her. One kiss, that was all.

He slid his hand around the back of her neck and gently pulled her closer—and she let him.

CHAPTER

18

THE FIRST seven floors of 738 Steele Street were garages, and every garage was filled to capacity with cars—cars to drive, cars to race, cars to sell, cars to hide behind. Not that anybody was hiding behind any of the cars on the fourth floor.

Hawkins had flushed three men out of the bays and was systematically herding them to their doom down on three. Creed was waiting for them there.

They'd cleared the building from the top down and left one asshole dead up on five, under a COPO Camaro Skeeter was rebuilding, a dead Indonesian pirate with a Jai Traon tattoo on the back of his hand.

Hawkins had rolled him over, rifled everything

out of his pockets, and wondered, really, what the guy had thought he was going to get away with, being in the wrong country, at the wrong time, in the wrong building, and going up against the wrong fucking guys.

There was never anything easy about hunting down men and killing them. Too many variables came into the mix. But doing it on home ground was as easy as it got. He and the other operators war-gamed Steele Street every week, in the dark, with and without night vision devices. Travis still stumbled over things sometimes, but he was the FNG, and he didn't live in the building. For the chop-shop boys like him and Creed and Quinn and Dylan—hell, they could do it blindfolded.

Skeeter had done it blindfolded.

Kid did it like a Marine.

And J.T. had done it like a coyote, the trickster, "mining" the trail behind him, setting traps, making them think, forcing them to get ahead of the game, to try and get ahead of him.

Hawkins took a breath and let it out, not letting his concentration waver—but it still hurt.

None of them had ever gotten ahead of J.T. It was the one thing they all knew, that the best of them had died. Tonight, though, only the bad guys were buying their last ticket home. They were good, but not good enough, not even close.

Hawkins saw a flash of movement at the stairwell and knew one of the Jai Traon bastards thought he'd just made his getaway.

Fat chance.

He let the next one go, too, then adjusted his position to get a clearer shot. When the last pirate made his move, Hawkins pulled the trigger on his suppressed MP5 twice, and once more for good measure. Two to the heart, one to the head.

"Four clear," he said into his comm unit. "Two to you."

"Roger" came the whispered reply, and Hawkins moved out.

TRAVIS wasn't going to kiss Gillian Red Dog Pentycote/Shore all night long, hell no, and he wasn't going to ravish her on the spot, not because by some fluke of an accident the two of them had ended up scrambled together in the front seat of a Honda Civic.

But neither could he quite convince himself to let go of her, not when kissing her lit up every cell in his body like the Fourth of July.

"I—you . . . we really shouldn't be, umm . . ." she said breathlessly, her voice sighing in his ear, her heart pounding next to his as he ran his teeth over her neck, gently grazing her skin.

He understood. He shouldn't have his hand under her shirt, and she really shouldn't be kissing some guy she'd just met like her life depended on it, but she was trembling, just a little, and clinging to him, a lot, like she needed something solid to hold on to tonight.

And he was solid, all right, like a rock. It had happened so damn fast, and she was bound to notice any minute.

"*Oh,*" she said, even more breathlessly, if that was possible, and he figured that was it. She'd noticed.

"Everything is okay. Honest. We'll be all right." Whatever the hell that meant. He didn't have a clue. "You're in charge here, whatever you want." Yeah, that sounded better, more of what he'd meant to say, and he meant *whatever*. He just didn't want to stop what he was doing. He knew that for sure, and he sure as hell didn't want her to stop what she was doing, so he slid his mouth over her cheek, heading back to her soft, soft lips.

This was all so very, very good, especially when she melted on top of him, letting go, making supergood body contact—and yes, it was that sort of response that had him thinking his dreams might come true.

He knew what he was supposed to be doing—and it wasn't this—but he could really use five minutes of R&R to get his head together. Ten minutes, really, if he could get it.

And maybe to get laid, if that was at all possible.

Under any other circumstances, he would have said no way in hell, but geezus, she was sweet, and so unbelievably responsive that honestly, he figured anything could happen—and he really should try and find out if it could.

Five minutes. He swore that was all.

Or maybe ten.

Because she was way more than cute. Every place he kissed her, she was beautiful, her face heart-shaped, her nose delicately sculpted and turned up ever so slightly on the end. She had a small scar on the bridge, and another across her left cheekbone, little nicks she could have gotten a thousand different ways, but which gave her sweet face a bit of an edge.

He liked it, the way he liked her soft curves, loose papers, and half-buttoned, half-zipped clothes. He loved being this close to her, wanted to get even closer, wanted to be on her, over her, in her.

Inside her.

Definitely ten minutes.

Oh, yeah. Ten, fifteen, twenty, thirty—if he could get even a little bit closer, he had a feeling his "God it would be great to take the edge off" sex was going to happen.

GILLIAN moved her head sideways to close the last scant inch of space separating her mouth from

Travis James's. His arms tightened around her. Her lips parted, his tongue slipped inside, and she fell straight into heaven—again.

Oh . . . my . . . God—she couldn't believe this was happening, heat washing through her, a sweet ache coming to life between her legs. She hadn't felt anything like it in so long, she'd thought that part of her had died with her marriage. But even during the best days of her marriage, she didn't remember anything ever feeling like this.

She opened her mouth wider, wanting more. No man could possibly taste this good, feel this good. She was ready to make a religion out of it—because this . . . this made up for everything, for months of being alone, for all the humiliation and hurt, for all those averted gazes and half-heard whispers, for the rumors and the even worse truth. For the smug look of satisfaction on Kimberly's face and the irritated indifference on Ken's—kissing Travis James made up for all of it. He was so strong and sure, molding her to him like he wanted her, only her, Gillian Pentycote soon-to-be Shore.

Ken would never believe it. She hardly believed what she was feeling, that anyone this amazing would want her so *physically*. She was the smart one, the brainy one, not the girl the guys wanted, but he was responding to her with every breath, with every touch, opening himself to her, practically begging her to explore, and there was nothing she wanted to do more than to feel the hard warmth of him, the lean toughness, to sink herself into the exquisite reality of his body.

Coming back to Washington, D.C., had been the right decision. She was so sure of it now. Giving up her academic position, starting fresh, setting herself on the track of a new and exciting career, practically becoming a secret agent of the government.

This was the life for her, necking in cars with exciting men—very exciting, almost too exciting. The way he made her melt was skirting toward the edge of something she wasn't sure she could handle.

But she could kiss him. There was no danger in kissing. And she could touch him, just a little, just enough to see her through.

A sigh left her mouth, so sweet. She pulled the band off his ponytail and slid her fingers up through the long, silky strands of his hair, pleasing herself and him. She could tell by his soft groan and the way his hand moved up again to cover her breast.

Dangerous ground, but so incredibly delicious, and it had been so long since anyone had touched her, and no one had ever touched her like this. The beautiful, beautiful angel boy was consuming her.

Groaning softly, she turned him deeper into her kiss, and he slid his other hand down around the curve of her waist, pressing her into his hips.

Oh, yes, she thought, feeling a new and deeper thrill shoot through her. *A thousand times yes.*

CHAPTER
19

RUNNING . . . *was not . . . a good . . . idea.*

Dylan doubled over, pulling free from Skeeter's hand and falling to his knees on Whitfield's lawn. The grass was cool, wet, the slight breeze a blessing— the pain crawling up the back of his skull just one more bad sign in a night that had gone to hell and wasn't coming back.

"Dylan. Get up. Come on. Help me." She pulled at him, trying to get her shoulder under his arm.

It wasn't going to work.

"I need a minute." Or an hour, day, week, month.

He'd made it to the catering van okay, except for those last few feet, but he'd still been high back then. Now he was low, bottomed out, sinking, and running was not working for him—at all.

"Come on. We're only fifty yards from the Mercedes. Then we're home free." She pulled at him again, and he gave it his all, staggering to his feet. Even half dead, he could do fifty yards, and he definitely felt half dead. The lovely rush he'd had inside Whitfield's vault had worn off with a vengeance. This feeling, this you're-going-to-die-feeling-like-a-piece-of-crap feeling, that was what he'd been expecting. It was pure Sumba, baby, especially with the addition of the jagged-pike-buried-in-the-back-of-your-skull feeling.

But he could do fifty yards.

He'd sure as hell done that Jai Traon tango back in the office, blown that sucker straight to hell. So there was one bright spot in the evening.

She brushed him off and straightened his bow tie again, because God knew, they were not the only people running around on Whitfield's lawn. There were hundreds. Besides the caterers and the valets, besides the drivers and the waiters, he'd seen SWAT, and EMTs, the D.C. Metro Police, Secret Service—they were the good-looking ones—and a couple of CIA guys—who were not the good-looking ones—FBI—the men in black, in short, everybody except the National Guard, and they were probably on their way. There was nothing like a couple of dead insurgents in a senator's house with a vault door hanging open to really rile up Washington, D.C.'s alphabet soup of agencies. Once that first subgun had gone off, it had been all over except the shouting—and the shouting was going on in full force.

But he'd gotten the job done. Skeeter had taken the Godwin file from him and stowed it inside her uniform. So now all they had to do was get to the Mercedes. He'd had the sense not to leave his jacket in the vault, so over all, he looked just like every other guy running around outside on the lawn in a tuxedo with a drop-dead gorgeous blond chauffeur holding him up. Right. All one of those guys.

Fifty yards.

He could do it.

TRAVIS tried not to groan again, and failed.

God, Red Dog was in so much trouble here. If she'd had any idea, she'd be crawling out the window and running for cover, instead of trying to immolate him on the spot.

But, man, her hands were small and hot and sliding over his chest, and he was down for the count, going under, so ready for her. He'd gotten hard the instant she'd opened her mouth on his, and every instant after had only made his arousal that much more intense. He was a guy. He knew about getting hard fast, but this was crazy.

And he liked it, a lot—crazy, hot, and sexual.

Even crammed into the front seat of a Civic, it was all going so incredibly well, like fate was saying "Take this woman and make her yours."

He could do it. Hell, with the kind of cooperation he was getting, he could do anything, and in half the space.

A small grin curved his lips. He loved a challenge.

One-handed, he gathered up her sensible khaki skirt, giving himself access to the satiny skin underneath, and it was all so easy. With his other hand, he slid under her sensible khaki shirt and unsnapped her bra. Then he moved his palm around to cup her breast, and she let him.

She not only let him, she sighed in his mouth, which was awesome. He deepened the kiss, loving the feel of her, the sheer mind-blowing softness of her skin. Sometimes sex was making love, sometimes it was sex, and sometimes it was sweet, and hot, and perfect.

This felt like one of those sweet-hot-perfect times, when two people were just so incredibly in sync, and yeah, he could get in sync with her in half the space, but with a little effort, they could have twice the space—front seat and back seat.

"Hold on, honey. We're moving."

Keeping one arm around her, he reached down and pulled the seat lever, taking them horizontal, and there she was, flat out on top of him—all of her, on all of him.

Life, he decided, was going to go on, despite ambushes and knife fights and any throats he'd slit. By some miracle, flying halfway across the country had gotten him the one thing he'd needed, a warm, willing, and wonderfully responsive woman in his arms—and Red Dog felt very willing, maybe even a little desperate, but he could relate to desperate. He knew what it was like.

"You okay?" he asked, not that the seat's ride down had been too wild. The inside of a Civic wasn't big enough to catch much vertical space.

"Um hmmm," she murmured between kisses, his kisses and hers. The girl was with him on this. She was with him all the way, and they were headed for the record. "Should we talk? I don't know, it seems that . . ."

"That we're moving at the speed of light. I know. Sure. We can talk." Whatever she wanted. He liked to talk, but not as much as he liked Gillian Pentycote. He wanted to take her right over the edge with him. He wanted her mouth on him. He wanted her panting. He wanted the heat.

He wanted to be inside her until she came. The need was driving him, and he couldn't remember anything like it ever coming on him so hard and fast.

Maybe he was feeding off the desperate edge he felt inside her. Maybe he was making it his own. Not that it mattered. Nothing mattered except what they were doing to each other.

He moved onto his side and let her slide down next to him in the seat. Then he took her face in his hands and just started from the top all over again. If she wanted to think, she was welcome. If she wanted to talk, he was ready, but he was going to talk while he took her clothes off, and all he wanted to think about was getting inside her.

This wasn't sex.

This was survival. He wanted to make love to her, and all she had to do was let him . . . let him—

"Travis? Mr. James?"

"Hmmm?" He slid his mouth across the top of her cheek and started unbuttoning her sensible khaki blouse.

"I'm sure we should . . . talk, I mean, I don't want you to think I do this with every guy who . . . who takes his shirt off in my car."

"Honey, I'm not thinking anything. At all. Guaranteed."

That got him another softly breathless laugh, and he grinned against her skin.

"You think that's funny?"

"I think this is crazy, to feel so crazy."

"Yeah. Me, too, and I'm loving it."

She laughed again even more softly, against his throat, and it was all the encouragement he needed. He moved his hands over her, cupping her breasts with his palms, trying to tell her with every touch how beautiful she was to him. Then he slid one hand down over the curve of her hip and back up under her skirt, and just let himself fall in love with the way she felt.

His friend Nikki, the artist who painted him, was always talking about his angles and his triangles, and how they all worked together artistically. She'd even taken photographs of him once and drawn triangles on them, showing him how all his parts fit together, big parts, little parts, his eyes, and nose, and mouth, his biceps, triceps, pecs, his quads, and his six-pack. She'd drawn over all of them, layering on triangles, explaining why those particular angles made him perfect.

Nikki was nuts.

Perfect was the curve under his hand, the utterly divine curve of Red Dog's waist down over her hip and around her ass, which was another particularly amazing curve. She was layered in curves. The only triangle on her was the one he slid his hand over at the juncture of her thighs—and it was perfect.

She gasped, a soft catch of breath, her hips lifting toward him—so sweet, and it was everything he needed to know. This was happening. They were going to take it home.

Deepening the kiss, he gently parted her with his fingers, and felt her groan in his mouth. He'd wanted to touch her so badly. He wanted to put his mouth between her legs and kiss her, French kiss her until she came. He wanted everything, and it was all within reach, because she hadn't pulled away, and she was wonderfully, amazingly, erotically wet.

TOO *far, too fast*, Gillian thought. Everything was going too far, getting out of hand, moving too fast, but she didn't want to stop.

Somehow, kissing had turned into so much more, and it all felt so incredibly right, to let this stranger take off her clothes and touch her everywhere. It felt like coming home after a long, long absence, and how could that be? She didn't even know this man.

"Skeeter said you were an angel." And Gillian was beginning to wonder if it was really true. Who but an angel could make her feel this way?

A small laugh escaped him.

He kissed her face one more time and lifted his head. A smile was curving his mouth. He was hot and hard against her, and he was smiling. That alone was beyond any experience she'd ever had.

"You're the angel, Gillian, not me." He leaned down and brushed his lips across her cheek. His hair was so soft, sliding down the length of her neck, across her collarbone, and drifting over her breast. Then his mouth was there, sucking on her.

When he brought his lips back to hers, they were warm.

"You're so beautiful, Gillian," he whispered against her mouth. "And tonight, you feel like a gift. I don't know how else to explain it."

He didn't have to explain. She felt the same thing, that he was a gift to her, something to hold on to, something to take inside herself—and she so wanted to take him inside her.

"Kiss me again," she whispered, pulling his mouth back to hers. "Kiss me."

TRAVIS did. He kissed her over and over, teasing her with his fingers, playing with her, until she melted with a soft sigh that went straight to his head. The sex was getting hot, but he wanted it hotter. Needed it hotter.

"Gillian, honey, I need you to—" He lifted her toward the backseat, and she immediately understood and scooted in that direction, and between the two of them, they managed to organize themselves across a very small space into a position where he could peel her panties off and indulge himself.

Every moment from then on moved at a luxurious pace, his whole world sliding wholeheartedly and without resistance into the sensations of heat and wonder and Gillian.

Her breasts, the inside of her wrist, her hips, her

stomach, between her thighs, inside her soft curls and all that incredibly soft, silky skin that drove her wild every time he teased her with his tongue—she tasted sublime everywhere, but even with him taking his time to explore every nuance of her response, she came much too quickly, in a small torrent of cries, more than half of which were his name.

"Travis . . . Travis—oh my, God, Mr. James."

He had never in his life had a woman call him mister anything while he was making love to her, and it was just quirky enough to count as kinky and be a little extra bit of a turn-on, which made him kiss her again, just because she was so sweet with the Mr. James.

It was definitely what he'd needed, and definitely where he'd wanted her, her hands tangled in his hair, her body pulsing with the pleasure he'd given her, his name on her lips, everything about her soft and hot and so ready to take him.

He reached down and unlaced his boots. When they were off, he unzipped his fly and pushed off his pants. Then he came down on top of her, slowly, being careful with his weight and sliding one of her legs around his waist.

She was easy to find.

With his mouth on hers, he pushed inside, taking his time, wanting to feel everything.

Geezus. He hadn't thought he could get any

harder, but with every inch that he went deeper, he proved himself wrong, and just like with her, he didn't think this whole "first time" was going to last nearly long enough to suit him.

Cradling her face with one of his hands, he reached for a handful of sweaters and T-shirts with his other.

"Lift up," he whispered against her lips, and when she did, he shoved the clothes underneath her hips.

Her lashes lifted to reveal soft brown eyes glazed with passion, and a slow grin curved his mouth.

This was a perfect angle.

"Hi," he said, slowly moving in and out of her, loving the mind-bending sensation of being inside her.

She was so lush, so beautiful—so soft and tight.

"Hi," she whispered.

Her mouth was wet, her hair a mess, her whole face flushed.

"Are you doing okay?"

"Mm-hmm." She nodded.

Still holding her gaze, he pulled partway out and slid up into her again. This was unexpected, this kind of bone-melting heat. He bent his head down and opened his mouth on her neck, grazing her with his teeth as he thrust into her again. Her skin was salty, damp, the taste of her melting on his tongue. He rocked into her, over and over, and she tightened her leg around his waist, her hands sliding through his hair, holding him to her . . . holding him. A soft gasp escaped from deep in her throat, and the sound sent heat sliding down his spine to settle in his groin, to settle in his balls.

Red Dog was his.

Her other leg came up around him then, locking him in place, and between one breath and the next, he slid into a fever dream—so hot, her mouth wild on his, her hips lifting toward him, moving with him, taking him to an edge beyond what he could see. The heat between his legs spread, becoming more intense, pushing him on, into her. The rhythm was mesmerizing, sweet sex all the way, harder and faster, until she arched against him, crying out, and everything inside him released, every ounce of him pouring into her, wave after wave of the hottest, sweetest pleasure.

God. He gave himself up to it completely, the sweat of their bodies, the female scent of her infusing his senses, filling him, dragging him under into her—only her.

CHAPTER

20

STANDING NEXT to Dylan at the edge of Whitfield's lawn, Skeeter stared at the Mercedes parked across the street and swore under her breath. There it was, right in front of her, and for all the good it was going to do them, it might as well have been a hundred miles away, with four flat tires, and no gas.

"I didn't know you knew those words," he said, his voice strained, which only made her that much angrier. He was in pain. It was all over his face, in the way he was holding himself.

She knew the words, all right, and as much as she'd like to rattle them all off again, cussing a blue streak wasn't going to change their situation—

which was royally screwed. The Mercedes wasn't going anywhere.

"We'll have to get a cab back to the hotel." And leave that gorgeous, kick-ass luxury sedan for Red Dog to pick up in the morning, but Skeeter would be damned if she left her gear behind.

"Then we'll have to move to another street," he said, "because there ain't *nada* coming down this one for the rest of the night."

He was right. The streets bordering Whitfield's mansion had all been blocked off, but the Mercedes hadn't just been blocked off—it was surrounded, corralled, buried in SWAT trucks, ambulances, cop cars, and nondescript sedans authorized to park in the middle of the street. Her plan for a quick getaway had backfired big-time. Everyone parked in Whitfield's driveway was being systematically searched, released, and directed out onto Q Street, and her getaway street had been turned into a federal and municipal employee parking lot.

It was her fault. She should have kept him moving, instead of stopping at the catering van, no matter that he'd all but collapsed at her feet.

Crap.

"Come on." She took him by the arm, giving him what support she could. She had a plan. She needed to execute it. Hanging around Whitfield's even a minute longer than absolutely necessary was only going to get them into a whole helluva lot of trouble.

There was a verge between the street where the Mercedes was parked and the next street over, a grassy, tree-lined stretch of parkway about twenty feet across.

"Can you hail us a cab if I leave you for a minute?" She was going to park him on the curb on the far side of the verge, then go back for the gear. There were dozens of official people around, and the quicker and more invisible she could be, the better. The one thing she didn't want to do tonight was answer any questions, not while she had the Godwin file stuck down her pants, a .45 holstered under her arm, and two dead tangos in the house behind her.

"Sure," he said, and despite the strain in his voice, she believed him. He was Dylan Hart. If he said he could do it, he could do it, even if he was starting to get a little bit of that falling-apart-in-her-arms feel to him again.

They reached the other street, and she propped him against the rear side panel of a nondescript Chevy. Then she crossed back to the Mercedes, popped the trunk, and grabbed her rucksack.

So far, so good.

She wasn't the only civilian whose car had gotten commandeered by circumstances, and she did her best to blend in and mill around with the rest of the people getting things out of their cars. A cop actually asked her if she needed any help when he saw her carrying her big rucksack. She just grinned, gave him a thumbs-up, and kept on moving—and she kept believing everything was going to be fine, until she cut back through the trees and saw Dylan sliding down the side of the old Chevy with one hand over his face and the other wrapped around his middle.

Oh, crap. She crossed the rest of the parkway at a run, dropping the rucksack at the curb and catching him before he landed in the grass or, God help her, slid under the wheels and into the gutter.

Hawkins would have her ass in a sling if she lost the boss in a gutter.

"Dylan. Dylan." She braced him as best she could, and tried to get her shoulder under his arm, and it was freaking déjà vu all over again. Could anything else possibly go wrong?

"Hey. Do you need some help?" a man called out from behind her.

"No. No," she said, glancing over her shoulder and seeing another cop following her across the parkway. "My client has just had too much to drink, that's all." She turned a little more to the side and gave the cop a cheerful smile.

"Here, let me help," the policeman said, reaching for Dylan. The cop wasn't much older than her, and too observant for his own good. "I don't know, ma'am, he looks sick to me, and he feels a little hot."

Yes, Dylan did feel hot, but an NG4 nuclear-fusion hot-flash relapse always tended to do that to a person.

Dammit. Wasn't the damn antidote doing its job? And what was she going to do if it didn't?

Hospital was the only answer to that one, even if they both ended up in Leavenworth.

"Oh, I've worked for him before, and he always gets this way." She tried to keep her tone light, but she was busy. She'd lodged her knee between Dylan's, and was leaning into him, using her thigh and her hip to keep him from falling, while trying to look nonchalant.

"This is our car," Dylan whispered so only she could hear, his face buried in the curve of her neck, where it was *not* supposed to be.

"This is our car right here," she said, babbling along without missing a beat and wondering what in the hell Dylan was thinking even as the words came out of her mouth. There wasn't a limo service in the country who tooled their clients around in a POS, a set of initials alternately defined as a Police Officer Special or a Piece of Shit. She meant the latter. "Thanks anyway, but I'm just going to take him home, you know, but thanks again anyway, for the offer."

"Open the car door," Dylan whispered.

Oh, right. He was a big help.

She wrapped her hand around the handle and pressed the button, but of course, the car was locked. In Washington, D. C., even the POSes were locked— and this beauty was a P O double S. It was missing paint, chrome, and part of its passenger-side rear-light assembly.

She smiled. "I'm just going to get my keys."

It was a simple thing, really, to lean up against Dylan, rustle around in her rucksack for a moment, and pop the lock on the car with her Slim Jim, without the cop seeing her slide the tool out of the bag and down inside the door frame, and then there she was, opening the door and stuffing Dylan inside, and all the while she was smiling and babbling and trying not to let on that she was stealing a car in front of a policeman.

"If you're sure you're okay?" the cop said.

"Positive." She smiled with all her teeth, like a freaking beauty queen.

The car ownership claim had to look a little doubtful to him when she leaned over Dylan and the whole front seat to unlock the driver's-side door, but she didn't let that throw her off her game.

"Bye," she said, getting back out and closing the passenger door, "and thanks again."

Without another look in his direction, she walked herself around to the other side of the car, hauling her rucksack, and by some miracle got it over the front seat and into the back—and she waited for him to leave.

And waited. Because POS or not, she had her whole crew and her gear in this damn Chevy now, and this was the car she was getting the hell out of

Dodge in, but not even she could hot-wire a car in front of a cop without him noticing, and grand theft auto was not what she wanted added to her rap sheet tonight.

From outside, she heard somebody call out a name, and miracle of miracles, the cop split like a hot stock—but he wasn't going to forget her, not if anyone asked. Cops were like elephants. She'd learned that lesson a long time ago.

Dammit.

"Dylan," she said, scooting over and smoothing her hand across his brow. His skin was surprisingly cool. "Dylan?"

His eyes were closed, his head resting on the back of the seat, his breathing easy, thank God.

"Dylan? Can you hear me?"

He let out a heavy sigh and opened his eyes. "Yeah. It's a little better. The Navy docs said the antidote might take a while to kick in, that it might fluctuate, but that the successive hot flashes wouldn't be so severe." He rolled his head to the side and met her gaze. "I think they were right. I'll have to give them a call, let them know. They wanted first dibs on the body if I kicked off, for the autopsy."

Yes, his breathing was definitely easier, but hers was suddenly quite shallow, the individual breaths sticking in her throat. Body. Autopsy. She was going to be sick.

She put her hand over her sternum and breathed through the slow pain building in her chest. He was giving her such a case of heartburn.

"Antacid?" he asked.

"Please."

He lifted his hips off the seat, dug a roll of antacids out of his pants pocket, and handed them over.

She took four.

"You might want to start this thing," he said when she didn't move.

"Yes," she said around a mouthful of tropical fruit–flavored chalk. He was right.

God, it was turning out to be a long night.

"We had an Impala like this at Steele Street once," he said.

Impossible, she thought. Nothing this ugly had ever graced the hallowed halls of Steele Street.

"Her name was Doreen."

Of course. Doreen. Now she believed it.

"Well, then come on, Doreen," she muttered, tilting sideways onto the seat and wedging herself under the steering column. Using her knife, she cut a couple of exposed wires, stripped them, then touched them together until she got the spark she needed. A quick twist, a little gas, and Doreen was ready to go, missing on two cylinders and sounding like she was gasping her last breath.

"I think she needs a tune-up," he said.

No doubt, but Skeeter thought a .50 caliber round to the engine block would be more humane.

TONY Royce was very unhappy.

He was stuck in a goddamn parking lot of limos and Town Cars, with a hundred fucking law enforcement officers crawling all over Whitfield's house and grounds, and he had two beat-to-crap pirates hiding in the back of his SUV.

Only two.

Apparently, the other two had gotten their fucking heads blown off. Or, actually, if he'd understood that incredible stream of gibberish coming out of Garin and Jai One, Kota's head had been blown off, Jai Two had been double-tapped in the chest.

Either way, they were both dead, both lying on Whitfield's property, and he could only hope neither of them had anything so stupid as an identifying piece of information on them—like his fucking name on a piece of paper safety-pinned to their T-shirts or something: *In case of emergency, call Anthony F. Royce, formerly of the Central Intelligence Agency, who brought me here tonight and is waiting for me in a black Land Rover, license plate number VM35723.*

It gave him an instant migraine.

Jesus Christ.

He should have known that even messed up and

running at half speed, Dylan Hart would be damn hard to bring down and more than capable of delivering his own quota of mayhem.

But the girl. *Goddamn*. She was supposed to be a fucking car mechanic, not a goddamn double-tapping, kick-fighting ninja.

She'd broken Garin's arm, and the bastard was back there groaning like a baby. Damn him. He'd better figure out how to shut himself up, or Royce was going to do it for him with a suppressed 9mm right between his eyes. The cops were doing a real shakedown in the driveway, and he'd be damned if he got caught because of some pansy-assed pirate.

He needed to call Negara's men at the Hotel Lafayette and warn them to be on their guard. When Dylan and his little kick-ass girlfriend got there, he wanted them ready.

And he wanted the girl. Any way he could get her. Negara's orders be damned. Women didn't set right with Royce under the best of circumstances. Under the worst of them, he had a tendency to want to put them in their place—the hard way.

And that's exactly what he was going to do to Skeeter Bang.

CHAPTER
21

TRAVIS WASN'T one to quantify his personal, intimate encounters with women, but *geezus*, he'd just had some of the hottest sex of his life with a woman named Red Dog in the backseat of a Honda Civic.

Really hot sex.

And that had been the backseat, the front seat, and half out the window.

The grin on his face was so big, it almost hurt.

He finished walking across the parking garage, until he reached the Civic. While they'd been waiting for the elevator to go up to the room, Gillian had realized she'd forgotten her glasses on the dash, so he'd come back to get them for her.

But the first thing he saw when he opened the door was her underwear—plain, white, one hundred percent cotton, and hanging off the rearview mirror.

His grin got even wider.

He didn't know how in the hell her underwear had ended up on the mirror, but he loved it. Her bra was draped over the passenger seat. He gathered both items in his hand and brought them to his face—*Gillian*. The scent of her was still warm on the fabric, still sultry, still enough to turn him on.

He'd love to see her in black lace.

Oh, yeah. Black lace, sweet ass, soft mouth, and all over him. God, he could be falling in love, and once Skeeter and Dylan got back from Whitfield's, he was taking Gillian Red Dog Pentycote and getting a room of his own.

It was such a good idea, so perfect, the whole night stretching out in front of them, he couldn't wait to get up to the suite and tell her about it, to ask her, *Please, please, please, Red Dog, spend the night with me.*

DOREEN was dying.

Fortunately, she was taking her own sweet time doing it, losing a bolt here, a clamp there, a couple more pounds of compression on one street, a few more inches of integrity out of the steering on another. The brakes she was pretty egalitarian with— she lost them at every red light. If there had been any cops around, Skeeter would have been in trouble, and it would have been all Doreen's fault.

Fortunately, there were no cops around—for a very good reason. There were neighborhoods in the District of Columbia where even the police feared to tread, and Doreen had found the granddaddy of them all. Skeeter didn't have a clue where they were or how in the hell they'd ended up north of Pennsylvania Avenue, west of Maryland, and east of civilization. She'd been heading for the Hotel Lafayette, or so she'd thought, but Doreen had a mind of her own, and it was wicked, wicked bad.

"This doesn't look like the way to the hotel," Dylan said.

By her count, that was his unhelpful comment number eight.

"I had to get off the highway."

"Why?"

"I thought the car was going to explode."

"Well, this neighborhood doesn't look very safe."

Number nine—but she wasn't counting, not really.

He pulled his Glock out of his pocket and checked the load, which perked up her outlook a little. His survival instincts were still working, and from the looks of where they'd ended up, they were going to need them.

"Why don't you keep an eye out for a service station?" she said. "Doreen needs coolant."

"Sounds like she needs a tune-up, rings, a muffler, and—"

"And like she's going to explode?"

"I still wouldn't have gotten off the highway."

Number ten.

"It looks like Armageddon out there," he said, but she wasn't going to count that one against him. He was right. More than right. In her book, it looked like Arma*freaking*geddon. She didn't know how she'd gotten so far off the beaten track so quickly.

They'd gone from "tony" brownstones to half-gutted buildings in the space of a couple of minutes. A fifty-gallon drum was on fire on the corner, but spookily, no one was hanging around it. She felt people out there, though, sliding through the shadows. She could see them clustered in dark doorways and the alleys—and every single one of them was watching the blond chick in the busted Chevy cruising down the street.

Dylan put his pistol back in his holster, which suited her fine. She didn't want him flashing any hardware. When she got out of the car, she'd be packing enough for both of them—and she was going to have to get out of the car. She could tell. It was only a matter of minutes before something terminal happened to Doreen. She just hoped to hell she found a service station or a garage before then.

At the next intersection, playing the brakes and the steering and truly feeling like she was piloting a bucket of bolts across a dark cosmic sea, she attempted a left-hand turn. Doreen didn't have any suspension left in her suspension, but Skeeter got the whole Impala around the corner. It was a miracle.

"I wouldn't have turned left."

Number eleven.

"There's a station up ahead on the right," she said, pointing it out to him.

"It looks closed."

And that was twelve—*very unhelpful*.

She didn't give a damn if the station was closed or not. It had a garage, and if she had to, she'd open the place herself, totally on the down-low, of course. The last thing she wanted was for anybody to call the police.

Right. Like *that* was going to happen.

Which was a helluva summation of the situation. In this neighborhood, at this time of night, with only a deranged partner and a broken-down rattletrap of a car, she didn't need saving by the cops. She just needed the hell out of Washington, D.C.

Her first choice of action would have been to dump Doreen and steal another car, but every car she'd seen for the last three blocks had looked just like the Impala or even sketchier. There had been two notable exceptions, and on her own, she might have attempted either one of them, but she didn't think she could manage Dylan, bust the locks on a Cadillac Escalade or a Jeep Grand Cherokee, and outshoot the drug-dealing posse that was bound to come down on her with their guns blazing for trying to steal their ride. Two out of three of those she figured she could handle, but not all three, and her fear was that it would be the managing-Dylan part that would get lost in the fracas.

And she'd be damned if she risked that.

So, it was either Doreen . . . or Doreen.

They limped and lurched into the service station and came to a stop on the garage side of the building, as far away as she could get from the sputtering neon sign announcing their arrival at George's Gas & Grub.

Lucky for her, she wasn't hungry.

"Okay, this is what we're going to do," she said, throwing Doreen into park and just letting her miss and hiss, and choke and rumble. God, she wished they were at Steele Street, with all those floors of sleek and mean automotive muscle. "You're going to stay in the car, and I'm going to fix this piece of junk in fifteen minutes or less."

She leaned over the seat, into the back, and pulled one of the UMP45s out of her rucksack. In this neighborhood, a subgun seemed like the minimum requirement for getting out of the car in the dark.

"No, you're not," he said, pushing himself upright. A wince crossed his face. "Stay put. I'll take a look under the hood."

She let out a small snort and changed the magazine on her .45.

"What?" he said, clearly offended. "You don't think I can fix the car?"

"Given enough time, enough tools, and enough parts, sure, you could probably fix the car." She slipped her Para back in its holster, then met his gaze straight on. "But I can do it without any of those things—no time, no tools, and no parts, and that's what we've got."

She reached for the door handle, and he reached for her, his hand going around her wrist.

"You're not going anywhere."

The hell she wasn't. "Look, Dylan, five years ago, maybe you could have given me a run for my money with a box-end wrench and a thirteen-millimeter deep socket—but not tonight. Not on this street, with this car, in your condition."

She started to pull away, but he tightened his hold—and her patience snapped.

"*Dammit*, Dylan . . . sir. We don't have time for—"

And he kissed her, just hauled her across the seat and laid his lips on hers and kissed her.

She saw it coming. My God, she saw it coming a mile away, and if she'd had an ounce of sense, she would have shut him down like a bad day at the track, but no, she let the train wreck happen, the whole thing in Technicolor slow motion—his mouth hot and wet, his desire for her overwhelming any common sense she might have thrown into the breech. He wanted her, and she'd wanted him for too long not to indulge herself.

Just once, she swore, letting his arms close around her, letting his hands slide all over her and trip her switches. He had good hands, strong, sure—and kind of fast. He was molding her to him, pulling her into his lap, and she decided, for a moment, to just let it all happen, because he was Dylan, and the night had gone all to hell, which she hated, and he was still all jacked up with NG4 and antidote, and she was more than a little scared for him.

So she opened her mouth over his, pushed her hands up into his hair, and kissed him for all she was worth. Because this was it, the chance she hadn't taken in the vault, and he was heaven to kiss. Absolute heaven. Nothing in her imagination had ever come close to the bone-deep thrill of actually having his mouth on hers, his tongue driving her to distraction and beyond. He was so intensely male, more than her fantasies had ever conjured, the taste of him, the feel of his skin along his jaw, the bare roughness where he'd shaved. She wanted to remember it all. She slid her hand into the open front of his shirt, because for just once, she could, and *oh, God*, she really wanted to remember this part, how he felt, his muscles hard, the hair on his chest soft.

She moaned, an inadvertent sound, touching him, and wishing she dared to touch him even more, knowing that soft dark hair covered him all the way to his groin. She'd seen him naked in the pool at Steele Street one night, coming across him by accident, one of the most amazing accidents of her life. She hadn't really stood there and ogled him, but she had looked, and lusted, and wanted him so badly it had hurt.

He was so heartbreakingly beautiful. There were no other words for him. He wasn't all rugged angles and tattoos like Hawkins, or one of *People* magazine's Fifty Sexiest people like Quinn. He didn't have any of the boyishness that still lingered in Kid's face. Nor was he wild around the edges like Creed.

Unlike all the other chop-shop boys, Dylan Hart had nothing of the street in him, and nothing "wild." He was cool, calculating, always in control. If Hawkins was the muscle of SDF, Dylan was the mastermind, and yet, physically, he had the same raw presence as Superman, all of it sculpted into layers of muscle and sinew—the power of long legs, corded arms, broad shoulders, and a back designed by God and perfected by lifting iron, getting strong, then getting stronger, getting tough, then getting tougher. It's what they all did. It's how Hawkins had trained her, how the guys stayed alive in the places they went, in doing the jobs they were tasked to do. And all Dylan's strength and power were finally in her arms, surrounding her, warming her skin on the outside and causing a meltdown inside.

He groaned, half lifting her, moving her across his lap, his mouth sliding to her neck, where he licked her skin, then sliding back to her mouth and sucking some more. It was the hottest, sweetest sensation, having him practically devour her, but no— *oh, freaking dear no.* Kissing him was wonderful, but straddling him was not a good idea, not a very good idea at all.

But his kisses had this way of disorientating her until she couldn't think straight, and he had a way of moving her to suit himself, lifting her and shifting his hips, and with her knee sliding one way, and her common sense going the other, she somehow ended up exactly where he wanted her, and it was amazing, and a little scary, and utterly mesmerizing to feel him between her legs.

She flashed hot, then cold, overwhelmed. He was fully, undeniably aroused. Dylan Hart, for her, and it made her head swim, and while that stunning information was transmitting to every cell in her body, he all but drowned her with a whole new database.

With more single-minded purpose than she would have thought he could muster, he started undoing his pants.

She felt his hands go between their bodies, heard the slide of his zipper.

"Dylan, uh . . ." "Stop" was the word she wanted.

Right. She was going to put a stop to this. It was insane to even be kissing him. Anything else was completely out of the question. They were in the parking lot of the freaking George's Gas & Grub, for God's sake, which was exactly what she was going to tell him, she was sure—except his hands were moving faster than she could get her thoughts to line up, and before she knew it, he'd pushed his pants and briefs down off his hips.

And he was hot, very hot, and very hard, and very naked, and very, very much between her legs. Her knees were on either side of him, the bottoms of her thighs were resting on the tops of his, and if it weren't for the incredibly annoying barrier of her uniform, they'd already be doing it.

Doing it with Dylan.

A frighteningly delicious shiver went straight down the middle of her and settled between her legs, right where they touched. It stole her breath. It made her consider crazy, crazy things.

No, she told herself. *Get a grip.*

"Dylan," she whispered against his mouth. "I . . . I . . ." She couldn't take advantage of him this way.

He'd never even noticed her until they'd been standing on that street corner in Georgetown, and he wasn't himself, not with the NG4 and that damned antidote in his body, but she didn't know what to say, and . . .

"Shhh," he murmured, stretching up to bite her lips, so gently, again and again. "You're thinking too hard. You don't have to think. I've got this covered."

Oh, right. He had it covered.

He was naked, and she was dying inside.

And neither of those facts were the ones she needed to address. She needed to address the fact that . . . he was drawing her tongue into his mouth and playing with her, sucking on her again—*oh, yes*, she really needed to talk to him about that, and she would, she swore it, as soon as she stopped melting, as soon he was finished doing it.

Doing it.

With Dylan.

Oh, geez.

And all the while he was slaying her with his kiss, his hands were unzipping her pants, helping her move her leg, sliding the pants down, slipping one leg off over her shoe, and then his hand slid back up her leg and slipped inside her underwear. He moved the tiny scrap of material aside, teased her, and *oh, God*, this is what happened when a girl's last line of defense was four square inches of black silk—*surrender.*

"*Dylan*," she gasped, and tightened her hands on his shoulders, which didn't slow him down in the least. "I'm not . . . sure about this."

"I am," he said without hesitation, his voice a soft growl.

He moved his hips underneath her, fitted himself to her, and any chance she had of salvaging a thought after that dissolved into a wave of anticipation and pleasure. She knew what was going to happen next. Of course she knew what was going to happen next. She wasn't an idiot or a virgin, and she knew she needed to get off of him *now*, before anything happened, because . . . because . . .

He pushed, and it was all over.

Heat. A tidal wave of it suffused her.

His head went back on the seat with a soft groan. His hands went to her hips, holding her to him, and he filled her, completely, hotly, sweetly.

"Dylan," she sighed his name, and a sob broke free from her throat.

"Ah, don't cry. Don't cry, sweetheart," he murmured. "This is good . . . all good. I swear, just don't . . . move. Not yet. Just let me . . ."

She wasn't going to cry, not really, and she wasn't going to move. She could hardly breathe, she was holding on to him so tight.

He shifted beneath her and let out another groan. "*Jesus*, you are so perfect."

Perfectly undone.

Perfectly insane.

His eyes drifted open, and his gaze met hers in the dim interior of the Impala.

"Skeeter Jeanne," he said softly, and pushed deeper.

Oh, God. He was a force of nature, a reckoning she had wildly underestimated in her fantasies. Neither of the boys she'd been with before had felt anything like this—but they'd been boys, not men. The difference was astounding. So help her, she could feel the echo of his heartbeat pulsing deep inside her, and it made him feel like a god.

"I'm . . . I'm overreacting." Synapses sizzling, sweat breaking out on her brow, hands trembling. Nothing should feel this good, this mesmerizing, this intense.

"No such thing," he said, reaching up and cupping her face with his hand. "Not for what we're doing. Do you know how long I've wanted you? Like this?"

She shook her head. No, she didn't know. She didn't have a clue, but if she'd had to make a guess, she'd guess from about the time the damned drugs had drop-loaded into his system back in the vault at Whitfield's—about an hour ago, max.

"Forever," he said. "Always."

Okay, that was considerably longer than she would have thought, especially considering that they had never hardly gotten past "Hello"—not that she really cared, not now, not when he was inside her.

With steady deliberation, he unbuttoned her uniform jacket for the second time.

"Demi-bra," he said when the jacket fell open and revealed the scrap of silk and hot pink lace. A smile curved his mouth.

She was coming undone. He was undoing her, inside and out, and it was better and more awful than she ever could have imagined. Better in the sheer, mind-blowing eroticism of having him look at her, of being with him, and worse in what she was afraid it was going to cost her.

"You're thinking again." He kissed her breast, ran his tongue over her, took her in his mouth, and she knew he was wrong. She wasn't thinking. She wasn't thinking at all—except about what he was doing to her.

Oh, God. She slid her hand up the back of his head, tunneling her fingers through the dark, silky strands of his hair, holding him to her breast, and she let her gaze drift over the planes of his face. He was so elegant—the refined shape of his nose, the clean, chiseled lines of his cheeks and brow.

Dylan. He rocked his hips up beneath her, and she slid down on him, the rhythm coming so naturally, the heated give and take of seduction.

Very heated. *God.* The last solid brain cell she had melted in the heat. Nothing she'd done had ever felt like this. He thrust into her again, his soft groan of pleasure washing through her, turning her on in places she hadn't even known existed.

"I . . . I think we're making love on the astral plane," she whispered. There was no other explanation for this otherworldly pleasure that was turning her inside out. It was so far beyond what she had imagined.

"Yes," he agreed, the word spoken against her skin. "Absolutely. On all the planes."

He was such a beautiful mess tonight, his clothes half off, which she loved, being able to run her hand over the soft hair covering his chest, to feel the hard layers of muscle underneath, to finally, after all these months and months of wanting him, have her hands on him.

Dylan. She leaned over him, releasing a sigh, letting her hair fall around them like a silver veil. She could feel him everywhere, buried so deep inside her, his mouth teasing her nipples, his chest beneath her hand—and his heartbeat everywhere, pulsing, sending a message to her soul.

She was going to regret this later, when he came out of his drug-induced haze and realized what they'd done. It was going to be impossible to be around him and not be able to have him like this, again and again and again, whenever she wanted, which was going to be a lot.

Oh, God, yes. She was going to want this a lot.

He smelled like sex, and felt like sex, and he was consuming her.

She would have to leave SDF, leave Steele Street and Superman, and Kid, and Creed. She'd seen the type of women Dylan dated on those rare occasions when he was in Denver, and she couldn't guarantee that the next time he brought one around she wouldn't accidentally snap her pretty little neck.

His dates were *always* beautiful, and *always* brilliant. It's like he put them through an IQ test or something.

But tonight he belonged to her, Skeeter Bang, street rat, gear head, computer nerd. He belonged to SB303, the spooky girl who loved him.

She wanted to tag him, mark him, claim him as hers for all time.

His hair was sinfully silky. He was usually so impeccably groomed, but not tonight. Swaths of dark, silken strands fell straight down on either side of his face, almost to his cheekbones. It was so sexy. He looked so rock-star cool.

Then he lifted his head from her breast, and she realized there wasn't a cool cell in his whole body. He was all heat.

For a moment, she simply held his gaze, his eyes so perfectly gray, his lashes so thick. In her comic book drawings, he was Kenshi the Avenger, a powerful dragon lord and wizard. For one solid year, she'd drawn Travis as Kenshi, and for one solid year, the character had been wrong. Travis had told her as much, but she hadn't been able to see it, until the night she'd darkened Kenshi's hair and turned it from a tawny mane into a straight fall of black silk, until she'd turned Kenshi into Dylan.

Travis didn't have a dark side, but Kenshi did, and so did Dylan Hart. What had happened to Wes Lake, a man incarcerated in the state penitentiary at the same time as Superman, had been a dark deed of justice wrought by a dark, ruthless hand, Dylan's hand. Even Quinn and Creed thought Dylan had contracted the hit that had killed Lake before the man could carry out his sworn vow to either sodomize or kill Hawkins, but she knew Dylan had done the deed himself, a promise kept.

She knew him, and she would have loved him for that one deed alone, for doing what had needed to be done, for saving Superman. It had been such a dark time.

In turn, years later, Superman had saved her, and tonight . . .

Tonight she didn't know who was saving who, but she felt redeemed from the hundreds of lonely nights she'd spent wanting him—and with him loving her, his body moving with hers, taking her someplace she'd never been, never imagined, to a completion she felt building to a peak under the knowing touch of his hands, the utter seduction of his mouth, and the naked, untempered physicality of sex, of him sliding in and out of her, deepening their connection with every stroke . . . with him loving her tonight, he looked like the very soul of salvation.

She let her head fall to his shoulder, felt him turn and open his mouth on her neck, his teeth grazing her skin, his tongue tasting her.

"I love you," he said, his voice hoarse with need. "I love you so much."

"Yes." She knew he did. For now, in this moment, he loved her. She felt it everywhere.

And when his love and his body finally took her over the edge, the sweet release of it stole her breath. It tied her to him with a power that went far beyond the boundaries of their skin, beyond the boundaries of reason.

CHAPTER

22

✦

PIRATES, Hawkins thought, *Jai Traon*. He'd gone up against Indonesian pirates once before, on an oil rig in the South China Sea, and all he could say was that these boys had obviously been out of their element on dry land—either that or they'd had the crap jet-lagged out of them. The Jai Traon on the rig had fought like sons-of-bitches and slid around like shadows.

Tonight, all the odds and determination had been on his and Creed's side, especially after Hawkins had gotten a look at the papers he'd found on the Jai Traon they'd left under the COPO Camaro.

He waited, utterly still, utterly silent, watching

Creed make his move on the last pirate. Out of the four men who had broken into Steele Street, two were dead, one was under Hawkins's knee, out cold and flex-cuffed, and the fourth was drawing his last breath.

Hawkins couldn't read Indonesian, but a few things defied translation and had to be written out in their original language—things like names. Like the names of everybody who lived at Steele Street, including the names Katya Hawkins and Cody Rivera, two names guaranteed to bring out Creed's finest qualities and most lethal skills. Hawkins had quietly suggested that they not kill one of the bastards so they could interrogate him, and the guy under his knee had pulled the lucky number.

Pirate number four was going to come up short in about five seconds.

Actually, it only took three. The man went down under Creed's knife in a classic Wingate maneuver. It was very smooth, very quiet, and very, very violent, Creed's killing strike coming out of the darkness, his right hand grabbing the guy around the face, his fingers spread, the strength of his hand and arm jerking the man's head to one side, laying wide the back of his neck and the small area where Creed silently jammed his knife up into the man's skull, severing his brain stem.

It was clean, quick—bloody, but not the mess of a gunshot killing.

The jungle boy didn't let the pirate fall, but rather lowered him to the floor. Then he wiped his knife across the pirate's shoulder and put it back in its sheath—a night's work well done, but not finished. There had been another bit of nontranslatable information on the dead pirate they'd left up on the fifth floor—an address in Prince William County, Virginia, across the state line from the nation's capital, where Skeeter and Dylan just happened to be stealing the Godwin file from Senator Whitfield.

Hawkins didn't believe in the tooth fairy, Santa Claus, or coincidences of any kind, and he needed to run the address through his computer and call Dylan and Skeeter while he did it. Something was definitely up with the damned Godwin mission.

Travis should have arrived in Washington, D.C., an hour ago, so at least they had another SDF operator on their side. Hawkins just hoped the three of them would be enough. He didn't care what Dylan had said, the boss was not at his best, not by a long shot. There was one other hope, though. It was possible that the number of good guys was four. There was a new girl at Grant's office, a Gillian Pentycote, code-named Red Dog by Skeeter, and he knew the general ran his staff through a training program. Hawkins hadn't gotten any evaluation reports on her, but maybe, just maybe, Red Dog could kick butt.

If Negara had set his men loose in Washington, Hawkins hoped so, for everybody's sake.

GILLIAN swiped the key card through the hotel suite's lock, watching to see if the light turned green, all the while humming. She'd been humming since she'd gotten on the elevator down in the parking garage—humming and smiling.

Oh. My. God. Sex was incredible, especially angel boy sex. So incredible, she wasn't sure she would ever be quite the same again—and she loved it. "Being the same" had been her third greatest marital crime, according to Ken. She'd always had her nose in a book, always been too serious, always been only about half put together with her clothes, and her glasses had always been broken, a phenomenon she hadn't understood any more than Ken. It was just one of those things. She'd no sooner get her glasses fixed in one spot than some other little part would let go.

Kimberly was a fashion plate, a clotheshorse, a shopaholic who spent more money on her haircuts than Gillian spent on groceries—which had been another point against her. Kimberly could cook, really cook. It had come down to a choice between a life of tuna casserole or baked sole, Ken had said, in what Gillian considered one of his more uninspired moments.

Kimberly had that effect on him, bringing out his least-inspired side, reducing him to an endless litany of clichés and shopworn opinions, and Gillian had warned him that uninspired clichés weren't going to do his career any good. They both knew he needed to be pushed to do his best work, and nobody pushed him more than Gillian—which had been her second greatest marital crime. He had his book now, and he was ready to slide into tenure. He didn't want to be pushed anymore, and he didn't want the competition of having a wife who was a little more brilliant at her worst than he was at his best. And that had been her greatest crime of all, being better than Dr. Kenneth Pentycote—even with her still being half a dissertation short of a doctoral degree of her own.

She swiped the card again when the light flashed red instead of changing to green.

Well, she was brilliant, all right, brilliant enough to change directions and try something new. Brilliant enough to get a job working for a man her father considered one of the great unsung heroes of America, a job where she got to load UMP magazines with .45 caliber cartridges, the kind of job where she picked exotic angel boys up at airports and ended up more than half naked in the backseat of her Honda.

Good Lord. Her smile broadened into a grin. What she'd done made her feel incredible, but that she'd actually done it made her head spin. What in the world had she been thinking? What in the world had Travis James been thinking?

And what, she wondered, were the chances of him thinking it again?

A small laugh escaped her. She felt so good—which elicited another soft laugh, because that's exactly what the angel boy had told her.

The light finally turned green on the third swipe. She grabbed the handle and opened the door, humming again. The door closed behind her as she dropped her purse on the entryway table. Then she looked up and realized, truly, just how incredibly brilliant she was—brilliant enough, she realized, seeing the three men coming at her with their weapons drawn, to get herself into more hot water than she would ever have dreamed possible.

SITTING in the front seat of the broken-down Impala, Dylan wanted to kiss Skeeter so badly, it hurt, but if he kissed her, he was going to devour her again, take her from the top down and drown himself in her. God, he was such a selfish bastard. He should never have let the situation get so far out of hand, especially since it didn't look like he was going to die.

Oh, yeah, that had been his bottom line.

Geezus, he was so fucked up, and yet it was the

god's truth, impending death and certain doom
were the only two justifications he would accept for
what he'd done. Unfortunately, he felt great, like he
was going to live at least another fifty or sixty years,
plenty of time to nurse his regrets into a colossal
case of guilt. Not that it was going to take anywhere
near that long. Five minutes out and he already had
a good jump on it.

He'd fallen off the edge, and that unnerved him
almost as much as what he'd done. It wasn't like him
to lose control, to break one of his own rules. He'd
been breaking the rest of the world's rules since he'd
been fifteen, but not his own, never his own.

Until now.

She was melted on top of him, totally relaxed,
about half undressed, her head resting on his shoulder, her breathing deep and even, but she wasn't
asleep. He could tell.

He dragged his hand back through his hair and
just held her with his other arm around her waist,
his fingers gripping her tighter than they should. He
knew it, but he couldn't help it. *Geezus*. It was
Skeeter, Baby Bang, and he'd had amazing sex with
her in the front seat of a Chevy that probably qualified as a toxic waste dump.

Someone should shoot him.

And yes, he knew the name of the exact someone who would be only too glad to do the job—
Christian. Cristo. Hawkins. Superman.

The whole situation made him feel a little wild, a little wildly crazed. *Fuck.* He let his gaze drift over the baby soft curve of her cheek, down the side of her neck, back to her shoulder, then lower, down the sleek, silky length of her upper arm.

Whitfield's had been a grade A disaster, complete with Negara's bastard pirates, and they were still out there, gunning for him, and for Skeeter, which was tearing him up. They shouldn't even know she existed, let alone have caught her with him.

It was going to go down as one of the best shots of his life, the one he'd used to kill that guy in Whitfield's office. His eyes had been crossed, he'd been so fucked up, and his arm had still been on fire, but he'd made the shot.

He let out a breath, and with an act of pure will kept himself from smoothing his hand down her arm, or up her leg and that amazingly erotic lightning-bolt tattoo. He'd been running with the wrong women if lightning-bolt tattoos turned him on—and they did. At least Skeeter's did.

But he kept his hand to himself. He needed to think, not start feeling her up again. He wasn't out of the woods yet. He could tell by the edge of faintness he felt skirting the borders of his brain—or maybe that was postcoital craziness. He felt that, for sure.

Ah, Skeeter. What in the hell had he done?

Honor, Loyalty, Duty. Those were the tattoos

inked down her arm. Her whole hip-hop crew had been tagged with the same symbols. Honor among thieves, he understood all too well, and he knew they'd been thieves as well as wallbangers. Loyalty he understood even more, especially for a crew of graffiti artists trying to paint the city without getting busted by the cops or capped by the gangs. Duty he understood best of all. It was the mantra his father had given him.

Honesty would have been another good one to add. He always was with himself, no matter what it cost. Tonight was no different in that respect, and he knew the problem wasn't that he couldn't love her. He did. The problem was that he didn't want to love her, and try as he might, he couldn't see his way around that one inviolate fact.

He didn't want this sick pain in his heart that said he'd put her in danger. He didn't want the heartache of knowing he really couldn't have her, not forever, if only because he knew himself, and he knew he would move on.

Oh, yeah, kissing her now, making love to her now was so perfect, but it wouldn't last. Nothing ever lasted for him, except the friendships he'd forged with the chop-shop boys. It's what he should have tried harder to have with her—friendship.

But, man, a friend didn't whisper your name when you pushed up into her, didn't melt you with a sigh when you took her breast in your mouth. A friend didn't get wet when you touched her, and didn't hold on to you when she came—hold on to you like you were the last solid thing in the universe.

Geezus, he'd felt her tighten around him, and he'd come all the way from the soles of his feet. The sides of his neck were hot, and the place at the base of his throat, just north of his heart and south of his brain, was pulsing. He'd just had her and his balls were still tight. He still wanted her.

He knew her down to the taste of her mouth and the scent of her skin, and everything about her said she was his. The soft place on the underside of her arm? *His*. The silky feel of her hair sliding over him as he'd thrust into her? *His*. The sound she'd made deep in her throat when she'd come undone? Most definitely *his*. *Only his*.

But she was so damn young, it was mind-boggling—and his mind was boggled enough, thank you.

CHAPTER

23

WITH A pocket full of underwear and a pair of taped-together glasses in his hand, Travis got off the elevator on the fourth floor of the Hotel Lafayette and headed down the hall to room 418. He didn't get too far before he noticed something unusual. Gillian had left the door ajar.

Or someone else had.

He didn't pause in his stride, but suddenly every warning signal he had went off. Continuing down the hall, he slipped the glasses into his jacket pocket, then reached behind his back and pulled the Springfield 1911 out of the paddle holster Skeeter had gotten for him.

Walking faster, every one of his senses on high alert, he racked a cartridge into the chamber. At the door, he stopped for a couple of seconds, listening and checking his line of sight.

The lights were on inside the room, but no one was talking, and there was no sound of movement.

Leading with the muzzle of the 1911, he slipped through the door. It took him all of ninety seconds to clear the three-room suite, including bathrooms, and it was clear. No one anywhere.

She could have gone for ice, but somehow he didn't think that's what was going on. Nothing in the suite was disturbed or particularly out of place, but it didn't feel right. Then he turned and saw the back of the door. A large circle had been drawn on the panels, with three long lines running through it. The message was clear, and it made his blood run cold.

Hamzah Negara's Jai Traon pirates had taken Red Dog.

SKEETER wanted to sigh, and she wanted to groan. Of all the damn things to have done, making love with Dylan Hart in the front seat of a broken-down 1985 Chevy Impala had to rank as one of the all-time bonehead moves of the century. Without all the heat and sex, and sex and heat, and all the sex absolutely *frying* her brain cells, she could see the incident for what it was—a mistake.

Colossal.

King Kong.

And she'd do it again in a heartbeat—which didn't address their current dilemma.

Somewhere between "Oh, my God, Dylan," and "Dylan, my God," Doreen had died, stone-cold-death died. She'd given her last, but not before she'd dumped them in a Washington, D.C., ghetto. Of course, all Skeeter had to do was call a cab, if there was a cabbie fearless enough to pick up a fare at George's Gas & Grub, smack-dab in the middle of the kind of no-man's-land where a different gang owned every street corner.

Even a moment's consideration of the fearless-cabbie possibility made it seem damned unlikely, which left her with only one place to go for help, the place she'd been going all day and getting everything she needed, the amazing Red Dog.

But before she could call Red Dog, she had to get herself off Dylan.

Right.

She didn't want to.

She wanted to stay where she was, plastered to him, lying on top of him, cradled around him. He was holding her pretty damn tightly, too, like he didn't want to let go of her, either.

I love you. That's what he'd said to her. *I love you so much.*

Well, she wasn't going to fool herself. Those particular words could mean a lot of things when a guy was inside a woman—and he'd definitely been inside her when he'd said them.

Dammit. How could she have been so addle-brained as to let things get that out of hand? And what were her chances, really, of them getting out of hand again, later at the hotel?

Slim, she decided. Except for holding on to her like he was never going to let go, he had hardly moved since they'd finished.

Plus, if she remembered correctly, and she *did*, they had another problem she didn't dare forget.

"How are you feeling?" she asked, and the question was neither polite nor rhetorical.

"Normal," he said, proving that he understood exactly what she'd meant. "Except . . . except I'm, uh, a little rattled."

"Rattled" was one way to put it, she guessed. Practically paralyzed with guilt was probably another way.

Double dammit. She knew him, too well, and he wasn't going to like himself for this.

Hell.

"Not too hot?"

"No."

"Not too cold?"

"No."

"Then we need to get moving," she said without moving so much as a millimeter.

This was it, her one chance to be with him, and it was hard to let him go. He was going to come to his senses, and her party would be over.

Honesty required her to admit that if her phone hadn't started ringing, she might have stayed exactly where she was for at least another week.

She pushed herself to more of a sitting position and pulled her cell out of her uniform jacket.

"Skeeter," she said, meaning to slide off his lap, but *geez*, he felt so good, all naked beneath her.

His gaze immediately fell to her breasts, which were at best only about half covered by her lace demi-bra, and suddenly she was all hot again—everywhere.

"Uh, Hawkins, hello, yes, good to hear from you, fine, sure." And then just as suddenly, she wasn't so hot anymore. She was cold, and focused, and listening to every word. "Prince William County. Yes."

She repeated the address out loud, nodding at Dylan, who was watching her with the same intensity she was giving Superman.

"Yes," she said, and repeated a series of directions aloud.

Dylan was getting it, understanding every word. She could see it in his eyes.

"I agree," she said. "I'll wait for Creed and Quinn, and then we'll go take a look. Just a second."

Another call was coming in.

She put Hawkins on hold, and fifteen seconds later knew there was going to be no waiting for anybody. It was Travis, and his message was succinct: Jai Traon pirates had been waiting at the Hotel Lafayette, and they'd taken Red Dog.

Suddenly, Skeeter's night was lying out before her just chock-full of opportunities for using that Knight Match SR-25 sniper rifle with the Litton Aquila 6X starlight scope attached.

CHAPTER

24

THEY'D BROUGHT him the wrong goddamn girl. Tony Royce could hardly believe it.

How in the hell, he wondered, could anyone possibly mistake this little bit of myopic, auburn-haired fluff for a street-tough, blond-haired Amazon like Skeeter Bang?

These idiots had seen the photograph. Negara had passed it around to everyone in his office before he'd deployed them for the night's work.

And they'd brought him Gillian Pentycote.

He tossed her wallet back into her purse.

He was disappointed, but Dr. Souk wasn't. The doctor was carefully checking all his metal clamps and leather straps, making sure each one was tight on her body, but not too tight. Each device needed to be capable of restraining her, but not likely to cause any unforeseen damage.

Foreseen damage was the calling card here tonight.

They'd gagged the woman, but Royce knew that particular leather strap would be removed, and soon. Dr. Souk's whole program of meticulously administered drugs and torture was designed to make people talk—and talk, and talk, and talk. Royce had heard people give up parts of their past they couldn't have consciously recalled to save their souls.

Not that he expected much of interest out of Gillian Pentycote, formerly of the University of Arizona Environmental Laboratory, and currently living in a condo in Arlington, Virginia.

Disappeared. That's all her family would ever know. That she'd disappeared one night, never making it home from whatever she'd been doing at the Hotel Lafayette. No one would ever guess that she'd ended up strapped to a dental chair in a secret clinic housed on one of Virginia's most luxurious estates, tortured to death by one of the world's most demented medical minds.

She knew, though. She was wild-eyed with the knowledge, and he took some hope in the fact. He'd love to see her fight for her life, even a little, rather than roll over and die without giving any show whatsoever. He'd never completely given in to his fantasies of terrorizing women, and he had to admit that he was more than a little excited to see what Dr. Souk came up with. In truth, he'd hardly given in to his misogynistic fantasies at all, making do at best with knocking a few women around, and a couple of times a little knife work. But mostly just knocking them around.

Women, he'd discovered at a young age, were no physical match for a man. It was ridiculous, really, how easy they were to break. Not ones like Skeeter Bang, which he knew was one reason he disliked her so intensely, but the smaller ones, like Gillian Pentycote, were pretty much at a man's mercy—not that there would be much mercy here tonight.

A smile slid across his face.

Not much mercy at all.

He loosened his tie and checked his watch. He guessed it would take about two minutes for Dr. Souk to find out what Ms. Pentycote had been doing in Hart and Bang's hotel room, and after that the real fun would begin.

RED *Dog*.

The name raced through Gillian's brain for about the millionth time—*Red Dog*.

It sounded cool, sounded strong, like the name of a steady person who could handle herself.

Red Dog.

She wondered if that's why Skeeter Bang had given it to her, so she'd have something to hold on to if things got tough.

Because things were tough for her right now, terribly tough. She was strapped into a dental chair in a white-tiled room that was so bright it hurt her eyes, and her heart was pounding like a jackhammer, and she could hardly breathe, and she had more than enough imagination to see where this was going.

There was a drain in the floor.

She'd seen it on the way in, when they'd dragged her into the horrifying white room, and her skin had gone instantly cold.

She was still so cold, terrified, trembling all over, and she couldn't stop, and no one seemed to care or even notice. Certainly not the guards standing around the room, or the iron-faced man in the cheap suit and loose tie who had been staring at her with unrepentant disgust since her arrival, and certainly not the pathetically thin, sallow-faced Asian man in the white lab coat who was picking and choosing his way through dozens of stainless steel instruments and laying them out on a white cloth on a steel table with wheels.

And the syringes. She didn't want to think about

the syringes. They were lined up, too, some filled with a clear liquid, others with red, and a few with blue. She didn't know why, but the thought of being injected with the colored liquids terrified her more than the thought of being injected with the clear liquid. Somehow, they looked like they would hurt very, very badly going in, especially the red one.

Or maybe the blue looked worse.

It was hard to tell with so much sweat running into her eyes, running down her face, making her damp in some places and downright wet in others. The white room was ice-cold, and she was sweating, and freezing, and shaking, and wanting so badly to just open her mouth and scream.

But she couldn't open her mouth, and she couldn't scream, and she was trying not to think about either of those things, because it just made her want to do them even more.

The leather gag was so tight between her teeth, pulling at the sides of her mouth. The metal clamps were so tight around her wrists and ankles, cutting into her skin. The light was so bright, hurting her eyes.

Red Dog.

The man in the white lab coat turned then and began pushing the steel table over to the dental chair, the wheels squeaking, the instruments rattling.

The iron-faced man had called him Dr. Souk.

Doctor. He didn't look like a doctor. He looked like a nightmare, a maniac, his glasses thick and dirty, his black hair the same, his lab coat stained. He pulled the table to a stop at the side of the chair and gave her an unreadable look. Unreadable except in its utter disregard for her as a human being. She was an organism to him, a living, breathing, flesh-and-blood lab experiment with enough sentience to fear and respond. His eyes were black, and cold, and intensely calculating, absorbed with the small pinch of her skin he'd taken between his fingers.

Red Dog had made love with an angel.

She watched him choose a syringe, the blue one. She watched him set the tip of the needle to that small pinch of her skin.

That's what she would think about—oh, God, help her, oh, God—Red Dog and the angel boy.

She felt the first prick.

. . . and the angel.

She felt the first sting of the liquid.

. . . angel . . . angel . . . angel . . .

And then she felt the pain.

CHAPTER

25

◈

Skeeter was not going to buy a Honda Civic.

Ever.

But Red Dog's had done the trick.

Travis had picked them up at the Gas & Grub, and she'd driven the baby POS to the very limits of its engineered capabilities to get them here.

They were parked on a hill overlooking Negara's ten acres of prime U.S. real estate, gearing up out of the trunk with all the goodies she'd stuffed in her rucksack. It was a free country, and Skeeter would fight to keep it that way, but it ticked her off that the likes of Hamzah Negara owned a piece of Virginia.

Indonesian warlords in Prince William County—
what the hell was next, she wondered.

Unfortunately, she knew the answer—Indonesian
warlords with Gillian Pentycote in their clutches.

She took a breath, reminded herself to stay calm,
to stay focused, to not give in to the wave of panic
trying to wash over her.

"I don't like the looks of that," Dylan said, pointing to an outcropping of trees two hundred meters
to the north of the mansion. "Something's up."

A glow was emanating from the center of the
outcropping, as if it were lit from within, or as if
there were a building hidden in the middle of it.

Skeeter didn't like it, either. She hated it, but unlike Dylan, she figured she knew exactly what was
up. Her "spidey sense" was humming in every direction with what was up. She glanced at Travis, and
worked faster, choosing one of the HK UMP45s over
the sniper rifle, and keeping her thoughts to herself.
This was going to be close-in work all the way.

Travis had a bra strap hanging out of his pants
pocket, and she'd noticed an empty condom wrap-
per on the console. Yes, sirree, it had been a busy,
busy night all around, and if there was one thing she
knew, it was that Travis James did not want to know
that his very recent lover was putting out a one
hundred percent pure vibe of sheer terror. Skeeter
could feel it. She could smell it, fear, sharp and acrid

and female, and so help her God, somebody was going to pay.

Goddammit.

She was sweating, like Red Dog had to be. She could almost hear the woman's brain going *snap, crackle, pop*.

What in the holy hell was going on in that building in the trees—and was it the same thing that had gone on with Dylan?

"This feels bad," Travis said, zipping into one of the tactical vests she'd had Red Dog load at the hotel.

"It is." She finished zipping her own tac vest.

"Let's move out." Dylan, typically, was carrying one thing, a .45, but at least this time he'd taken all the extra magazines.

WELL, so far, the night was a bit of a disappointment, Royce silently conceded. Gillian Pentycote had passed out. Just like that. Without a whimper.

Well, not much of a whimper. Not enough to do him any good.

Negara had come in, taken one look at the slip of a woman, and left again, pure disgust on his face.

Royce didn't blame the man. Ms. Pentycote wasn't Skeeter Bang. She wasn't enough bait to draw in the big fish, and she wasn't nearly the challenge Dylan Hart had been. Hart had fought. He'd not only fought the guards, he'd fought Souk, he'd fought the drugs, and Royce had to admit, he'd done a damn fine job of all of it.

Of course, in the end, he'd given everything up. Well, almost everything. The damned White Rook was still a mystery.

And the woman in the chair was a disappointment. The whole night was a disappointment. He'd played his Godwin trump card, and Hart had still eluded him. Skeeter Bang had eluded him. Two Indonesian pirates had died at Whitfield's, which should give the authorities something to chew on for the next few years, and he doubted if Negara would hear from the men he'd sent to Denver ever again.

Those boys were gone. Royce felt it in his bones.

Gillian Pentycote wasn't going to last much longer, either. Dr. Souk was trying to revive her, but she'd gone completely limp. No challenge, no torture, no pain, no watching her squirm and scream. Souk had all but killed her with his first volley. It wasn't like the bastard to be so damn careless.

Wait a minute.

Her fingers had moved.

Royce pushed himself off the counter and walked closer to the chair. Maybe this was going to get interesting after all. Souk had taken the gag off, so if the woman did come up with something to say, or another whimper or two, at least they'd all be able to hear it.

Staring down at her, he waited, not particularly patiently, for something else to happen. When it did, he grinned.

She clenched her hand into a fist. Tiny blue veins stood out all along the tender inside of her arm. Then she made a strangled sound.

That was good, he thought. Whatever was in the blue syringes hadn't outright killed her. She was coming around.

A spasm hit her next, making her jerk from one side of the chair to the other, her legs going stiff, her head going back, and his grin broadened. Dr. Souk hadn't lost his touch.

The doctor walked back over to his supply cabinet and pulled out a few more items. When nothing else happened with the woman for the next couple of minutes, Royce decided to help things along a bit.

Raising his arm, he backhanded her across the face, a blow that snapped her head to one side, but garnered him no other reaction—dammit.

Then her eyes popped open.

For all of five long seconds, she held him with her wild gaze, and then she opened her mouth and let out a bloodcurdling scream.

———

AGAINST Dylan's direct order, Skeeter was already flat out on the run when she heard Gillian scream.

Goddamn, she thought. *Oh, goddamn.*

Travis was pacing her, and they both increased their speed, breaking every hostage-rescue rule in the book. Speed and violence of action were supposed to happen after the team was in place, after the operators had infiltrated, gathered what information they could about their enemies, and readied themselves for the takedown.

Skeeter was starting the party early.

She dropped to one knee behind a tree at the edge of the clearing around the two-story building and swung up her subgun. Floodlights illuminated the grounds, giving her all the advantage she needed. She dropped the guard on the south side of the building with a suppressed burst as Travis took out the man standing in front of a set of double doors.

No other movement was visible, and the two of them moved out. With so much light on the outside of the building, they didn't waste any time getting inside. They slid in the door, and Skeeter took out the man inside with a quick single suppressed shot. A number of doors lined the main hall, but with Gillian still screaming and other people yelling, there was no mistaking which room they were in.

The screams were awful, unbearable.

Skeeter felt Travis pull a flash-bang off the back

of her tac vest, and she let him move forward. She would follow him into the room, covering the left side as he cleared to the right.

Dylan, she knew, would remain outside in the shadows, hidden in the tree line, his pistol trained on the doors. Anyone who tried to get in the building would never make it past his Glock. Anyone who tried to get out, besides her, Travis, and Gillian, would have to cross through the same deadly line of fire—and they wouldn't make it, either.

Speed was of the absolute essence. If reinforcements arrived from the mansion, the rescue mission could easily turn into a standoff, with all the odds on Negara's side.

Travis threw open the door to the room and tossed the concussion grenade inside—and all hell broke loose with a blinding flash and an earsplitting bang. They cleared the room in seconds, acquiring targets almost instantaneously, one after another, until the tally was filled—four guards dead, a man in a white lab coat dead, Gillian still screaming, and standing over her, a man Skeeter had instantly identified and not shot. In the split second of his reprieve, he'd dropped behind a dental chair bolted to the floor, and Skeeter had signaled to Travis to hold his fire.

But all the while, her brain was working at light speed and coming up with answers that made too much sense not to be acted upon.

Dylan's capture in Jakarta had been an inside job. The Godwin job had been a setup. Indonesian pirates at Steele Street was nothing short of bizarre—and all of it could have been arranged by the CIA, or by someone who had recently left the CIA, someone like Tony Royce, who had plenty of motivation for destroying SDF.

Travis had moved toward Gillian even as Skeeter made her own move toward the chair, taking small steps, making sure her feet never crossed, moving fast, her gun up, ready. God, the room reeked of negative psychic energy, of horror and death. But her concentration was all on Royce, until the hair rose on the back of her neck.

She swung around, her finger pulling up slack on the subgun's trigger and squeezing off a round. The Jai Traon coming through the door went down, and she was hit by someone from behind.

Twisting, she dragged her combat knife out of its sheath on her vest and slashed upward, making contact. The sling on her subgun tightened around her left arm, leaving her to fight one-handed, until she made her second slash, and her attacker screamed—Tony Royce, blood gushing from a head wound, his hands over one side of his face, covering his right eye as he backed away.

Travis had one job during the fight—get Gillian and get out.

Another pirate came through the door, and

Skeeter pulled her sidearm and shot him dead. Shouts from outside told her their time was up.

Scrambling to her feet, she ran from the room, covering Travis's retreat. He was carrying Red Dog and running sure and steady for the trees. Dylan fell in with them as they passed his position, while behind them, more and more men from the mansion were racing toward the building.

CHAPTER

26

———◆———

TONY ROYCE, Dylan thought, stepping aside as another CIA agent crossed by him to get to the other side of the hall. The small building on Negara's estate was crawling with agents and operatives from half a dozen agencies housed on both sides of the Potomac. Most of them were in the hallway, looking through the windows, while a couple of specialists were inside the white room, collecting evidence. There was even an older guy from the State Department, the last person Dylan would have expected to see.

He watched the white-haired man write something down on a piece of paper and hand it to his aide. Then the State guy looked up and caught his gaze.

Dylan understood.

The mansion and grounds had been abandoned by the time the authorities had arrived. The warlord had moved quickly. The sun was barely breaking the horizon. With General Grant out of the country, it had taken Dylan longer than he was happy with to make contact with the kinds of people who could expedite and execute a full-scale takeover of an exclusive estate deeded to a foreign corporation with strong ties to a previous administration. Especially since it had taken a ridiculous amount of time to make it clear that the abduction and subsequent torture of one small woman on the estate grounds had anything to do with national security.

But even the lowest of the official low understood the importance of apprehending anyone involved with the fiasco at Senator Arthur Whitfield's reception for the British ambassador. Of course, the only crime against the state committed at Whitfield's had been committed by Dylan, a fact he was keeping to himself.

It was a complex situation, the irony of which was not lost on him.

In an even more bizarre twist, the rumor running through this crowd of alphabet-soup agents was that Vice President Hallaway's fingerprints had been found at Whitfield's, on the biometric lock to the senator's safe.

Skeeter had obviously been a busy girl and was finding all sorts of uses for her newfound "fingerprint" collection. Grant should have known better than to give her something she could really get herself in trouble with. On the other hand, given what Dylan knew about the names on the Godwin file, which included Hallaway's, he figured the whole damn, crazy night had come full circle. Except for all the bad guys getting away. Negara had flown the coop, and Tony Royce was not dead on the floor.

Skeeter had failed to deliver a killing strike, and she wasn't happy about it. He'd been with her and Travis at the hospital while the doctors had been working on Gillian Pentycote, and they'd gone over every detail of the attack, analyzing her moves, deciding what she could have done differently, how she could have killed Royce in the split seconds allotted for the job.

Tony Royce. A lot of things made sense now that hadn't before, including, possibly, what had happened to J. T. Chronopolous in Colombia. J. T. and Creed had been taking up the slack on a CIA operation when they'd been ambushed, and Dylan had often wondered how much of that disaster could be laid at the Agency's door.

He was guessing plenty.

Tony Royce was going down, if Dylan had to

track him to the ends of the earth, and Negara was going down with him—all Dylan needed were the orders, and there were ways to get those.

He wasn't a rogue, and he wasn't a vigilante, and none of what he did was personal. Every dead bastard SDF had left in Colombia had been authorized and covered by the mission's Rules of Engagement. Tonight had been the same. He'd been tasked with stealing seventeen million dollars for the U.S. government and given plenty of latitude to accomplish the goal—and he had.

He looked back through the window, his gaze raking the white room. Whatever had been in the Navy's antidote had worked. He was back to what he was comfortable being—a coolheaded, cold-hearted, calculating son of a bitch. Skeeter and Travis had made a mess of the white room. There was blood everywhere, and a whole lot of other stuff running down the walls, and none of it bothered him, not even the damn chair.

It was eerie, how exactly Dr. Souk had re-created this room to match the one on Sumba, but Dylan guessed if he'd been a psycho medical-sadist, he would have done the same thing. And yeah, he probably would have used a dental chair, too, just to up the terror factor.

Fuck. He rolled his head to one side, stretching out the kinks.

So everything had worked out fine, everything

was good. Gillian Pentycote would undoubtably recover from her ordeal. Travis was going to get promoted to full operational status, and Skeeter was . . .

Skeeter was . . .

Fine, he decided, a great girl. Hot, lovely, gorgeous, spooky, and out of his system. He'd had her. It was time to move on, just the way he'd known it would be.

Once was enough.

And if he'd said a few things, done a few things, well, he'd been jacked up on NG4, and she knew it as well as he did.

And those female abandonment issues left over from his childhood and his truly horrendously crappy relationship with his mother—well, those were still in the vault, still his, still safe and sound and keeping him out of trouble.

No harm, no foul, no commitment, no error. Especially no commitment. Things were back to normal. He was back to normal, and what he normally did in situations like this was get a new assignment and go make the world safe for another week, until the next disaster hit the fan. With everyone else at Steele Street starting to settle down and look like goddamn Ozzie and Harriet, it was why he was the boss.

He checked his watch. If he could move things along here, he could catch a flight out of Dulles and be in another country by lunchtime.

Yeah. That sounded good. He always thought more clearly when he was out of the country.

He looked over at the white-haired man and caught his attention with a slight nod. In answer, White Rook's gaze landed briefly on the outside door, then returned to his aide.

Fine. Perfect. All systems go. If Dylan wanted orders to kill Tony Royce and Hamzah Negara, White Rook was the guy who could give them.

CHAPTER

27

Two months later—Mexico

SHE WAS leaving.

That was impossible.

From where he was sitting in a pool of hot Mexican sunshine, watching the waves break on the beach below his cabana, Dylan read the fax transmission again.

Skeeter Jeanne Bang was leaving Steele Street. She was packing up her spaceship apartment, her ungodly amount of junk, and her bags, and she was leaving.

She'd gotten a better offer, the fax from Hawkins said, an offer from the freaking FBI, which was ridiculous. She would never be happy with the FBI.

He set down his tumbler of Scotch, then picked it back up and took another swallow.

Skeeter couldn't leave Steele Street. The whole damn place would fall apart if she did, and everyone knew that—so why in the hell weren't they doing something about it?

Did he have to do everything?

No.

Okay, that had been a stupid question. He didn't do crap at Steele Street, except stay away from it.

Looking up, he lifted his tumbler and signaled his houseboy for another refill.

There had been a time—oh, say, two months ago—when he would have had a woman, a lover, to pour his Scotch. But he hadn't had a lover in, oh, say, two months, and even then, he'd only done it once, and before that, he hadn't done it in months, and sometimes he wondered if he was ever going to "do it" again. It was so goddamn stupid. It was just sex, for crying out loud, not rocket science.

So why wasn't he getting any?

And why was he drinking so goddamn much Scotch all the time?

He'd killed Negara—or actually, Kid had. Dylan had spent the last eight weeks collecting intelligence for a hit on the warlord, and two weeks ago, he'd contacted Kid and had him fly from Paris to Jakarta for the final run-up to the mission.

With Kid on his rifle, and Dylan on a pair of

binoculars, they'd lain in the fetid jungle of Sumba day after day after day, waiting for the exact moment when Kid could line up his bore with Negara's heart. It had been an immensely satisfying experience.

Tony Royce was still at large. The man had completely disappeared, and not even Dylan's best rats had been able to find him. He'd show up someday, though, and when he did, he was a dead man.

None of which addressed his current problem— a spooky girl with a lightning-bolt tattoo who had blown his mind. For the life of him, he could not seem to get her out of his head. She was just there, inside him, all the time, smelling like sugar, and melting all over him, and all around driving him crazy.

He waited while the boy filled his tumbler, then he took another long swallow. Scotch was not Skeeter, but at least it numbed his brain long enough to get some sleep every now and then. Not much sleep, and not very now and then, just occasionally, but not occasionally enough. He was a wreck, and it was time to face some facts.

Once had not been enough.

It was as simple as that. He needed to do it with her twice, maybe three or four times, and he couldn't do that if he was in Mexico, and she was leaving Steele Street.

He had to go home.

He started to take another swallow of Scotch, but set the tumbler back on the table instead and pulled out his cell phone.

There was a flight out of Cabo San Lucas in two hours, and with a little luck, he was going to be on it.

Leaving, his ass.

She couldn't leave.

He was the one who left—always.

CHAPTER 28

It was, without a doubt, the most amazing thing Dylan had ever seen at Steele Street—Superman, walking the hall with a small pink-blanketed bundle in his arms, crooning.

Hawkins looked like hell. The baby looked . . . small. Dylan tried to think if he'd ever been in the presence of an infant before, and decided this was a first. He'd seen them on television, of course, and in the movies, but he'd never actually been in the same room with one.

Alexandria Kleir Hawkins.

While he and Skeeter and Travis had been shooting it out with pirates in Washington, D.C., that night, and generally making a big deal out of everything, Hawkins and Creed had killed three of their own, kept one for interrogation, and then taken Katya to the hospital for the night's truly big event.

Alexandria had dark hair and the tiniest hands he'd ever seen. One of them was wrapped around Hawkins's finger, and there was room to spare on both ends. He hadn't realized Hawkins's hands were so large—or that babies were so . . . small.

"Are you sure you know what you're doing?" he said, stepping out of the elevator on the eleventh floor. Skeeter's floor. He hadn't even been up to his place on thirteen. He'd dropped his luggage in the office on seven and hauled his butt up here to eleven.

Hawkins looked up and smiled, and Dylan had to wonder how someone who looked so exhausted could also look so sappily happy.

"Are you sure you know what *you're* doing?" Hawkins said—except he didn't say it exactly. He kind of sang it in the same tone of voice he'd been crooning in, and he did it without missing a beat or a step. He was still walking, walking, walking, one short jiggly step after another, the baby bouncing up and down on his arm. Her head and her back were resting in his hand and along his arm. Her butt was about halfway to his elbow, and her little legs were dangling down on either side of his forearm.

"I don't think you're supposed to hold them like

that." *Geez*. Shouldn't there be a professional around for this, or at least Katya?

"And I don't think you have any idea how pissed off Skeeter is at you," Hawkins crooned, the sound of which was just weird enough to push Dylan a little more off center, which was the last damn thing he needed. "I told her you were coming."

Great.

"Should I go get a Kevlar vest?"

"No. Just remember she leads with her right." Hawkins came to a stop next to Dylan, but he didn't actually stop. His feet weren't moving, but the rest of him was—his arm swaying from side to side and going up and down, his body rocking back and forth—and the baby lying there, sleeping, looking utterly content, with the sweetest little smile Dylan had ever seen on the teeniest lips he'd ever seen.

It was weird, but she looked like Hawkins, the badass Superman. No shit. Her dark hair was all wild and sticking up like Hawkins's, and the two of them had the same exact eyebrows, except hers were in miniature.

Geez. Hawkins had a baby. He'd known it was coming, and known it the night it had happened, but it was still amazing to actually see the reality.

"You've got spit-up on your shoulder."

"I've also got the code to Skeeter's door. Come on. I'll let you in." Hawkins started that damned disconcerting jiggly-step walking again, heading back down the hall.

"She's beautiful." Dylan might not have known anything about babies, but he knew beautiful when he saw it.

"You should see her when she's awake," Hawkins crooned. "She's so cool."

Cool?

"She's limp. I don't know if you hypnotized her or what, but she's gone." And like all women, she trusted Superman implicitly. Her life was literally in his hands, one hand, and the girl was completely blissed out.

"Aaaa-lex-annn-driaaaa," Hawkins sang. "Daddy's little kick-ass pummmmmmmpkin."

Geezus. Steele Street really had slipped into the Twilight Zone, and personally, Dylan didn't think anyone under ten pounds could kick anybody's ass.

Then again, even at eight weeks, it looked like Alexandria Hawkins had already kicked Superman's ass, but good.

Two minutes later, he was face-to-face with his own kick-ass pumpkin, but his little squash really could get the job done, and then some.

Yeah, she'd been expecting him, all right. He could tell by the ice-cold unwelcome frozen on her face. The girl was not happy to see him.

He was hoping to change her mind with the ring in his pocket.

Yeah, a ring. A diamond ring.

He'd actually gotten it a few weeks ago, on a side trip he'd taken to Hong Kong while trying to track down Tony Royce. It had been too good a deal to pass up.

Right.

That's what he'd told himself at the time, that dropping five figures on a perfect diamond set in platinum was a smart move, the thing to do.

It was unnerving, really, what a good deal he'd gotten. Too many more good deals like that one and he'd end up with a harem.

Or not. Because the look on Skeeter's face was saying "fat chance," whether he whipped out a ring or not.

"Hi." He'd decided a simple opener was the best. At least it had sounded good in the elevator.

"Who let you in?"

Ouch.

"Hawkins. He's, uh, walking the hall and burping the baby."

She softened a little at the mention of the baby, moving aside enough for him to get out of the main gangway. Her whole loft had been reconfigured with foam and paint and ingenuity into a fair replica of the *Millennium Falcon*, complete with a hydraulic hatch, otherwise known as the front door, and a gangway, otherwise known as the entry hall. The jungle she was growing for Creed in the loft below hers had "Jumanjied" itself through the floor in a few places, but he managed to negotiate the works to get himself into her living room . . . into hot water up to his neck.

"We got Negara, Kid and I, a week ago, on Sumba." That was his big news.

"Yeah. I heard." She turned and walked over to her computer desk, showing absolutely no interest whatsoever in his big news.

"It was a helluva shot, if Kid hasn't already told you about it."

"He did."

Of course he had. She and Kid had probably talked about the shot dozens of times in the last week.

He needed to do better, or he was going to end up back out in the hall.

"You were a great help that night, in Washington, D.C." He followed a short ways behind her, watching her, carefully, looking for a sign, any kind of a sign that she was glad to see him.

"Yes, I was," she agreed, giving herself full credit for a job well done, which was exactly what she deserved, right along with a heavy dose of abject groveling at her feet—her black patent-leather, thigh-high, spike-heeled, boot-clad feet.

He could see it all so clearly now. He'd been an idiot to run off and leave everything at such loose ends.

She boosted herself up on the edge of the desk and just sat there, looking at him, her eyes clear and blue and completely unadorned by any damned mirrored sunglasses.

He guessed they'd both moved on from old habits.

He let out a heavy breath, ran his hand through his hair, and looked around her loft. He was nervous.

That was a first, a damned disconcerting first.

"Skeeter, I . . ." His voice trailed off. He didn't know what to say.

Another first.

He dragged his hand through his hair—again. *Christ*. He had to do better than this.

"You're a complete jerk, Dylan."

Okay, he wouldn't have said that, not exactly, but she wasn't too far off the mark.

"I'm sorry." That was a good place to start, way better than him being a jerk. "I should have . . . well, I've been thinking . . . and what I thought was that you were too young . . . for me, I mean."

"You were wrong."

Past tense. That wasn't good. "Don't make this easy on me."

"I won't."

Okay, he deserved that.

"Are you armed?" It seemed a reasonable question after what he'd seen in Washington, D.C.

"Of course."

Of course.

"So what should I be on the lookout for? Combat knife? Butterfly Sting? A Remington .45 caliber hardball?"

Lightening the mood could only help, and he was ready for anything, except what she used.

Slowly, but unmistakably, her lips started to tremble, and her nose turned pink.

Emotion.

Hell. That was a surefire killer. He'd never hold up under emotion.

"Skeeter, honey." He moved in closer, heedless of the danger, and cupped her face. She was so amazingly soft, and if she was going to do him in, a couple of feet of distance wasn't going to make any difference.

"Dammit, Dylan. You cut me out of the hit."

The hit?

She was on the verge of tears because of the hit?

Oh, man, he was on a helluva lot shakier ground than he'd thought.

"Kid's the sniper, babe, not you." He smoothed his thumb over her cheek.

"Then you haven't been paying attention."

Of course he hadn't been paying attention, he'd been . . . thousands of miles away for eight weeks, and before that for seven months, as far away as he could get. He'd only come home to die, and he hadn't done that, and in the middle of not dying, he'd made love to her.

She was right. He was a complete jerk.

"Kid's been training you on the long gun. That's . . . uh, great." He needed to get used to this if he was going to be hanging around Steele Street, if he was going to be hanging around her—which he guessed was one way to put it, one kind of stupid way. He had a freaking diamond ring in his pocket. "Hanging around" didn't begin to cover what he had planned.

"He says I'm a natural."

"Of course you are." He'd seen her move. He'd seen her think under pressure, under fire. He'd seen her plan and outfit a mission. And he'd seen her save Gillian Pentycote. "How's Red Dog?" The two women were friends, and he should ask. He should have asked about Gillian a long time ago.

Her gaze fell away, and beneath his hand he felt her jaw tighten again.

"Not so good," she said. "She doesn't know who she is. She never regained her memory."

Oh, Christ. He should have known that. He should have done a follow-up.

"I didn't have any memory loss." Unfortunately. There were things that had happened on Sumba that he wished he *could* forget.

"Dr. Souk gave you NG4. Gillian got the XT7. Plus, you're a lot bigger than she is, and male. The drugs reacted oddly on her. Even the lab rats who work with the stuff have been surprised by her reaction. Memory loss hasn't been associated with that class of drugs in any of the clinical tests."

"What are her chances of recovery?"

"Memory-wise, no one is taking a guess," she said. "But in every other way, she's doing very well, even great. Physically, she's stronger than she's ever been, in perfect health."

"I'm sorry, Skeeter." He'd lost people out of his life, but never because of amnesia.

She gave a small shrug. "We're still friends, just different friends than we were before. Kid is training her, too."

"Ah . . ." That was pretty alarming. "Kid is training an amnesiac to be a sniper?"

Geez, he really did need to spend more time at Steele Street, just to get everybody back on the straight and narrow, if nothing else.

"Yes. She's very, very good. Better than me, and Travis is working with her, too, using some of his sexual imprinting techniques."

And that was even more alarming. He'd heard about the FNG's sexual imprinting business, and although Kid was completely sold on the whole idea, Dylan had to wonder what the guy was up to.

"Travis is having sex with an amnesiac?" God, somebody really did need to take the place in hand, get back on the reins, and Hawkins was obviously way too preoccupied to do the job. Coming home was starting to feel more and more like the right thing to do.

"Not sex. I don't think so. He's trying to get her back in tune with her feminine side, and he buys her underwear."

"Underwear?"

"Lots of underwear." She nodded, and a small smile curved her lips. "She seems to like it. She always takes it, but she won't let anyone get too close to her, not physically close, and not emotionally close, either."

What an opener she'd handed him. This whole getting-close thing was his problem, the real reason he'd come home.

"I have a woman I'd like to get close to, emotionally and physically."

Her smile slid away, along with her gaze. "You never did before."

No, he hadn't. Not ever.

"Well, I think that's because I've had this ongoing conflict with my mother—" He stopped cold, more than a little surprised at himself, not quite believing he'd actually said that.

"Who you haven't seen in seventeen years, but I can understand that," she said, her voice softening. "It must have been a shock when she married so quickly after your father's death."

And he *really* couldn't believe she'd said that.

"A bit," he agreed, and wondered if it was getting warmer in her apartment.

"Liam Dylan Magnuson, that was your father's name, right?" She looked up, her one eyebrow quirked in that way that made her look cutely confused.

"Right." Very right.

"Your name, too, right?"

Yes again. She was batting a thousand.

"He was the second Liam Dylan Magnuson. I'm the third." Or rather, he had been. He'd left that behind him a long time ago. "You really shouldn't know all this, Skeeter." The greatest investigators on two continents didn't know this stuff—and they'd been looking.

"If we're going to have any chance at all, Dylan, I need to know everything."

She was right, but he was still a little shocked about how much she already knew. The whole "if we're going to have a chance" thing sounded good to him, though. Damn good.

He looked down at her very demure, librarian-approved, short-sleeved, white cotton shirt with its little stand-up collar. It was amazing, really, how sexy a librarian-approved shirt could look when paired with black patent-leather boots and a black patent-leather miniskirt. She was every boy's bad-girl fantasy—and if she thought they had a chance, he was taking it.

He'd been crazy to leave.

"I'm an idiot." Hindsight was so perfect.

"Yes."

"Are you going to agree with everything I say?" It was an interesting possibility.

"No."

"Can we finish this fight in bed, then?" He didn't mean to be obvious, but that's exactly where this was headed, sooner or later, and he was pushing for sooner.

"I'm still angry with you." And she had every right to be. He was angry with himself, too. But she smelled good, and felt better, and he'd been without her for two months.

"We could be angry in bed," he said hopefully, slipping his other hand under her right knee and lifting it to his hip, pulling her closer to the edge of the desk and making room for him between her legs.

A small laugh escaped her, which he took as a very good sign.

"Are you listening to yourself?" she asked, her arms sliding up around his neck, her right leg tightening around his hip and sending a hot thrill straight to his groin.

"No." He was beyond listening. All he wanted now was her. So he kissed her, softly at first, loving the feel of her mouth, the sliding of her hands through his hair, and absolutely loving that her prim little shirt had only four buttons, four, inconsequential, easily done away with buttons.

He smoothed his free hand up the satiny skin of her torso and cupped her breast. Her bra was lace. He could feel the delicacy of it with his fingertips.

"We should talk," she whispered.

Of course they should.

His mouth came down on hers again, open, his tongue delving deep as he took her in a hot, heavy kiss, a wet and wild kiss.

"Good idea," he said when he lifted his head. "Let's talk in bed."

Swinging her up into his arms, he headed up the short flight of stairs to the platform where her bed was perched like a . . . like a he didn't know what.

"What is that?" he asked.

"A 1960 Chrysler 300F Letter Car. Johnny and I chopped it, and I had a custom mattress made to fit the interior."

Which was exactly what the contraption looked like, amazing, all sweeping fins, chrome grille, whitewall tires, red taillights, and Mardi Gras green paint—and like a lot of fun with the right girl.

Lucky him, he had the right girl in his arms.

Then he remembered the ring.

Damn. How could he have forgotten the ring?

He stopped what he was doing, and she looked up at him, breathlessly beautiful. He had one hand up her skirt, her blouse was already unbuttoned, and her white lace bra was so sheer, he could see through it—and he'd stopped. Was he nuts?

No. He wasn't nuts. This was important. The whole thing was important. Doing it right was important.

He let her feet slide to the floor, and she gave him a quizzical look.

"What?" she asked.

Okay, this was it. Now he was nervous.

He pulled a small velvet box out of his pocket.

"Dylan?"

He knew it was crazy. She was Baby Bang, the Goth princess of every dark street in LoDo. She was chain mail and black leather, switchblades and trouble, and so help him God, she was supposed to be his.

He opened the box, and the light hit three carats' worth of diamond set in platinum. It was the most traditional wedding ring in the world. It reeked of stability and fiftieth wedding anniversaries. It proclaimed itself to the world as the rock upon which vows were never broken. It was a testament of his love. Proof of his commitment.

And from the look on her face, he could tell it was absolutely exactly what she'd needed to get from him.

CHAPTER

29

＊

Holy freaking *cripes*. Skeeter swore to God she was never going to move again. She was limp, worn-out, and completely in love, and she would have kept her promise not to move, so help her God, if he hadn't hit the "shimmy switch" again.

The old Chrysler roared into Magic Fingers mode, the whole mattress vibrating to the pre-recorded pitch and rumble of the most perfectly tuned set of headers she'd ever heard, the pipes that had been bolted onto Jeanette the Jet, a long-dead but well-loved 1969 Camaro who had given her all one night in Denver's old Stapleton Airport.

"I can't believe you did that again." It was about

his tenth time. "If you don't stop, I'm going to be carsick."

He just grinned. "I can't believe you hooked a giant vibrator to the mattress. It's amazing."

"Didn't you ever stay in one of those cheap hotels with the coin slot on the side of the bed, where it keeps shaking as long as you keep feeding it quarters?"

She lifted her hand into the air and just enjoyed the absolutely spectacular sparkle and shine of a huge diamond set in platinum.

Skeeter Jeanne Hart. Oh, yeah, she liked the sound of that.

"Honey, I've never been within a hundred feet of a cheap hotel."

She slanted him a quick glance, her brain suddenly, acutely "on," all traces of lethargy instantly banished. This was an opportunity. This was as good an opening as she was ever going to get. So with the two of them humming along with the Chrysler 300 and Jeanette, she asked the million-dollar question.

Actually, the five-million-dollar question.

"Whatever happened to the money from Magnuson International?"

It was a bona fide bombshell of a question, and absolutely nothing happened when she dropped it, not for one long endless minute after another. He just lay there next to her, breathing softly.

Thinking.

He had to be thinking.

Finally, when she couldn't stand it any longer, she tilted her head to look up at him.

And he was looking back, a bemused expression on his face.

"How long have you been carrying that information around?"

"A while."

"You're pretty good, aren't you?"

"Pretty good," she conceded—carefully. He'd kept his secrets for seventeen years, and she'd been throwing them around pretty easily tonight.

"Hmmm, Magnuson International," he said, rolling onto his back and stretching out beside her. "That was a while back."

She wasn't buying it.

"It was also a helluva lot of money." The bed finally stopped vibrating. "You couldn't possibly have forgotten what you did with it."

"But you couldn't find it?" He glanced over at her.

She shook her head. "Nope, and I looked everywhere."

"You've been a busy girl, haven't you?"

She gave him a little lift of her shoulder, then looked at him from under her lashes. "I could get busier."

That got his attention. She could tell by the sudden darkening of his gaze.

"How busy?" he asked.

A grin tugged at her lips. "Pretty busy," she promised, sliding her hand down the length of his chest.

"Magnuson International," he began, his own grin curving his mouth.

"I want the whole story," she warned.

"Okay." He started again. "The whole story. My father started the company in his early thirties, just before I was born, and by the time I was fifteen years old, I was practically his right-hand man. We spent a lot of time in Europe and Asia, with Dad putting together investments, evaluating companies, making money, and making his clients rich."

"Including White Rook," she interjected, taking a pretty good guess. Some of the pieces at least halfway fit together, and White Rook had to come into the story somewhere toward the beginning. White Rook had been behind the creation of SDF. She knew that much.

One elegant brow arched in disbelief. "You found White Rook?"

She shook her head. "Not really. I know there *is* a White Rook, someone at the State Department, but I don't know who it is."

He rolled onto his side, facing her, and propped his head up with his hand, giving her a very considering look.

"Neither do I," he said after a moment.

No way.

"You don't know who White Rook is?"

"He's a phone number at the State Department, and a face I know by sight but never shows up anywhere officially, or unofficially, for that matter—and I mean *never* shows up. Believe me, I've looked. I was first contacted by him in Moscow, and couriered documents for him for over a year before the CIA got ahold of me. It could have been all downhill after that, but strings were pulled, and then I was released and turned over to General Grant."

"And started SDF."

He nodded. "Christian and I weren't supposed to survive our first mission, a delivery into Beirut. The brass figured we could get in and hook up with the right guys, but that we'd get whacked getting back out."

The creeps.

"But you didn't." Not her guys. No way.

He laughed, a soft chuckle. "Christian had just barely gotten out of prison. To say his nerves were a little raw is an understatement. Those guys in Beirut couldn't scratch their butts without Hawkins knowing two minutes in advance where it was going to itch."

Which was interesting as hell, and information she was glad to have, but there was still that five million dollars out there somewhere.

"So how did you get the money, and what happened to it?"

"Well, getting it was . . . uh . . . easy," he said, his voice trailing off a bit, his gaze shifting down their bodies and following the movement of her fingers over his lower abdomen. "Are you going to be doing much more of that?"

"Probably."

"Could you do it a little lower?"

"Probably."

When she didn't, he looked back up at her, an unspoken question on his face.

"The story," she reminded him. "Magnuson International. The five million."

"Right." He started in again, grinning. "My father gave it to me. I don't know if he had a premonition or what, but the day he died, we were in Geneva, and he transferred five million dollars of his personal Magnuson International account into a private account with my name on it. I sat on the money for weeks after I buried him, waiting for my mother to come—but she never did. She was too busy getting remarried to Magnuson International's vice president in charge of operations. So I took the money, invested it in Russian oil and gas futures, and then I disappeared."

And that was it, the last mystery of Dylan Hart. She was blown away.

"I knew your father had a heart attack in Geneva, but nothing in the papers mentioned his son being there. No wonder you're—"

"Such a coldhearted bastard?" he filled in for her. Then he touched his fingers to her lips, silencing her, before she could say anything. "No. We're not getting sidetracked with the psychoanalysis of Dylan Hart. I love you, Skeeter, and there's no way I can lie here next to you and pour out my poor little brokenhearted-boy story. I walked away from my dad with five million dollars and an incredible education. You walked away from yours missing a pint of blood and needing twenty stitches, and if we have to talk about all of this now, not to mention our maternal abandonment issues, I'm going to be too angry to make love to you again."

"Oh," she said.

"Oh," he confirmed.

"Can I ask one more question?"

He narrowed his gaze. "Only if it's about what position we should try next."

"Why Denver?" she asked. "You could have gone anywhere."

A broad smile curved his mouth. "From all the places I'd been, Denver, Colorado, looked like the absolute middle of nowhere, the ends of the earth, but still with phone service and running water. I figured no one would ever find me here. And no one ever did. From L.A. to Chicago, the Steele Street boys pushed more stolen cars through the pipeline than any other chop shop in the western United States, and no one knew I existed, until we got busted, and that is the whole story." He leaned down and gave her a soft kiss. "The *whole* story, busy girl."

She grinned at him and let her hand slide lower and wrap around him. His eyes drifted closed on a groan. Then he kissed her again and moved his hips forward, thrusting into her hand.

God, he was beautiful—and he was hers.

"You know, honey," he murmured between kisses on her mouth, and her cheek, and her ear, and that very sensitive spot on the side of her neck, "I think we could get into Guinness."

"You do?" She was melting under all those kisses and the very gentle exploration he was making with his fingers between her legs.

"Um-hmmm. I think if we can do this two more times without having to get up for food, we can set a record."

"You want to get into Guinness?"

"No," he admitted, lifting up enough to smile down at her. "I just want to do it two more times."

Then he kissed her, starting at her shoulder and the top of her lightning-bolt tattoo. Kiss by kiss, he worked his way down the length of her back, over the curve of her hip, and down her thigh, to the one place where the lightning bolt was broken.

He stopped and kissed her twice on the spot.

"I should kick Superman's ass for taking you into a war zone." He laid another kiss a little bit lower.

"I'd like to see you try." She rolled from her side onto her back and grinned up at him.

"You don't think I can kick Superman's ass?"

She shook her head, still grinning.

"I kick Superman's ass all the time," he assured her, then went back to kissing her leg, following her tattoo. By the time he got to her ankle and started licking his way back up the inside of her leg, she was in meltdown mode.

"You're getting me all hot and bothered," she said, trembling just a little as he licked the inside of her thigh. Then he licked inside her—for a long, long time, running his tongue over her, all over her, until she came. Again.

Oh, God. She was limp, her body on an overload of little soft explosions.

"So you're hot and bothered," he said, resuming his leisurely path up her body, working his way all the way up, until he was kissing her throat, and her cheek, and her eyebrows. "What do you want to do about it?"

He lifted his head to meet her gaze, and she knew he knew. She could feel it in the hot and welcome pressure of his body seeking entrance into hers. She could see it in the darkening of his eyes and in the not-so-innocent curve of his smile.

"Screw you," she said.

His grin turned absolutely wicked, and he leaned down to whisper in her ear, *"Make me."*

ABOUT THE AUTHOR

Tara Janzen lives in Colorado with her husband, children, and two dogs, and is now at work on her next novel. Of the mind that love truly is what makes the world go 'round, she can be contacted at *www.tarajanzen.com*. Happy reading!

If you loved

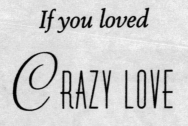

RAZY LOVE

You won't want to miss

RAZY SWEET

The final novel in

Tara Janzen's sizzling series

COMING IN FALL 2006

Read on for a sneak peek
at this heart-stopping page-turner

CRAZY SWEET

ON SALE FALL 2006

Red Dog was here—back from cheating death one more time. The roar and rumble of the pipes on the car pulling up outside Beck's Back Alley Bar were unmistakable, headers and the dual exhaust of the bad girl's ride, tuned to perfection and guaranteed to shake glass in four directions.

Travis James let out a heavy breath and knocked back a shot of tequila before he turned to face the front door. He hated to miss her entrance. Watching Red Dog walk into a room was the best floorshow in town—in any town.

"Geezus," the guy sitting at the table behind him said when the door opened.

Oh, yeah. She had that effect on him, too—all the time, every time.

He chased the tequila with a swallow of beer and let his gaze drop down the length of her body. She was so bad, she was good. Good like seven-dollar-a-shot-mescal, and exquisitely, classy bad.

Dangerous.

A sheer red silk muscle shirt didn't leave anything to the imagination, especially not the size, the shape, or the delicacy of the black lace bra she was wearing underneath it.

He bought her a lot of black lace.

Her worn denim jeans had silver studs running down the right leg and were so tight, they should have come with a warning label. A small chamois fanny pack was slung around her waist. Pale ostrich-leather cowboy boots covered her feet. Stacked heels, pointed toes, and worn vamps, they'd seen a lot of long days in a dozen Third World hellholes over the last two years—the two years since Red Dog had created herself from a blank slate and a heart hungry for revenge. She was five feet five inches of pure, unadulterated, ass-kicking girl, and every day she pushed him. She pushed him hard.

Sometimes he wondered if either of them would survive the trip she was on.

"I'd sure take a piece of that," the man at the table continued, his voice hoarse in a way Travis understood only too well—which did nothing to improve his mood.

"Forget it," another guy said. "That one would just as soon gut you as fu—"

Travis reached back, grabbed the last man by the scruff of his collar, and hauled him around until they were face to face.

"Don't," he said, very clearly, very succinctly, and very, very calmly. Rising from his barstool, he pulled the guy's face even closer to his. "Don't say it. Don't think it."

Fear flashed through the man's eyes, and Travis understood that, too. It had been a hard two years since the night Red Dog had lost her first life and started on her second, and those two years, on the front line with Special Defense Force, a group of black ops warriors based in Denver, Colorado, had changed him. Only one person ever mistook him for anything close to an angel anymore.

Letting go of the man's shirt, he started toward the end of the bar and the woman standing there, waiting for him.

Gillian Pentycote—that had been her name before Dr. Souk, a maniacal physician in the employ of a drug lord, had shot her full of an experimental "truth serum" called NG4 and stolen her memory. By the time Travis and his friend Skeeter B. Hart had gotten to her, there had been nothing left but her screams and four images burned into her brain—only four.

His steps faltered for the barest fraction of a second, less than a heartbeat's worth of pause. Walking on, he wiped the back of his hand across his mouth.

The faces of the two men who had hurt her were half of her short-changed memory bank: Dr. Souk, his dark and dirty hair, wire-rimmed glasses, and open-mouthed death shock when Travis's .45 caliber slug had punched a hole in his chest—a memory Travis wouldn't wish on anybody, let alone a woman, even one with Red Dog's resume; and Tony Royce, the CIA agent gone bad who had set her up for the torture she'd endured strapped into Souk's dental chair.

Tony Royce, whose face Skeeter had cut open with her knife.

Tony Royce, who had escaped that night and disappeared.

Tony Royce, who Red Dog hunted with a vengeance born of desperation.

It was her desperation that kept Travis always on edge. She was a gun for hire. She went to bad places and did bad things to bad people, and so far, every time she'd come back to him. But time was running out. He felt it with each passing day, with each mission she survived. He felt it when they worked together, and he felt it when she went out without him, like she had this time.

"You're late," he said, coming to a stop in front of her and taking hold of her arm. Contact, that's what he needed, physical contact.

"Things came up." The huskiness of her voice told him how tired she was, how run down.

"Four days late." He tried to keep the frustration out of his words, and failed.

"El Salvador is kind of a long ways away." She ran her hand back through her short auburn hair, sending a little more of it sticking up on end. She was a wild girl, the wildest.

El Salvador?

"The mission was in Panama," he said, his jaw tight. Fucking El Salvador?

"I took a side trip."

Which was the last goddamn thing he wanted to hear. Her "side trips" only had one motivation—Tony Royce.

"What did you find?"

"Nothing. It was a rumor."

And that was a lie. He could tell by the way she avoided meeting his eyes.

He tightened his hold on her. He wanted the truth. He needed to know, but she never gave him what he wanted, and barely gave him what he needed. She had a head full of bits and pieces, and that's all she ever offered of herself—except in bed.

Geezus.

Sex wasn't love, though, and it wasn't trust, and though he didn't know a damn thing about love anymore—and in retrospect doubted if he ever had—he did know about trust—and he wanted hers. It was the only way he could ever keep her safe.

She'd been laying a trap for Royce since she'd walked out of rehab, and any day, the bastard was going to catch the scent and come after her. It was what she hoped for, what she prayed for, that the man who had stood over Gillian Pentycote and watched her lose her mind would come for the woman she'd become. That Royce would come for Red Dog.

It was all she wanted, and the only thing he feared—that Royce would find her somewhere, sometime, someplace when he wasn't by her side. Some goddamn place like El Salvador.

A moment passed. Then she lifted her gaze to his, and looking down into her eyes, he suddenly didn't give a damn if she lied, and he didn't care that she pushed him hard and kept him on edge. Tonight, she was back. She was safe. And even if she didn't know who she was, she knew she was his.

"Take me home, Angel," she whispered, closing

her hand around his shirt and leaning against him, tearing him up and turning him on at the same time. "I'm tired. The Panama deal, it was rough."

Angel—that was her third memory, the way Skeeter had described him to her. And she remembered his face, the face of the man who had made love to her that night, before she'd been abducted, before Souk had injected her—before her life had taken a sharp left into hell.

Take me home.

It was the one thing he could do—take her home . . . and take her.

Still holding onto her arm, he turned her around and started for the door, but she stopped after two strides and looked up at him again.

"Don't you have something for me?" she asked. She always asked, and he always had something for her, whatever she wanted.

But he knew what she meant, and he reached into the front pocket of his jeans. Inch by soft silky inch, he pulled out a scrap of black lace.

"A new bra?" She reached for the small piece of lingerie.

"No, baby. Panties." Super-short, boy-cut underwear, the bit of stretchy lace would sit low on her hips and curve up over her ass, leaving a lot of bare bottom for his profound personal enjoyment—and she thought he bought the stuff for her.

Yeah. Right.

With a smile that damn near slayed him on the spot, she took the underwear and shoved it into her own pocket. "I hope they fit."

They fit. He knew the shape of her body better than he knew his own. Their relationship was very "hands on"—his hands on her, and his hands were the only hands on her, ever. Nobody touched Red Dog except him, not even her mother, which broke the woman's heart, the way everything that had happened to her daughter broke Lydia Shore's heart—especially what her daughter had become.

Mercenary. Contractor. Whatever anyone called it, the job was the same. A week ago in Thailand, he'd heard the word assassin connected to her name, along with a price tag that guaranteed Gillian could provide for herself in whatever manner she chose, for as long as she chose to stay in business.

Assassin? Maybe. Unsung hero, just as likely, especially considering the kind of men Red Dog took down. It was all a matter of semantics and point of view. There wasn't an SDF operator at Steele Street or a combat soldier in the employ of Uncle Sam who hadn't been tagged an assassin by somebody, somewhere. But Red Dog wasn't an SDF operator or a U.S. soldier. By most standards, she was unemployable, except in the niche Christian Hawkins and Kid Chaos had trained her to fill.

Sometimes lately, Travis wondered what in the

hell Superman and the Boy Wonder had been thinking, but in the beginning, he'd understood what they were doing only too well. She'd been so lost when she'd first come out of her drug-induced coma, so detached. Hawkins had given her something to hold onto: physical training. Her memories were gone, but she was alive. Her body worked, so Superman had worked her hard, made her fight for herself. Then Hawkins had given her to Kid, and Kid had taken her to a Department of Defense—DOD—remote training camp high in the Rocky Mountains and taught her how to fight for her country.

Panama had been the seventh job she'd taken that hadn't included him—and it was her last. He was finished with not knowing where in the hell she was, or what in the hell she was doing, or even if she was alive. Nothing felt right, not when she was out on her own.

And then to disappear off the face of the earth—well, hell, that was way more than he had the strength to endure anymore, especially when he was in goddamn Thailand, thousands of miles away.

It was General Grant himself who had hired her to work with C. Smith Rydell in Panama, the newest member of the SDF team, and it was Grant who had called Hawkins and congratulated him on his protégé's latest successful mission. So if everything had gone so well and the job was finished, Hawkins had wondered, why in the hell hadn't she come home?

Travis had wondered the same damn thing when Superman had called him, and by nightfall he'd been on a plane home.

Fuck. Four days—that's how much time had passed between when she'd left Smith in Panama City and when she'd checked in with Hawkins and told him she was headed back to Denver. Four days—plenty of time for her to have gotten herself into more trouble than she could handle.

Going to El Salvador. Alone.

He needed to clip her wings, lock her in, tie her down, whatever it took to keep her in his sight. The DOD didn't give a damn if she lived or died, as long as she accomplished her missions, but he cared—too much.

Sliding his hand to her waist, he started toward the door again. Beck's Back Alley Bar was in an industrial section of north Denver called Commerce City, tucked between the refineries and the factories on a strip of street eight blocks west of the Steele Street Commerce City garage. The garage was an annex to the SDF headquarters in LoDo, the only place in Denver with enough security to suit him. Hawkins and the boss of SDF, Dylan Hart, had both offered Gillian one of the upper floor lofts at Steele Street, but the bad girl wasn't looking for security. She didn't want to be hard to find.

Quite the opposite, and it unnerved the hell out of him.

"Give me your keys," he said, opening the door for her and heading toward the 1967 Pontiac GTO parked in front of the bar. Chrome bumpers, bright trim, and six coats of wet-sanded and polished Signet Gold paint gleamed in the summer sunlight of late afternoon. Coralie was her name, Corinna's sister, and with a 360-horse Ram Air 400 under the hood and a four speed Muncie on deck, she was as bad as the girl who drove her.

He unlocked the car and handed Gillian in before giving back the keys.

"Straight home?" He wanted to make sure.

"Straight." She nodded, sliding into the butter-soft, custom black leather interior.

"Five minutes, then." It shouldn't take more, not in Coralie, but he never took anything for granted, not with her.

"Two, if we blow the lights," she said, glancing back up at him.

He grinned and shook his head.

"Not on my watch, babe. Five minutes." He turned and headed toward his Jeep.

Behind him, he heard the GTO start up, the deep rumbling purr of her engine and headers echoing in the back alley. Coralie had been a gift to

Gillian from Dylan, a classic piece of muscle for the woman they'd all been too late to save. The boss had been the target that night, not a sweet faced, tousle-haired, thirty-year-old "wannabe" assistant trying to work her way up the ladder in General Grant's office.

She still had a sweet face, sweetly exotic, except when seen from the bore end of an M40 rifle or her TC Contender single shot pistol. "Sweet" wasn't the word that came to mind in those situations. She had a Glock 17 long slide reworked to a .40 Smith and Wesson in her fanny pack, and a seven-inch Recon Tanto sheathed in her boot—razor sharp. He'd seen the clip of her folding knife hooked over her pants pocket. He knew if he looked, he'd find a 12-gauge tactical shotgun under Coralie's front seat, a flat black beauty called Nightshade that Gillian kept loaded with double-ought buck and rifled slugs.

Two knives, a shotgun, and a semiautomatic pistol, just to visit the neighborhood bar. Nobody touched Red Dog. No man could get a hand on her, not on his own.

But Royce wouldn't be alone when he came. The ex-CIA agent had recruited a dozen of the most notorious mercenaries operating on the international scene to headline his underworld organization, every one of them a hardened criminal, the kind of men who would kill each other for the right price. The DOD had dubbed them the Damn Dirty Dozen, and they were on wanted lists from London to Laos, their reputations the stuff of people's nightmares.

Travis knew each of them by name, face, and rap sheet. He'd made it his business to know, and if Tony Royce had moved into El Salvador, they'd been there with him—with Red Dog not nearly far enough behind.

She was going to get herself killed, unless he got to Royce before Royce got to her—so he hunted. He followed the mercs, he followed the money, he followed the deals, always looking for the man who stayed hidden behind it all—Tony Royce. Two weeks ago, a source had pinpointed the former government agent in Bangkok. But when he and Kid had gotten to Thailand the trail had been cold, and it had stayed cold—until now.

Gillian was wrong. El Salvador wasn't far away, not at all. Travis would be there in a matter of hours.

Rounding the tail end of his Jeep, he glanced down at his license plate—SRCHN4U—and a brief smile twisted his lips. He'd spent his whole life searching for something—the astral plane, the perfect meditation, the solution for other people's problems—but nothing had ever compelled him with more deadly and serious intent than the search for the man who had destroyed Gillian Pentycote's mind and turned her into a highly professional, highly paid covert operator who only knew herself by the code name Red Dog.